JEEVES
AND THE
KING OF CLUBS

BEN SCHOTT

An homage to P. G. Wodehouse
authorised by the Wodehouse Estate

WITH AUTHORIAL ENDNOTES

I.

WEDNESDAY

I was idling away the pre-cocktail ennui, flicking cards into the coal scuttle, when in buttled Jeeves with the quenching tray.

'Your whisky and soda, sir,' he murmured, placing a perfectly judged tumbler at my elbow.

I thanked him with a nod, sinking with ease the six of hearts. 'Be it ever so humble, Jeeves.'

'Sir?'

'There's no place like home.'

'As I am led to believe, sir.'

'I mean, Monte Carlo is all well and good.'

'Sir.'

'But there's only so much baccarat a man can play.'

'Sir.'

'So many promenades he can toe along the front.'

'Sir.'

'So many snails he can winkle out with one of those contraptions.'

'*Pinces à escargots*, sir?'

'Before, one morning, he takes a long, hard look in the mirror and asks: I wonder how Mayfair is muddling along without me?'

'I see, sir.'

'After a while, abroad is always so dashed *abroad*, what?'

'It does have that quality, sir.'

'Thank you for your postcard, by-the-by.' I indicated a seaside panorama mantelpieced between the snuff-boxes. 'I trust the gods smiled down on you in Herne Bay?'

'They did, sir.'

'Could you see the breeze and taste the sun?'

'I could, sir.'

'Did the shrimps jump eagerly into your net, with lemon wedges clamped between their tiny teeth?'

'Almost, sir.'

'Well,' I said, accidentally consigning a joker to the log-basket, 'you seem suffused with joy, jollity, and song, and eager to bop life squarely on the conk.'

'You are too kind, sir.'

'Supper in an hour, would you say?'

I flicked the nine of diamonds, which ricocheted alarmingly off a lampshade. To my amazement, Jeeves snapped the errant card from out of thin air, and then coughed very slightly.

'Concerning supper, sir ...' His answer was a question.

'I'm always concerned about supper. Wouldn't trust a chap who wasn't.'

'I wonder, sir, if I might absent myself this evening?'

I have to admit this rather put a damper on my mood of domestic tranquillity. Master and manservant had just been reunited after a fortnight's dislocation across the Channel, and now welcome's red carpet was being rolled up from under my travel-weary dogs.

'Really, Jeeves? On my first night back?'

'Sadly, sir.'

'I thought tomorrow was your evening for cribbage and gin?'

'It is, sir, and I must apologise for the belated nature of my entreaty, but I have only just received a telegram from Lord MacAuslan urgently requesting an interview.'

'So that was the knuckle at the knock?'

'It was, sir.'

'Hang on a sec – Lord MacAuslan? Am I dreaming, or didn't you used to valet for him?'

'I did, sir, some years ago, prior to his lordship's departure for Berlin.'

'I say, Jeeves, I'm not sure I like the sound of this. I mean, lord or no lord, you don't go snaking another gentleman's personal gentleman just because you're sick of German sausage.'

'Quite so, sir. However, I infer from the content of the telegram that re-employment is not his lordship's motive. And, if you will permit me, I have no desire to return to Lord MacAuslan's service.'

'Too much tartan?'

'Yes, sir. And I felt his lordship's fondness for the music and dance of the Scottish Highlands was perhaps a little vigorous for the domestic setting.'

'So what gives?'

'Without further information, sir, I would not like to hazard a guess.'

Disappointed though I was, it would have been unreasonably petty to confine the man to barracks merely to peel the spuds for my supper. We Woosters are capable of more than 'the frivolous work of polished idleness' – despite what many an aunt has accused, more often than not in writing.

'Very well, Jeeves. But inform Lord MacAuslan that he owes me a snifter.'

'I am most grateful, sir. In anticipation of a favourable response, I took the liberty of laying out some cold game pie, and have iced a split of the '99.'

'Champagne, eh?'

'Yes, sir. I thought it might prove a benison.'

'Bung it back in the icebox, Jeeves. I'll biff off to the club and scare up some supper there.'

'Very good, sir,' he said, replacing the nine of diamonds into the ivory card case with a pleasingly agile flourish.

It was a ravenous Wooster who stepped out that warm summer's evening, strolling up Hay Hill and down Dover Street towards the Drones. So it came as something of a blow to find the club's windows tightly shuttered and its oak firmly sported. I knocked to no avail, when it struck me – the place must still be padlocked for its annual wash and brush-up.

I try whenever possible to escape these weeks of sorrow and lamentation by booking a foreign jaunt to coincide with the fortnight that the Drones Club ceases to buzz. This summer it appeared, for reasons inexplicable, I had undershot my target by several days. Was it, I wondered, a leap year? Expocketing my club diary I found the following annotation:

During the summer closure, members may obtain
reciprocal hospitality at the Athenaeum.

The heart sank.

It is custom and practice for London's finer clubs to stagger their summer holidays, alternately admitting members from cousin establishments so that the denizens of clubdom can always drink port in a storm. Bitter experience over many years, however, had taught most club secretaries that reciprocity with the Drones is precisely the specimen of good deed that never goes unpunished.

One memorable August, expatriated Dronesmen took umbrage at the less-than-generous measures dispensed by the barmen of The In & Out club on Piccadilly. They extracted their revenge one moonless night, dismantling a two-seater Rover Nine owned by the president, lowering each part into the basement through an unlocked cellar hatch, and rebuilding the vehicle atop the green baize of the billiard table. By way of nailing their thesis to the door, they topped up the car's petrol tank with *crème de menthe*.

This year, it seemed, the Drones had been spike-bozzled by every club of note, and we were left seeking alms from the Athenaeum – the Club of Last Resort.

With a resigned sigh I set the compass south, crossed Piccadilly, and descended St James's Street – dawdling briefly to window-shop the shoes in Lobb, the hats in Lock, and some dusty burgundy in Berry Bros. Tipping the trilby to the guardsmen outside St James's Palace, I perambulated along Pall Mall to the corner of Waterloo Place where, opposite Edward VII's newish statue, loomed the Athenaeum's hulking cream edifice.

'Good evening, sir,' an elderly doorman intoned. 'Are you the guest of a member?'

'Actually, I'm a reciprocal, in exile from the Drones, here to see about some supper.'

'Your name, sir?'

'Wooster-comma-Bertram.'

He ran a quill down to the 'W's and then, with a look I've heard described as 'old-fashioned', gestured wearily across an expanse of chequerboard marble towards the coat-racks.

Hatless, gloveless, caneless, and thirsty, I made my way to the bar, only to be met by a sepulchral chill and the forlorn glance of two dog-collared sky pilots nursing a single schooner of sherry.

The barman was languidly polishing a silver tankard with the calculated malice of an Australian leg-spinner.

'Salutations, barkeep! How's business?'

'Business, sir, is slow,' he replied, menacingly. 'Business is often slow.'

'Nobody in from the Drones?'

His insolent eyes traversed the almost empty room. 'I can't see any, sir, can you?'

A wise king once observed that the saddest words in the English language are 'Shall we go straight through to dinner?'

And so it was, with unslaked melancholy, that I turned on my heel and ankled across the hall to the coffee room.

I was accosted at the threshold by the maître d', who was equipped with one of those accents so madly French you feel sure they are working it for a bet.

'*Bonsoir*, monsieur.' He bowed low from the waist. 'Will monsieur be dining alone?'

Behind him stood table after table of dark-suited singletons. In front of each man was a low, metal music-stand that splayed open the spine of some or other book. The diners stared down at their texts as if blinkered, forking mouthfuls as they read and only occasionally missing their mouths and spearing their cheeks. Of amusement, bonhomie, repartee – nothing was doing. The mournful tableau was animated intermittently by tongue-moistened fingers turning sun-faded pages.

'What about the club table?' I enquired.

Mine host glanced ruefully towards 'Temperance Corner', where three men were eating in slow communal silence, while a fourth slumped napping like a dormouse.

I craned my neck around the corner. 'I don't suppose there's anyone in from the Drones?' The desperation in my voice was, I fear, not well disguised.

At this, the maître d' perked up. 'Ah! Monsieur should 'ave said. This way, if you please!'

He guided me energetically past a brace of bishops towards the far wall, where a brass handle projected from the painted wood panelling.

'We find that many of our *réciproques* prefer a livelier *ambience*, monsieur,' and, with that, he flung open the hidden door with a theatrical swagger.

There was a terrible roar of voices combining, perhaps, the innocent enthusiasm of the Last Night of the Proms with the bloodthirsty vim of a Light Brigade charge.

Some primitive instinct, doubtless acquired from a wily forebear at the Battle of Crécy, prompted me to duck – thereby narrowly avoiding a bread roll hurled with practised accuracy at the Wooster bonce. Every eye turned to follow this well-buttered missile as it arced upwards in a graceful parabola, paused for a second at the crust's crest, and descended into the main dining-room towards a military gent with a walrus moustache.

The moment of impact was spectacular. The roll landed bang on the bullseye of a bowl of vichyssoise, creating a tidal splash that comprehensively bespattered the old boy's arms, chest, neck, and face.

The silent room fell silenter still. Even the Drones mob was struck dumb.

And then there was a delicate but distantly audible 'plonk' as the military man's monocle fell into his claret.

Normal service was soon restored by the unmistakable yodel of Catsmeat Potter-Pirbright – 'Oh, I say, that one had jam on it!' – followed by the deafening whistles and hoots that characterise Dronesmen at the trough.

Concluding that discretion was the better p. of v., I slid into the private room, closed the door behind me, and braced myself to accept the poggled abuse of my fellow Eggs, Beans, and Crumpets.

Before I sat, though, I hailed a hovering steward. 'I say, might you pop out to the old campaigner who was inadvertently drenched by my friend, and suggest that the Drones Club settles his bill? It's the least we can do.'

'Certainly, sir. I am sure Colonel Stroud-Pringle will be grateful.'

A quick perusal of the panelled room confirmed what I already feared: the last available seat was at the head of the table. This was far from cheering, since Drones tradition dictates that the presiding chair of the 'club table' should only ever be taken by the Youngest Member. Should an old hand sit in this sacred spot through absent-mindedness or inebriation, or because it is the only unoccupied pew, an immediate forfeit is imposed. Depending on the whim of the members present, transgressors can be 'Wined' – obliged to present a case of champagne – or 'Dined' – compelled to eat some horrendous admixture of condiments.

Only a few months back, Pongo Twistleton began speaking in tongues after being obliged to ingest a half-pint beaker filled with mustard, Tabasco, Patum Peperium, and an intensely venomous bloater paste.

Fortunately, the chaps that night were thirstier for champagne than they were hungry for punishment. And so, to the chant of 'Wine him! Wine him!', I summoned some magnums of fizz for the mob, and the saddle of lamb for myself.

The stuffier gentlemen's clubs frown upon members swapping seats during meals – it confuses the staff, and results in some unsuspecting teetotal vegetarian finding his quarterly account jammed with charges for club claret and rump steak. At the Drones, however, members play 'club table musical chairs' by 'cutting in' – as at a dance. The *de jure* procedure is to catch the eye of another member and make a scissoring sign with your fingers. The *de facto* method is to lob cubes of sugar at him until he relents. By the end of most meals, the Drones Club communal table is in a Mad-Hatterish state of confusion.

It was by the more graceful scissoring technique that, at the smoking stage of supper, Montague Montgomery cut in to sit next to me. He was bearing two glasses of Madeira and, so it seemed, the weight of the world.

'What-ho, Bertie. How do we find you?'

'Moister than an oyster, Monty.'

'That's splendid,' he sighed. 'Very splendid. Splendid indeed.' He sipped his wine sheepishly. 'Splendid.'

I'd seen this ovine look before, and steeled myself to take the hardest of lines. 'Moolah or matrimony, Monty?'

'A bit of both, as it happens.'

'How much, when, and for whom?'

'Two thousand pounds—'

I spluttered.

'As soon as poss …' he paused '… for Florence Craye.'

My splutter collapsed into full-blown asphyxiation.

I appreciate that not everyone will have tracked the travails of Bertram Wilberforce Wooster in fastidious detail. Even one's most loyal readers must occasionally tuck back the bookmark and protest that enough, for the time being, is jolly well enough. Yet I like to think the name Florence Craye is sufficiently infamous for foghorns to sound up and down the coastline, warning all shipping of hazardous breakers ahead.

Lady Florence, daughter of Percy Craye, Earl of Worplesdon, is, as the punchline goes, a 'curate's egg'. Tall, blonde, and unquestionably willowy, she has a profile that, if not a thousand ships, certainly propelled a punt or two down the Cherwell. Behind these superficial charms, however, lurks a mind like a steel trap.

To girls like Florence, you see, chaps are projects. Whereas angelic souls are content to let sleeping Dronesmen laze, Florentine Furies demand they beg, roll over, and perform all manner of demeaning tricks. When it comes to romance, as I can attest, their *modus operandi* is: 'Find a feller you really like, and change him.'

So, if you see a dashing blade groaning under a weight of dusty books, or staggering from an especially Teutonic opera with a pounding museum headache, it's a racing cert that Florence, or one of her ilk, has dispatched him on a mandatory course of self-improvement.

Sadly, this made Monty an ideal candidate for her attention, since even his boonest companions could not deny that here was a man in dire need of intellectual refurbishment. It's not that he isn't tall, rugged, and gallant. It's just that he's not the brainiest dog in the shop, and seems quite content to remain so.

Monty took advantage of my pulmonary incapacity to press his case. 'Florence has stolen my heart, Bertie, and I am powerless to resist.'

By this time, I had just about regained control of the breathing apparatus, and I fixed on my chum the beadiest of eyes. 'Powerless, Monty, but poverty-stricken.'

'Circumstances are straitened, it's true. And I do find myself somewhat on the back-seam.'

'But how can such a distressing damsel require such a quantity of loot?' I feared the worst. 'Oh Lord, Monty, it's not ...?'

'It's love, Bertie, but love unrequited. Although she is the apple of my eye, to her I am no more than a pip. I need to make a dramatic gesture, and for that I need spondulicks.'

'*My* spondulicks,' I corrected.

'Well, yes. She has a new play opening next week, *Flotsam*—'

'*Flotsam*, Monty? *Flotsam*? Who titles a play *Flotsam*? Is this a joke?'

'No, it's the sequel to *Spindrift* – and one of her angels pulled out this very morning. If she can't make up the difference quicksharp the theatre stays dark and the ghost don't walk.'

'Sounds ideal.'

'Don't say that, Bertie – it's a marvellous production. I've been sneaking into rehearsals for the last three weeks, and *Flotsam* has "box-office smash" written all over it.'

I explained to Monty, with the patience of Job, that we'd been up this garden path before. Florence, as they say down New Scotland Yard, has 'form'. Last time it was for *Spindrift*, when she attempted to extract a thousand pounds from your present correspondent and, if memory serves, many others. Her backers have a habit of retreating at speed, and I struggle to find fault with their cowardice.

'This is different,' protested Monty. 'If I can raise the stakes she needs by tomorrow afternoon, the play will be saved, and I will be her saviour.'

'Oh, you will, will you?'

'Certainly. And, as the first-night curtain falls, I will bend the knee and pop the question.'

It was time to call a halt to this reverie of falling, bending, and popping before Monty did himself a mischief. 'My dear thing, this simply won't do. You can't fund hopeless theatrical ventures by touching old school pals for brass. I hate to play the candid friend, but what you need – and I'm sorry if this comes as a shock – is Gainful Employment.'

Monty bristled. A nerve had been touched. 'For your information, Bertram, I have three jobs.'

I was inclined to take such braggadocio *cum* a hefty *grano* of *salis*, since the majority of Dronesmen suffer from advanced cases of ergophobia – a sloth-inducing affliction that is as crippling as it is contagious. Medical Science has hitherto been reluctant to recognise ergophobia as a genuine diagnosis, but if Medical Science ever popped into the Drones Club on a weekday afternoon, then Medical Science's bow tie would spin round and round in amazement.

'Three jobs, Monty? Three? More than two and fewer than four?'

'In the mornings, I am a board-walker.'

'Eh?'

'A board-walker. I roam the streets with a sandwich-board advertising a tobacco concern.'

'Oh.'

'Later in the day I bottle-wash at the Lamb and Flag in Covent Garden. And four nights a week, I major-domo at the Hot Spot off Bond Street. Tonight is one of my nights off.'

I was dashed impressed. Very few of my chums ever manage to hold a position for long, and I'd never heard of a Dronesman simultaneously trousering three packets of pay.

'Surely, Monty, such frenzied activity leaves you inundated with ducats.'

'That's what I thought! But you'd be surprised. Taxes, taxis, unavoidable expenses – it all adds up.'

'You take *taxis* to wash bottles in a pub?'

'The Tube really is fearful, especially in the crush.'

'You're hardly making rigid economies, Monty. Being chauffeured to work is the acme of squander-mania.'

'Believe me, Bertie, I'm chopping peas! But my outgoings have temporarily overwhelmed my incomings, and my meagre allowance.'

A thought struck me, the way they do when the filbert is whirling. Monty hailed from one of the finest families; he had an accent fruity enough to spread on a muffin, and his fondness for double-breasted suiting meant he was rarely dressed in anything less than a full acre of tweed. I knew for a fact that the dinner jacket in which he was currently attired had been bespoken on Savile Row, no less, for I was with him at its bespeaking.

'Don't you rather stand out?'

'Oh, the togs?' He laughed. 'I don't wear this, if that's what you're thinking.'

'And the voice? Surely that queers the pitch?'

'I never use my real voice, Bertie! I use Sharp-Shine Joe's.'

'Who, pray tell, is Sharp-Shine Joe?'

Sharp-Shine Joe, it transpired, was the knives and boots man at Monty's childhood home – Widcombe Hall – who, in return for help with the laces, taught the young master the 'ifs' and 'buts' of Cockney rhyming slang. For Joe was not simply born within earshot of the bells of St Mary-le-Bow – a prerequisite for any true Cockney. Oh no, Joe was born inside the church itself, on Christmas Eve, during Midnight Mass, upon the straw of the Nativity. This evidently explained his name, since Joseph was a shade more realistic than Balthazar or, one supposes, Jesus.

Monty shifted in his seat, lopsided his jaw, and relocated his vocal cords towards Cheapside. '*Anyways, guv, Sharp-Shine Joe was Cockney from loaf to Bromleys with the lingo and kabac genals down cold.*'

'*Kabac genals?*'

'Back slang! You need to be *pu to the kalat*, Bertie.'

I shook my head. 'Surely, Monty, such nonsensical imposture can't work?'

'*Guv, I can flash the patter like a top* – but,' he relapsed into his languid Etonian drawl, 'it does get a bit exhausting. And sometimes one forgets to switch off the Billingsgate blarney, which can prove a tad awks-ma-lawks.'

'So,' I said decisively, in an attempt to retune the radio and acquire a clearer signal, 'despite working three jobs, and jabbering like a costermonger, you find yourself, cash-wise, in the soup?'

'Breaststroke in the bisque.'

'And you want *me* to bung *you* two grand – *two grand* – so you can fund a play – *of all things* – written by – *of all people* – Florence Craye?'

'Be a sport.'

'A sport I will be. A sap I will not.'

I took a swig of Madeira, and he gave me a pleading look. The chap had fallen into a vat of molasses and I felt honour-bound to hoist him out. The Woosters have a Code, you know, and that Code is carved in stone: Never let a pal down.

'However, Monty, given our long history, and on the strict understanding that this is the final time my benevolence is tested by thespian larceny, the Bank of Bertram is prepared to advance a modest sum.'

He braced himself. 'How modest?'

'A grand.'

'Could you stretch to a grand and a half?'

'Not without snapping. A thou – and that is my final offer.'

'Guineas?'

I gave him the desiccated stare that had once been fixed on me from the bench by a particularly Draconian beak. 'Pounds, Montague. Sterling.' I took out my chequebook. 'Payable to you, or to the *Flotsam* sinking fund?'

'Oh, no. Cash please. The folding stuff.'

'Cash? Surely you jest? What kind of swindle is this?'

'Theatre folk have their ways, Bertie. Best not to rock the boat.'

'Dubious, Monty, distinctly so. You may be surprised to know that I rarely haul that quantity of treasure about my person.'

'Banks open bright and early tomorrow morning.'

I sighed. 'Very well.'

'And then you can meet me in Cambridge Circus. It's where I walk my sandwich.'

'Well, at least I will get a laugh out of this ludicrous transaction.'

'I say, that's dashed kind. When Florence agrees to tie the dissoluble knot, as surely she must, you shall be my best man.'

'If you'd threatened that earlier, Monty, I'd have ponied up the whole sub-cheese to avoid it.'

*　　*　　*

It was well after midnight when the door of 3A Berkeley Mansions yielded to its master's key, and I was more than a little surprised to encounter Jeeves at full attention in the hall, wearing an expression of crispness unsuited to the hour.

'Good evening, sir. I trust you had an enjoyable supper?'

'Not too shabby, I suppose, if you don't mind chewing the cud with a gang of ballyhoos. Next time, I shall eat my chop alone.'

'Very good, sir. There is a visitor, sir, in the sitting-room.'

'A visitor? Who trespasses at this time of night?'

'Lord MacAuslan, sir,' he murmured in a confiding tone. 'He's here on official business.'

'Sounds ominously like the tax man. Lead on, McJeeves!'

MacAuslan is one of those chaps who, from the nursery, had established firm ideas about What's What, and stuck to them like gum. Most of these ideas, I seemed to recall, were related to Scotland. I'd first met him at a Burns Night supper, many years ago, where he'd prepared the haggis, piped it in, addressed it, and then, there being no takers, eaten the entire monstrosity himself.

Since that meal I had somewhat lost his spoor, though he appeared often enough in the pages of *The Times* even for me, a more devoted reader of *Sporting Life*, to be aware of his influential yet understated presence on the international stage.

And here he was, in the flesh, leaning against my mantelpiece like an elongated exclamation mark – sharp-eyed, pencil-thin, and sporting a three-piece suit of radioactively vibrant tartan.

'Mr Wooster,' he purred in his Edinburgh Morningside burr, 'it is exceedingly kind of you to tolerate an intrusion at this late and lonely hour.'

'Not at all, think nothing of it. Has Jeeves supplied you with branch water?'

He lifted a tumbler of whisky in salute.

'So what can I do for you? If it's about Jeeves—'

He cut me off. 'Mr Wooster, my mission is confidential. I would say clandestine, but ...' He gestured towards his suit. 'I am here as a representative of His Majesty's Government to beg of you a favour.'

'Beg away.'

'I gather you are acquainted with the seventh Earl of Sidcup?'

'Roderick Spode? You gather well. Although it's a deuce ticklish acquaintanceship. He's convinced I'm some kind of womanising kleptomaniac and has, on several occasions, attempted to have me locked up.'

'So I have heard. Most unfortunate. Well, not to put too fine a point on it, HMG is concerned about Lord Sidcup.'

'HMG is wise. Spode is a carbuncle.'

'He is also a fascist. Or an aspiring fascist. At the very least, he associates with fascists.'

'You only have to see his upswing with a mashie to spot that something is dreadfully amiss. No follow-through whatsoever. Shocking.'

'As you may know, Mr Wooster, I travel regularly between Berlin and Rome as part of the British "trade mission".' His eyebrows acted as quotation marks. 'Europe is an increasingly disturbing place. The seeds of discord are being sown, and we expect to reap a dark harvest.'

I blinked.

'We believe, on sound evidence, that Lord Sidcup is giving succour to countries that may soon be our enemy – and is receiving succour from those countries in return.'

'Right. Well, that sounds manifestly offside.'

'Are you aware of Lord Sidcup's political organisation?'

'The Black Shorts? That bunch of knobbly-kneed misfits who follow Spode around in distressing footer-bags, saluting like marionettes and claiming to be Saviours of Britain?'

'Quite so. However, Lord Sidcup and his gang of so-called Saviours are curiously well funded, and not all of these funds originate from the country which they claim to be saving.'

I have to admit, the napper began to reel. Perhaps it was the Athenaeum's antique food, or the 'Emerald Goddess' that Boko

Fittleworth had concocktailed using only green liqueurs, but I simply couldn't see Roderick Spode as an enemy of the King. Certainly he was an enemy of good taste, good manners, and good tailoring: bicycling around the countryside dressed in baggy black shorts and haranguing the populace about the purity of British vegetables. But hang it all, Roderick Spode was an obvious buffoon.

MacAuslan gave me a knowing look. 'You're thinking: How can we be concerned about such an obvious buffoon?'

'You read my mind.'

'Well, we are. Very concerned. And to clip his treasonous wings we require your help.'

'Treason? Really? Are you sure you don't require Jeeves?' People usually ask for Jeeves in such situations, even though the Wooster cranium is habitually fizzing with stratagems and spoils.

'Your help *and* Jeeves's, I should have said.'

At that moment I had the kind of flash that would have made Archimedes fling his loofah. 'I say, did you know—'

'That Lord Sidcup secretly owned a ladies' lingerie shop on Bond Street called Eulalie Sœurs?'

I deflated. 'You did.'

'We did. Sadly, ever since Lord Sidcup sold the business what leverage that minor social embarrassment may once have given us has since evaporated.'

'Ah.'

'But we do have other lines of enquiry, assuming you are willing to assist?'

'Decidedly willing,' I nodded. 'And eager to help His Maj in any way I can, so long as it does not impinge too momentously on the social calendar.'

'I am so pleased. We felt sure you would be amenable.' He located a fob-watch in one of the many pockets of his tartan waistcoat and consulted it with a frown. 'I have detained you long and late enough. Perhaps we might continue this conversation on Friday morning? Say ten o'clock at the Cabinet Office? You might bring Jeeves along too.'

'Really?'

'If you'd be so kind.'

'Right-ho. Anything to oblige.'

2.

THURSDAY

I've said it before, and I'll say it again: you'd have to be loco in the noggin to employ Jeeves *and* own an alarm clock.

On the rare occasions I am burdened with an ack emma appointment – a round of golf, perhaps, or an early train to Ascot – Jeeves wakes me in excellent time to prepare for the daily grind. More often, though, when the pre-lunch diary is unblemished by obligation, he engineers his ingress to coincide with the specific moment my eyelids flutter back to life. It might, I suppose, be uncanny if it wasn't so dashed harmonious.

'What says the enemy?' I yawned luxuriously.

'Nine o'clock precisely, sir.' He drew back the curtains to reveal an expanse of blue sufficient, as they say, to make a pair of policeman's trousers.

'I see the day looks zesty.'

'Decidedly, sir.'

'Excellent. I have to zip to the bank this morning to extricate Monty from the bouillabaisse, and deposit my casino winnings. I can amble over in the sunshine.'

'Very good, sir. I shall lay out the light charcoal flannel.'

'Really? I was thinking of buzzing the Bees.'

This was Wooster shorthand for Bags, Blazer, and straw Boater – the ideal get-up for a faultless summer's day – but, by a minute quiveration of his eyebrow, I could tell that Jeeves was far from impressed.

'Very good, sir. Although you may be more comfortable in the light charcoal flannel.'

And with that he oozed away to draw the bath and decant the salts.

When it comes to clothing, gentlemen's personal gentlemen have a comprehensive vocabulary of euphemisms. 'Bold' translates as 'ostentatious', 'lively' as 'clown-like', and 'striking' as 'obscene'. To this, they add a repertoire of frowns and winces whenever their sensibilities are offended by, for instance, a nifty and not inexpensive scarlet silk cummerbund.

Naturally, specific outfits are required for specific events (hatching, matching, dispatching), and specific locations (the opera, Lord's, Bosher Street Police Court). The only acceptable way to stand out, as far as valets and dog shows are concerned, is to combine sartorial purity ('true to pedigree') with fastidious uniformity ('best in breed').

For reasons obliquely connected with the Gold Standard, Jeeves has an unswerving respect for financial institutions, which he places in the same vestimentary class as churches. It's not that he's a slave to Mammon, you understand – though he speaks fondly of an age when gentlemen's clubs ironed banknotes and boil-washed coins. It's just that he could never countenance entering a bank dressed in anything less elevated than the nines.

All of which is to say, having bathed long and breakfasted well, I set out that sun-drenched morning attired in the light charcoal flannel.

*   *   *

The counting house entrusted with the Wooster sock is Trollope & Sons, a stately institution on Fleet Street, more akin to a club than any modern financial concern. As the old joke goes, there have been Trollopes in the family for generations – certainly since 1720, when my ancestors parted company with Hoare & Co. after an unhappy crossing of wires concerning the South Sea Bubble.

It's hard not to love Trollope's – even if the place gets a touch Gilbert and Sullivan around the fringe. The double-height banking hall is illuminated by enormous candlelit chandeliers, and each of the duty-clerks stands to attention behind a mahogany escritoire, in full court dress: velvet coat, silk waistcoat, satin breeches, and silver-buckled shoes. I have it on good authority that the uniform used to include a silver ceremonial sword, and often think of petitioning for the return of this tradition.

I approached my regular clerk, Niven.

'Stick 'em up!'

'Good morning, Mr Wooster. How may I be of service?'

'I'd like to withdraw a thousand pounds, please.'

'Certainly, sir. One moment.'

He beetled off to the senior clerk's desk, conferred for a moment on the telephone, and beetled back with said senior clerk in tow.

'Good morning, Mr Wooster.'

'We've done all that.'

'The manager would like a moment of your time, sir, if that would be convenient?'

'Buffty? But of course! I always have time for Buffty. He probably wants a racing tip.'

'If you would follow me, sir.'

He led me through an important-looking door and down a long, dark corridor lined with shelf upon shelf of ancient ledgers, the combined contents of which bore witness to the financial travails of Europe's grandest dynasties.

I was shown into the manager's office where I was greeted by a tall, gaunt, impatient sort of cove who moved in a nimbus of Turkish cologne.

'Good morning, Mr Wooster,' said this beaky bird, preening his Vandyke beard.

'And a frabjous day to you, Mr ...?'

'*Sir* Gilbert Skinner. The chairman of Trollope's.'

'Oh, what happened to Buffty?'

'Mr Buffton-Acton has parted company with the bank.'

'Retired? He wasn't that old, was he?'

'No.'

'Oh, *I see* – sticky-fingers! I must say, I'm a little surprised – he didn't look the type. But, with all this temptation to hand I can see how even a saint would slip. I mean, take Raffles.'

'Mr Wooster! I assure you that nothing of the sort took place. Mr Buffton-Acton, if I may speak plainly, was deemed inadequately aligned with the bank's pressing commercial imperatives.'

'Sounds painful.'

'As a result, I have temporarily assumed his managerial responsibilities.'

'Lucky you.'

'Please be seated, Mr Wooster. I don't have all day.'

Gone were Buffty's clubbable leather armchairs. In their place stood a single and pointedly uncomfortable metal stool that, several inches too low, obliged me to gaze up into Sir Gilbert's cold, damp eyes.

'I gather you wish to withdraw a substantial sum of money,' he said, with the more-in-sorrow-than-in-anger tone of one about to punish the entire Lower Sixth for committing yet another Sports Day Outrage.

'That's right. A thousand quid.'

Buffty would have doled out the lolly in a trice, and insisted we spend a chunk of it on an early lunch at Ye Olde Cheshire Cheese. Sir Gilbert, by contrast, was deeply disappointed. This new breed of bean-counter never fails to inform you of the good deed they are doing by handing back your hard-won plunder.

'Is there a snag?' I feigned concern. 'Did Buffty clean out the vaults? Should I pop back when you've had a whip-round?'

My levity produced nothing more than an acerbic, gummy smile. 'Very amusing, Mr Wooster, I'm sure. I merely wanted to introduce myself, inform you about Mr Buffton-Acton, and warn you personally to be on your guard for counterfeit banknotes.'

'Funny money, eh?'

'We are advising caution with various denominations. Tens, twenties, and fifties.'

'And how does one spot these lills?' I asked, deploying the forger's argot I had read about in *The Mystery of the Pink Crayfish*. 'Is there a fatal flaw? There's always a fatal flaw. Is the watermark insufficiently translucent? Or are they printed on the wrong kind of rag?'

'There appears to be nothing distinguishing about them whatsoever.'

'R-ight. So, you want me to keep my eyes peeled for flawless reproductions of twenty-quid notes?'

'Also tens and fifties. The utmost vigilance is called for.'

The man was clearly cuckoo. Why they had replaced affable Buffty with this overzealous abacus surpassed all understanding.

'I shall do what I can, Sir Gilbert. No man can promise more.'

'Might I enquire what the thousand pounds is for, Mr Wooster?'

Such rank impertinence demanded nothing less than the truth. 'I'm going to invest in a new play.'

'Ah, of course,' he smiled thinly, assuming this was yet another of my flippancies. 'If you could just sign here ... and here ... and initial here ... and here ... and finally, here ... and here ... and here.'

'In some countries we'd be married now.'

He wasn't in the least amused, and was keen to tell me why. 'I have introduced much stricter standards than you would have been used to under Mr Buffton-Acton. We need to avoid even the faintest suggestion of impropriety, irregularity, or jiggery-pokery.'

I resisted the urge to tell him that I'd won a princely sum on Jiggery-Pokery only last month in the Eclipse Stakes at Sandown Park.

Sir Gilbert unlocked a small japanned cash-box and counted out a stack of fifties, like the owner of rare corpuscles resentfully donating blood. 'I trust this will tide you over for a good while to come,' he sniffed.

'Hold on. How do I know this isn't the snide scratch you've just warned me about?'

'Mr Wooster!' Sir Gilbert was aghast. 'This is Trollope's. *Our* banknotes are above suspicion.'

I was almost back on Fleet Street when I recalled the second reason for my visit, and whirled round to relocate Niven.

'Was there something else, sir?'

I took an envelope from my jacket pocket, and handed it over. 'I'd like to deposit some francs.'

'I see, sir.' He leaned in closer. 'Forgive me for asking, Mr Wooster, but might these funds be the proceeds of gambling?' He tapped the corner of my envelope where it was embossed in gold with the insignia of the Casino de Monte-Carlo.

'If by proceeds you mean winnings, then yes. *Chemin de fer.* I had a fairly spirited run.'

He looked concerned.

'Does this present difficulties, Niven?'

'Not exactly, sir, except that we have been instructed to report all such transactions to the chairman.'

'For what possible reason?'

Niven lowered his voice to a whisper. 'The chairman is a man of high ethical standards, sir. Sir Gilbert doesn't approve of gambling, amongst many other things.'

It would not be an exaggeration to say that I tottered a little at this news. What had Trollope's become? Buffty would cheerfully propose the most trivial of wagers, from the number of the next omnibus to drive past the bank, to the duration of the Chancellor's Budget speech. His party trick is to guess the height of any top hat – which he accomplishes with unerring accuracy, carrying around a short tape measure during the Season to settle any disputes.

'Thank you, Niven,' I said, re-jacketing my francs with not a little consternation. 'Your candour is much appreciated. If Sir Gilbert has seen fit to enter holy orders, I shall take my ill-gotten and evidently filthy lucre elsewhere.'

I stalked out of the bank in mid-dudgeon, with the firm intention of forsaking Trollope's for the more accommodating embrace of a Hoare.

Monty and I met, as planned, on the south-east corner of Cambridge Circus. He had warned me that he'd be 'filling the sandwich', but it was still quite a shock to espy his head emerging out of a colossal wooden sign that declared SMYTH'S FOR SNUFF in foot-high letters.

'What-ho, Bertie!'

'Snuff, eh, Monty?'

'It's "The Pinch With the Punch!" don't you know. Care for a snoot of Golden Lavender?'

'No, thank you.'

'How about Irish High Toast?'

'I think not.'

'Cock of the North?'

'Never before lunch.'

Monty glanced about feloniously. 'Do you have the needful?' He rubbed his thumb against his index finger, like a bookie.

'I do.'

'I say, Bertie, you are a brick.'

'I'm a blockhead, if anything.'

I handed Monty the stack of notes, which he stuffed clumsily into a trouser pocket.

'And now,' he announced, 'for the swap!'

'What swap? You have the cash.'

'The costume swap. You in the sandwich, me a free man.'

'What are you blithering about?'

'Bertie, listen, the money is one thing, and I thank you for it, but it needs to be delivered to Florence *instanter*. Chop-chop. No time to lose. And, since I am contracted to hawk tobaccy from breakfast till teatime, I require someone – you, that is – to take my part for a while.'

'No, no, absolutely not. This is a favour too far.'

'But, Bertie, you've already relinquished the cash. If you don't help now it's a *sine quid non*.'

'Oh! *Sine quid non*, is it? Really, Montague?'

He stuck to his guns. '*Sine*, Bertie, *quid non*.'

His Latin was as fatuous as ever, but his logic was tiresomely sound – he did, after all, have my splosh.

'You win,' I groaned. 'What does it involve?'

'Oh, there's nothing to it. You walk around Cambridge Circus, clockwise or anti – absolutely your choice – ensuring that at all times you can be seen. No sitting down and no leaning against anything. If you sit, stand, or pause for too long, you become what is known as a "permanent advertisement", and the rozzers will nab you.'

He crouched down until the wooden boards formed an inverted 'V' on the pavement, and wriggled out of his shoulder straps. Seeing I had scant choice, I ducked into his place, adjusted the harness, and rose with considerable effort to my feet.

'I say, it's deuced heavy!'

'You get used to it after a while,' Monty reassured, unconvincingly. 'It'll be as the zephyr before long.'

'I don't think I'm cut out for the sandwich.'

'It could be worse. You could be toad-in-the-hole.' And he pointed to a poor wretch shuffling towards Seven Dials entombed in a four-sided box emblazoned on each panel: GOLF SALE! GOLF SALE! GOLF SALE!

'What about the accent, Monty? Do I have to be a Cockney?'

'Not for this one. Pretty much everyone ignores the sandwich, except for the occasional joker who shouts "Pass the mustard!"'

'Charming.'

'Well, I'll be toddling off to the theatre. Back in a couple of hours. Have fun!'

I stood staring at him, attempting to account for this rapid reversal of fortune, but he shooed me away.

'You have to keep moving, Bertie. It's the law!'

Reasoning I would anyway be counting the minutes until he returned, I opted to patrol clockwise, alternating Shaftesbury Avenue with the Charing Cross Road, and passing under the neon lights of the Palace Theatre every fourth crossing. I quickly discovered that Monty was right: 'meating the sandwich' renders one practically invisible to other pedestrians, who bump and what-the-hell you with blind impunity and angry impatience.

There was only one other peripatetic placard with me in the Circus – a splendid old boy in a smart peaked cap who held aloft a sign that promised LESS PASSION FROM LESS PROTEIN. Since he was rotating counter-clockwise, the two of us fell into a companionable contrapuntal rhythm, exchanging nods of professional acknowledgement as we passed.

What little novelty there was soon wore off. After fifty or so Circus-navigations, I took a breather against a lamp-post until I spotted a copper heading towards me with an expensive gleam in his eye. Back in motion I developed a hypnotic rhythm, and was soon in a fugue-like state, daydreaming of ways to revenge myself on Monty, when all of a sudden I looked up from the pavement and found myself eyeball-to-eyeball with Aunt Dahlia.

'There you are, Bertie! And about time too.'

'Dearest Aunt, what *can* you mean? Did we arrange to meet?'

'Certainly not!' she yawped, affronted by the very idea. 'But I felt sure we'd bump into each other, and I was right. London's such a little village, isn't it?'

'Up to a point, aged thing. There are, in fact, many millions of us.'

'I only count the people who matter, Bertie. And there are precious few of them.'

Aunt logic is an immovable object; aunts themselves an unstoppable force.

'You are quite correct,' I acquiesced. 'And here we both are. Although, why *are* you here? You loathe the metrop, especially in the dog days.'

'I am here to see doctors.' She gave me a hard stare. 'And by this stage, I think I've seen them all.'

'Oh, I am sorry. Everything tickety-boo?'

'Like a clockwork ghost. I shall outlive you, Bertie, if it kills me.'

'That's the juice!'

'And now, I want you to join me for lunch at the Ritz. I have a favour to extract, and I require you diverted by food.'

'My dear old thing, I'm not sure if you've noticed but I am presently otherwise occupied.'

She stepped back, gave me the up-and-down, and for the first time took in my strident promotion of snuff. Without missing a beat she concluded the grandest course of action was a brazen *nolle prosequi*: 'Occupied, indeed! What piffle. You exist purely for pleasure, Bertie. Now please be so good as to hail for us a taximeter cab, we're already late.'

Of all the aunts that grip for dear life to the Wooster family tree, Aunt Dahlia is very much the cream of the crop: not simply a good egg, but an egg that, more often than not, emerges from the frying pan sunny-side up. It's true that Mrs Thomas Portarlington Travers of Brinkley Court, Market Snodsbury (for that is her formal, postal title), exhibits an infuriated bluntness that would shrink Attila the Hun – but we should not judge her too harshly for she is, after all, an aunt. And, as I have often had cause to observe, aunts aren't gentlemen. Indeed, Aunt Dahlia embodies the milk of h. k. when set next to my Aunt Agatha, who sacrifices livestock by the light of the moon and chews broken glass to sharpen her tongue.

So, when Aunt Dahlia demands of her nephew a taxi to lunch, said nephew jolly well sets about hailing one, with only the faintest of misgivings.

*   *   *

It can't be every day that the cloakroom of the Ritz is asked to mothball a sandwich-board, but they accepted my burden without demur. After a brief confab, it was decided that the advertisement most resembled not, as I suggested, a wooden overcoat but, rather, a folding umbrella. And so it was that twelve foot of lumber was neatly stacked alongside its rainproof kith and kin. I was even presented with a numbered octagonal token with which to identify my 'umbrella' on collection.

Aunt Dahlia, meanwhile, had launched herself across the hotel lobby like a galleon's figurehead, leaving in her wake the jetsam of other, more timorous guests. Given her principled refusal to make appointments of any kind, the maître d' could hardly have expected us, however he hid his lapse of telepathic presentiment admirably and whisked us without delay to a prestigious table overlooking Green Park.

'This won't do at all,' Aunt Dahlia declared, choosing instead an identical table with an identical view, before changing her mind once again and relocating, with some fanfare, to our original spot.

Like most aunts, Dahlia has as little time for menus as she does for reservations. 'I will have consommé followed by lightly poached salmon,' she boomed at a passing steward, who was delivering a tray of brimming coupes to a table across the room. 'He will have the same.'

'Now look here, old stick, some of us have been tramping the streets all day. Some of us need real sustenance.'

'I think you have had quite enough sustenance for the time being, Bertie. You won't mind me saying this, I'm sure, but you are presently looking rather well-upholstered.'

At this, I bridled. 'The Wooster frame, I would have you know, is celebrated for its aquiline silhouette. Hubbard and Legg have cut my suits from the same patterns since I was at Oxford and, give or take a cream horn, my weight has never strayed north of ten stone nine.'

There was a pause. Aunts, I have learned, never admit defeat. In the face of overwhelming forces, or incontestable facts, they simply change tack. Had Napoleon been an aunt, he would never have done anything so vulgar as to 'retreat' from Moscow. Rather, he would have framed his return to Paris casually as a question of clothing and etiquette, noting it was unseasonably cold for October and declaring that – like fish and family – armies of invasion go off after three days.

'That is as maybe,' said Aunt Dahlia, airily. 'But you are looking more than usually seedy. Some simple fare will do you the world of good. Heaven only knows what you shovel down at that adolescent club of yours.'

Seeing from my icy visage that my *amour propre* had been poked, she relented ever so slightly. 'All that having been said, because you are soon to do my bidding, we shall share a bottle of dry hock, which my doctors warned me especially to avoid.'

Over coffee, Aunt Dahlia served the meat of the meal.

'I want you to come down to Brinkley Court this weekend, Bertie. I have a task for you.'

'I'm not going to like it, am I?'

'Don't be pert. Brinkley is heaven at this time of year, and Anatole is returning from his fortnight in Grenoble, so your gluttony will have free rein.'

She was right, of course – Brinkley Court is a jewel in Worcestershire's crown, and what Bradman is to the bat so Anatole is to the egg-whisk. Anyone who has tasted his *Sylphides à la crème d'Écrevisses* or *Timbale de ris de veau Toulousaine* knows for certain that Man did indeed eat angels' food and, more often than not, helped himself to thirds when the angels were busy with the dishes.

'If you're serving up Anatole, I feel sure that I, and my well-upholstered gluttony, will be able to accommodate your whims.'

'Excellent. Now, what do you know about sauces?'

'Saucers? Nothing whatsoever.'

'Sauces!'

'Oh. Well, I know that what's sauce for the goose is sauce for the gander, if that assists the court?'

'It does not. I am speaking of pickled seasonings, spicy preserves, and zesty catsups.'

'I see.'

'You have heard of Lea and Perrins, I assume?'

'Naturally. It is the sauce of sauces. Accept no imitations. And it is a key component in Jeeves's patent post-hangover pick-me-up. I could swear it has shamanistic powers. The initial effect, you see, is slow—'

Aunt Dahlia swept me aside. 'Lea and Perrins is a Worcestershire sauce. It was invented in Worcestershire, and it is made in

Worcestershire. It is because of Lea and Perrins that Worcestershire is synonymous with sauces.'

There was no arguing with this, so I didn't.

'And, beamish boy, Brinkley Court is located in ...?'

Her pause for effect was marred somewhat by the absence of any effect.

'Worcestershire! You are slow, Bertie. It's a wonder you manage to dress yourself.'

I was about to mention that Jeeves had, in fact, decided on today's light charcoal flannel, but thought better of interrupting an aunt on the fold.

'Don't you see, Bertie? I have created, and intend to sell, a Worcestershire sauce to rival Lea and Perrins.'

'Right-ho.'

'And I shall call it ... Brinkley Sauce.'

I was baffled. 'May I ask why?'

'For money, you dolt! Do you have any idea how much profit Lea and Perrins rakes in each year?'

'Not the foggiest. How much?'

'Well, it must amount to a fortune. And a fortune I need. The money I made from selling *Milady's Boudoir* failed to go far, and your Uncle Tom, bless him, insists on spending more on his silver than on the leaking roof. The Brinkley Sauce millions will not go unspent, I assure you.'

I could see the denouement arriving like a Number 9 omnibus.

'Dearest Aunt, if you think I am going to break into Lea and Perrins, steal the recipe—'

She raised her hand. 'Don't be an ass. Why would they keep a secret, eighty-year-old recipe anywhere where it could be stolen by someone as bungling as you? Indeed, what is this talk of stealing? Really, Bertie, I worry you pollute your feeble mind with too much cheap detective fiction.'

This was a little strong, since I had undertaken any number of pilferous enterprises on Dahlia's direct orders, but I declined to take the bait.

'Very well, if not theft, then what?'

She hooded her eyes in thought, and I could almost hear the cogs creaking as she decided whether I was to be trusted with whatever pottiness she was cooking up.

'No. It's too soon. You'll have to wait and see.' She rose from the table with the cumbersome majesty of an unmoored Zeppelin. 'I shall expect you at Brinkley Court tomorrow in time for supper. Bring an eagle's eye and a lion's appetite.'

Thus dismissed from Aunt Dahlia's presence, I tramped wearily homewards and, too tired for the key, leaned on the doorbell like a drunkard at a bar.

Jeeves unlatched the timber. 'Good afternoon, sir.'

'Ditto,' I sighed, heading to the sitting-room.

'Wearisome day, sir?'

'I have been ambushed by Monty and bushwhacked by Dahlia.'

'Is Mrs Travers well, sir?'

'Rude health is not the half of it. Her constitution is positively profane. In consequence, I am in urgent need of a wink of the balmy.'

'Very good, sir. When would be a convenient time to wake you?'

'If I've not stirred before five, smash a vase.'

I sank into the nearest armchair, conjoined the lids, and was falling into a hypnagogic bliss when the telephone erupted.

Moments later, Jeeves emerged. 'Mr Montgomery desires to speak with you, sir.'

'Gah!'

'I advised him firmly that you were not at home, sir, but he was resolutely disinclined to accept my word.'

I groaned to my feet, paced to the phone, and plucked the receiver. 'Sleep no more!' I cried. 'Montgomery doth murder sleep.'

'Lunch at the Ritz, eh?' he smirked down the line.

'I say, that's dashed clever! How did you know?'

'Did you forget anything, Bertie? Some trifling piece of luggage, perhaps?'

'Egad! The sandwich-board.' I trousered my hand and discovered the octagonal cloakroom token still in my pocket.

'Yes, Bertie. The sandwich-board. The Ritz telephoned G. Smyth of G. Smyth and Sons, and J. Smyth, a son of G. Smyth and Sons, telephoned me.'

'Golly. Is family Smyth furious?'

'As a matter of fact ... no. Funny thing. They saw the light side of it, and were tickled moderately pink that I had been flaunting their wares in such a swank joint. Naturally I pretended it was all my doing, not that they needed much convincing, I mean what kind of half-wit shoulders another man's sandwich-board?'

'I can't imagine. So you haven't been given the boot?'

'*Au contraire, mon ami.* I've been instructed to pick my own top-class routes, and I've been given a pay rise.'

I remembered the pay rise I had just given him. 'And how did it unfold with Florence? Did the cash unharden her heart?'

'Touch and go, old bean, touch and go.' He exhaled like a pneumatic tyre. 'More go than touch, I fear. But we shall see.'

I pictured my investment fluttering away on the breeze, and was mollified only by imagining Sir Gilbert's disapproving face.

Monty brought me back to my senses. 'Look here, Bertie, are you free tonight? It's one of my evenings at the Hot Spot, and I feel that I owe you a drink.'

'I dare say I could manage to accept a tipple from you.'

'Splendid! Come and wash your neck any time after nine, but ask for "Mr Mickey", not Monty – the Hot Spot's one of my Cockney jobs.'

I replaced the receiver, and called out to Jeeves. 'Might we disconnect the apparatus for an hour? Either that, or I will sleep on the roof.'

* * *

The Hot Spot is a bijou nightclub off Bond Street, owned and managed by a couple of Dronesmen – which is presumably how

Monty secured his job. Intimate booths hug the walls, and tables surround the stage-cum-dance-floor, which is 'in the round' with a bridge leading off backstage. The band overlooks the action from a minstrels' gallery, and they usually play with tolerable gusto.

When I finally spotted 'Mr Mickey' he was working the room with the oiled self-possession of a music-hall compère. At every table he paused to shake a hand, share a joke, murmur a confidence, top up a glass, summon a waiter, or ignite a cigar with his ever-present gold lighter. He was, in other words, charm incarnate and utterly unrecognisable from the dissolute knut who had once been rusticated for bicycling round the quad wearing nothing but the Dean's wife's hat.

Eventually his zigzag passage through the throng delivered him to the bar, where I was sipping something chilled.

'I say, Monty, you're a natural: the very model of the modern nightclub maître d'.'

'I know!' he preened. 'I fashioned myself on a Cockney Ronald Colman, and everything just came naturally.'

'Is it always so sardined in here?'

'Always! You'd think *we* had Prohibition. Look here, Bertie, what are you doing for lunch tomorrow?'

'Nothing. I have a morning appointment and a fitting at three but, other than that, am anchorless until I motor down to Brinkley Court.'

'There you are wrong, for tomorrow you lunch at Quaglino's with the light of my bushel, Florence Craye.'

'Really, Monty? I think you might be mistaking me for someone you once saw in the mirror.'

'Be a pal, Bertie. My heart hangs perilously in the balance, and things could go either way. I need you to serenade my praises to the woman I love.'

'Oh, no. I refuse to play Cyrano de Belgravia to your Whatsit de Something. Have you seen the dignity of my nose?'

He flicked his lighter meaningfully, like an arsonist with unfinished business in a hayloft. 'I did think you'd want to nursemaid your investment, that's all. I mean, it's entirely up to you – but a thousand quid is a lot of paper never to see again.'

That's the confounding thing about money – its power evaporates as soon as you chuck it away. Monty had bitten my ear for a free loan and was now extorting usurious interest.

'Very well, Montague, but you know this is a shakedown?'

'"Mr Mickey", if you please. But really, I'm dashed grateful. Florence is a tough banana to peel, and if anyone can make her see the sense in me, it's you.' Before I could answer he was back in character. 'Look, guv, I've got to mingle, but why not roost for a spell and ogle the fillies?'

He snapped his fingers at the barman, and indicated with a rococo hand gesture that I should be bought the same again, on the house.

'What time at Quag's tomorrow?' I asked.

'One o'clock. And don't be late – you know what she's like.'

My second snifter had just been delivered when, from behind me, two soft hands reached round to blinker my eyes.

'Peekaboo!' trilled a voice that might have sounded like the choir angelic to some, but to me foretold nothing but doom. 'Guess who?'

'Madeline Bassett – as I live and breathe.'

'Bertie Wooster, you darling man, what a scrumptious surprise!'

'What, indeed.'

Madeline Bassett is the Charybdis to Florence Craye's Scylla. Just as deadly to the seafaring community, but offering a subtly different form of death by drowning. Whereas Florence dashes you on the rocks of her intellectual disapproval, Madeline engulfs you in a sentimental whirlpool of froth.

Despite being educated at the girls' school equivalent of Dartmoor Prison, Miss Bassett is as soupy as New England clam chowder. She steadfastly believes, for instance, that four-leaf clovers are leprechauns' parasols, rainbows are sky-bridges for unicorns, and that every time a kitten sneezes a new star joins the firmament. All of which might be mildly endearing in homeo-pathic doses, but very quickly has the tendency to become fatally saccharine.

'Lovely, lovely Bertie! Have you missed me?'

'As the slaves miss Pharaoh.'

'Is your heart still shattered?'

'Like the splinters of Don Quixote's lance.'

'Like the what of who?'

'One of Jeeves's. Beats me.'

'Oh! How is Jeeves? Does he miss me too?'

'As keenly as a blade, I'm sure. Though not as keenly as I.'

'I'm so pleased. Now what are you doing here all alone, Bertie? Drowning your sorrows, I expect. That was always your way.'

'Not at all. Simply savouring a splash, and taking in the show. A pal of mine works here.'

'How extraordinary. I didn't think anyone you knew had a job of work. I'm here with Roderick. He's just gone to make a telephone call.'

'Oh, so you and Spode are back on?'

Madeline presented her hand, as if to be kissed, and waggled her fingers to flaunt a diamond ring the size of a plover's egg. 'We're engaged all over again, Bertie! Isn't it wonderful?'

'It's more than wonderful, Madeline, it's ... indescribable.'

'You are so brave to be happy for us, when it must mean wretchedness for you.'

'Absolutely! Sharp misery has worn me to the bones, and all that.'

In truth, I was not for a second convinced. Madeline and I have been engaged four times, according to the latest official estimates, and her betrothal to Lord Sidcup has seen more near-fatal falls than the Grand National. So, despite her diamond ring and dimpled smile, I vowed to remain on my guard until she and Spode were safely behind a well-sliced wedding cake.

I signalled the barman, and ordered myself another stiff one.

'I'm so glad I spotted you, Bertie. I'm in a bit of a pickle, you see, and I need a man's perspective.'

'I feel uniquely qualified.'

'Roderick is always buying me little things, tokens of his love.' She waggled her plover's egg once more. 'And I want to get him something special in return. I've given him teddy bears, daisy chains, and heaps of adorable billikens, but I wonder if I'm missing the *masculine* angle.'

'It sounds as if you might be.'

'You're a dear friend of my sweet, precious Roderick—'

'Well ...'

'What would he like best?'

'Thumbscrew, brass knuckle, wooden cosh,' I muttered *sotto voce*.

'What was that? A cosh?'

'A snuff-box!' I improvised. 'He's always banging on about how much he likes snuff.'

'Is he? I didn't know that.' She wrinkled her nose like a disapproving rabbit, before suddenly brightening up. 'But I expect every man has his little vices.'

'I wouldn't call snuff a vice,' I protested.

'It's not exactly a virtue, Bertie, is it? Now, where does one purchase snuff-boxes?'

'I acquire mine from Lambert Lyall of Bond Street, just round the corner.'

'Would you help me pick one out? It would mean ever so much to Roderick. And of course to me.'

This was, frankly, an appalling idea. Shopping is an essentially solitary pursuit, and were I forced to choose a companion with whom to trudge from counter to counter, the name Madeline Bassett would fail to make even the list of injured reserves. That said, the closer Madeline got to Spode the further she was from shattering my bachelor's serenity. And, it occurred to me, marriage to so tinkling a cymbal might be the only thing capable of muting Lord Sidcup's sounding and treasonous brass.

I bowed to the intolerable. 'I expect I could tutor you in the noble art of snuff-boxing.'

'Yay!' she yipped. 'What about Monday morning? Does Monday morning suit? Of course it suits! You never have plans before lunch. Shall we say ten thirty at Brown's Hotel? Splendid. Ten thirty. Brown's. Look, it's in my diary now. In pen!'

The Bassett can move at tremendous speed when she wants, and I saw that my fate had been sealed in a child-like hand with bright green ink.

'Very well,' I capitulated. 'Monday morning.'

'I expect you to be bright of eye and wet of nose.'

'Let's set the bar at dressed and sentient, shall we?'

'Lovely, lovely, *lovely* Bertie!'

'Right then,' I said, anticipating Spode's approach by the itching of my thumb. 'Time for me to skidoo.'

'Won't you stay and say hullo to Roderick?'

'Sadly, tomorrow requires me to be the early bird.'

'Going to catch a juicy worm?'

Visions of Lord Sidcup in his revolting black shorts swam before my eyes. 'I think tomorrow's prey can confidently be described as such.'

I was draining the remnants of my cocktail when I heard a familiar, unwelcome voice.

'WOOSTER!'

He often spoke with the shift-key down.

Spode in theory is one thing; Spode in the flesh, quite another – and flesh really is the operative word. The seventh Earl of Sidcup is a sore for sighted eyes. It's as if evolution took a wrong turn, got stuck in a cul-de-sac, and just threw in the sponge. Even in the warm, flattering glow of the Hot Spot, the man was the stuff of nursery-rhyme nightmares.

'Evening, Spode. Always a pleasure.'

'I wish I could say the same, Wooster. What, may I ask, do you think you are playing at? Apart from squandering precious oxygen and bothering my fiancée.'

'If anyone can call themselves the bothered party, Spode, it is I.'

'Faugh!'

'It's no use faugh-ing. I was minding my own, scrutinising the floor show, when who should appear but Madeline.'

'It's true, Roderick. I saw him across the crowded room, and thought: *Hullo! There's Bertie. All alone. Looking so sad. I must go and comfort him.*'

Spode was evidently torn between taking the word of his best-beloved and setting about my torso with the nearest bar-stool to hand.

'And what a comfort you are, Madeline,' I said. 'We've been catching up on old times, Spode.'

'Old times, is it?' he sneered. 'You mean the assault of police-men and the theft of their helmets? The burglary of priceless silver antiques? Frequenting illegal bars? Obstructing officers of the law? Dognapping? Cat stealing?'

This was a cruelly uncharitable selection of my former mis-deeds, many of which are firmly outside the social (if not legal) statute of limitations. I ordered a beverage to fortify the life-force, and opened up a fresh line of attack.

'I heard a rumour, *Lord* Sidcup, that you were trying to renounce your peerage in order to stand for Parliament as common-or-garden *Mister* Roderick Spode.'

He gave me a look of pure hatred; the kind of look a cat might give having been prematurely let out of a bag.

'Oh *no*, Bertie,' said Madeline, taking Spode's hand in hers, 'you must be mistaken. Roderick would *never* renounce his title to become a silly old MP. He knows how much I long to become Lady Sidcup.'

'And who can blame you?' I said. 'The name conjures such soaring poetry.'

'Of course, my angel,' Spode soothed unctuously, 'there's no question of anyone renouncing anything. I did, perhaps, wonder whether I could pursue my political campaign more effectively from *inside* the House of Commons . . .'

His voice faltered as Madeline's knuckles whitened around his.

' . . . but now I see that would be most unwise.'

Madeline unclenched her vice-like grip and patted Spode's hand tenderly. 'Lady Sidcup,' she purred. 'Lord and Lady Sidcup.'

The conversational ball was back in Spode's court, and he positioned himself for a smash. 'You know, Wooster, seeing as you are here—'

'I was just leaving.'

'Seeing as you are *here*,' he insisted, 'there's something you can do for me.'

'A favour, Spode? This is exceeding bold.'

'More of a warning, really. I am an angel in the new play by Florence Craye—'

'You have invested in *Flotsam*?' It was impossible to hide my incredulity.

'Oh, so you've heard of the production?' He groomed the edges of his repugnant little moustache. 'How very *interesting*.'

I had no idea where he was going with this, but I didn't like the scenery one jot. 'It's hardly a secret, Spode. *Flotsam* is up in lights outside the Gaiety Theatre. Not that Florence Craye's work is anything like my mug of hemlock.'

'I expect not. Serious art must soar above your comprehension.'

'Untrue, Spode. When it comes to the theatre, Dronesmen stick to light musical comedy and high-minded dramaturgy.' I kindled a soothing cigarette. 'We seldom dally with the middlebrow.'

'Middlebrow?' he seethed. 'How dare you? *Flotsam* plumbs the very depths of the human soul.'

'It does, Bertie,' Madeline simpered, her eyes misting with tears. 'It's terribly, terribly, terribly moving.'

'Oh, come now. Did you see her first one? *Spindrift* was utterly boggling from prologue to curtain call.'

'The thing is, Wooster, I've been informed that *Flotsam* may well be visited by the "first-night wreckers". And, on hearing this news, I naturally thought of the Drones Club lizards – and, more specifically, of you.'

First-night wreckers are the terror of any fashionable première. A claque of rabble-rousers congregate in the pit to ridicule poor performances or fluffed lines with the honking and hissing of demented geese. Sometimes they do it for a lark, sometimes they are in the pay of blackmailers who squeeze the theatres for 'protection'. A few producers pay off these extortionists, but most sit bouncers in the front rows to quash troublemakers on sight. Clearly, Lord Sidcup – the Saviour of Britain – had appointed himself just such a bouncer.

'Wreckers? I think not, Spode. I have no intention of suffering the work of Florence Craye, and am confident that any play called *Flotsam* will be quite capable of wrecking itself.'

'Let me simply say this,' he warned, jabbing his finger at my chest; the man can hardly speak without jabbing something at someone. 'I shall be at the theatre next Tuesday, and I shall have my eyes peeled. If I see any sign of first-night wreckers, or whistlers, or hissers, I shall hold you, Wooster, personally responsible.'

'Well, that seems perfectly reasonable, Spode, since I obviously wield supreme command over every irresponsible youth in London.'

'You know what I mean to say, Wooster.'

'And I mean to say: Good night. At least to you, that is. To Madeline, I say merely: Toodle-oo.'

I finished my drink, ordered another, finished that, and left.

3

FRIDAY

'Grrgghh.'

'Indeed, sir?'

'Grrrggghhh.'

'Very good, sir. One moment.'

Some minutes later, Jeeves floated back to the bedroom and I peeked out from under the soft, dark safety of my pillow.

'I think this may prove palliative, sir.'

I stuck out my arm and he handed me a tall, cool glass, the contents of which I gulped down urgently.

The effect, as usual, was gradual. It began at the extremities and converged at the core with the awesome impact and unstoppable consequence of a hand-grenade tossed casually through the skylight of a fireworks factory.

My taste buds, which had been thickly carpeted overnight, were newly alive with sensation. My pulse, which had been plodding along in the doldrums, was back to its familiar foxtrot. My ears were unmuffled, my eyes were unglued, and my fingertips were tingling with insistent sensation. The overall effect was akin to being plucked from the third circle of Hell and transported on eagle's wings to Paradise.

I sat up.

'It is safe now, Jeeves, to unleash the curtains.'

'Very good, sir. And good morning, sir.'

'Was today's magic potion different from previous magic potions?'

'Sir?'

'The fuse seemed a touch longer and the eventual detonation a tad more volatile.'

'The drink is somewhat instinctive, sir. The fundamentals remain consistent, but there is always the question of how best to equilibrate the ingredients.'

'Which are?'

He wasn't falling for that old trick. 'I shall prepare your bath, sir.'

Years of observation and sly enquiry have unearthed some of his secrets. A raw egg, easy to spot. A healthy glug of Lea & Perrins, one can tell from the colour. And I'm fairly certain a dash of red pepper, and a squeeze of citrus. But there are other powerful components lurking in the substrate, and it is these that deliver the merciless uppercut to an unsuspecting temporal lobe.

No matter how heavily I tax the barman the night before, the morning after is guaranteed to be a snap. I can't for the life of me fathom how chaps can enjoy a carefree night on the tiles without the safety-net of Jeeves's pick-you-up to cushion their inevitable fall. Some chance their luck with the hair of the dog; I have always entrusted my soul to Jeeves's hoof of the rhino.

'What's the forecast?' I called out.

'At present, sir, cool, dull, and drizzling. Though I am confident the rain will disperse shortly before luncheon, and the barometer suggests optimism for an agreeable afternoon. Would you care for some tea?'

'I think coffee is required this morning, and of the fiercest. I need my senses cuffed into shape before we meet with MacAuslan and discover what His Majesty's Government has in mind for the perfidious Spode.'

In our taxi over to Whitehall I petitioned Jeeves for some advice.

'Don't ask me how, but Monty has bamboozled me into lunching with Florence Craye in order to plead his cause.'

'I'm very sorry to hear that, sir.'

'He's in love, she's in limbo, and I am stumped for ideas on how a match might be struck.'

Jeeves considered the matter. 'I know Mr Montgomery only slenderly, sir, but would I be correct in thinking he is not an avid reader?'

'Monty is to reading as Mozart was to golf.'

'Whereas we know, sir, that Lady Florence is a dedicated bibliophile.'

'A bookworm death-watch beetle.'

'Such disparity in intellectual acquisitiveness does suggest one course of action, sir.'

'I'm all ears.'

'Are you familiar, sir, with Mr Bernard Shaw's play *Pygmalion*?'

'Where Henry Higgins teaches Eliza Doolittle to become a lady?'

'Yes, sir. Although in this instance, the roles would be inverted.'

'You mean: Florence, *qua* Higgins, teaches Monty, *qua* Eliza, about the numberless mental wonders to be unlocked with an ever-so-'umble library ticket?'

'Just so, sir.'

'I like this strategy, Jeeves. I like it muchly. It combines all the merits of Monty-proof simplicity with the blue-chip credentials of a literary big cheese. I predict Florence will swallow the bait George, Bernard, and Shaw.'

We arrived at the Cabinet Office as Big Ben chimed ten, and were met on the steps by a dapper clerk who escorted us wordlessly to an elegantly appointed room on the first floor. As before, Lord MacAuslan was elongated against a mantelpiece like a prime example of Euclidean geometry. Above him hung a vast ornamental mirror that reflected the many hues of an entirely different, though equally breathtaking, tartan suit.

'Gentlemen, welcome. Please make yourselves comfortable.'

I took an armchair by the fireplace, Jeeves stationed himself by the door.

After the usual pleasantries and how-d'ye-dos, Lord MacAuslan got down to the matter in hand.

'Mr Wooster, you will have heard of the Official Secrets Act ...?'

'Er – no.'

'Really?' He had evidently assumed his question to be rhetorical, and was fairly startled by my lacuna.

'Just goes to prove how effective it is, what?'

'Possibly. The Official Secrets Act of 1920 draws on earlier Acts from 1911 and 1889 …' He hesitated, studied me closely, and, after an uncertain glance at Jeeves, continued. 'Suffice to say, everything we discuss in this room is to be treated as an official, state secret.'

'Right-ho.'

'Perhaps I might ask you a second question: What do you know of the Junior Ganymede Club?'

'This time,' I said, 'I can be of use. The Junior Ganymede is Jeeves's club. It's an association of butlers, valets, and gentlemen's personal gentlemen. They flock together on Curzon Street to chew the fat, perform charitable works, and wangle the finer points of contract bridge.'

'Have you heard of the *club book*?'

You could hear his italics, and I felt an icy caterpillar of fear ascend my spine.

Under Rule Eleven of the Junior Ganymede's constitution, every member is required to divulge into the 'club book' the antics, oddities, and doings-derring of his various employers. No transgression is too small (or compromising) to be included and there are, I'm told, severe penalties – even unto expulsion – for failing to spill any salient beans.

As well as offering a fount of gossipy amusement for the long winter evenings, the book's main purpose is to provide confidential references for valets and butlers contemplating a new position. Would they, for instance, care to work for the duke who forbids the use of hot water between February and November? Or the marquess who habitually wears ungazetted military decorations? Or the baron who telephones his castle on days he is absent merely to hear the screech of his peacocks?

Although Jeeves assures me that the club book's numerous volumes are securely under lock and key, and that its myriad secrets are safe with his fellow members, I remain deeply uneasy. To me, the Junior Ganymede book is no less than a Pandora's box of scandal lurking like a keg of gunpowder between the pages of *Who's Who*.

'Well, I know that the club keeps a book.' I paused, attempting nonchalance. 'I gather there may once have been a line or two devoted to me.'

'Eighteen pages, sir,' interjected a disloyal voice from the sidelines.

'I say, MacAuslan, if it's about that time—'

'No, Mr Wooster, I assure you it's not.'

Lord MacAuslan abandoned his perch and sat down opposite me. 'The book is only the beginning, Mr Wooster.' He leaned over to address Jeeves. 'Might you give us a little of the club's history?'

Jeeves stepped modestly forward. 'I'd be happy to, m'lord. The Junior Ganymede Club was founded in 1878 by the Earl of Winchester, who had recently been appointed Secretary of State for Foreign Affairs. As you will recall, the Russo-Turkish War had just ended, and diplomacy – especially as it concerned the Balkans – was at what some have called a crossroads.'

Lord MacAuslan shot me a knowing look. For want of anything better to do, I shot one right back.

Jeeves continued. 'The Foreign Secretary felt keenly that British statecraft was insufficiently informed as to the intentions of antagonist nations, and, indeed, certain allies. As a consequence, he set about establishing various novel lines of intelligence.'

Jeeves hesitated, clearly seeking permission to continue. Lord MacAuslan nodded his consent.

'Steps were taken to collect and collate information from private individuals who had dealings with foreign commerce, academia, journalism, and even tourism. However, the Earl knew well how the muse of history could be influenced informally, behind the doors of private houses and the gates of country estates. As he said, if foreign visitors are discussing politics over the port, or on the moors during a shoot, who better to hear about it than the staff? The Earl consulted with Fairweather, his man at Swanmore Castle, and together they founded the Junior Ganymede. A property in Curzon Street was purchased and converted into a clubhouse, and the country's most senior butlers and valets were invited to join.'

Jeeves paused briefly, before adding a coda. 'And, as I'm sure you know, sir, the club's name draws on Greek mythology. Ganymede was a Trojan prince, described by Homer as "the loveliest born of mortal men". He was abducted by Zeus and transported to Mount Olympus to become cup-bearer to the gods.'

'The original gentleman's personal gentleman,' said Lord MacAuslan, taking up the conversational reins. 'So you see, Mr Wooster, the Junior Ganymede leads a double life. It remains a genuine social club for those in the upper echelons of service –

but it is also a conduit of unique intelligence to His Majesty's Government.'

I was, quite simply, agog. 'You mean to say, there's a gang of butlers and valets roaming the halls, sniffing out secrets like the Baker Street Irregulars?'

Lord MacAuslan smiled. 'I like to think of them as the Curzon Street Perfectionists, but your comparison is apt. Secret intelligence is premised on inconspicuous access. Sherlock Holmes's urchins could roam the dens and rookeries of London, effortlessly mixing with and eavesdropping on the criminal underworld. Similarly, the Junior Ganymede has unfettered admission to the country's most consequential drawing-rooms, dining-tables, libraries, and bedrooms.'

He stood and returned to his mantelpiece perch, like a harlequin flamingo. 'Over time, the Junior Ganymede's tentacles have extended far and wide, and nowadays the club gathers information from across the domestic class.'

He counted off on his fingers: 'Private secretaries, estate stewards, drivers, grooms, gardeners, gamekeepers, porters, doormen, pageboys, stable boys.'

He replenished his digits: 'Waiters, chefs, cooks, nannies, housekeepers, kitchen maids, laundry maids, nursemaids, charwomen, cleaners … Have I missed anyone, Jeeves?'

'Pigmen, m'lord, have been unusually accommodating.'

'Ah, yes, pigmen. Naturally, very few of these people have ever heard of the Junior Ganymede, and none has an inkling of what they might be part of. Isn't that so, Jeeves?'

'Yes, m'lord. The secret has remained admirably close.'

'Below-stairs, back-room, garden-gate, and kitchen-door chatter percolates up to the butlers. They filter out frivolous gossip and pantry politics before passing on what they consider germane to senior Junior Ganymede officers, like Jeeves here. These officers communicate with the Cabinet Office, which in turn coordinates with the Foreign Office, the Home Office, the War Office and,' he paused, 'the Prime Minister.'

Observing my look of bewilderment, Lord MacAuslan made a long arm and, with a slender finger, pressed a small ivory button set into the wall.

A distant bell rang.

Moments later the door opened, and in stalked a military gent with a white walrus moustache and a face like thunder. He took one look at me, and snorted. 'Oh, it's you, is it?'

'Colonel Stroud-Pringle, may I present Mr Bertram Wooster?'

'We've met.'

I rose to my feet and stuck on the bravest face at my disposal. 'What-ho! Colonel.'

'The events of Wednesday night, young man, warrant a little more than "What-ho!"'

'Oh.'

'And a great deal more than "Oh". I sit on the Athenaeum's general committee, and I counselled strongly – *strongly* – against offering summer reciprocity to the Drones Club for precisely the reasons that you and your companions demonstrated not forty-eight hours ago.'

'Just a little high spirits, Colonel, after a few large spirits. You know how it is.'

'I do not, Mr Wooster, "know how it is". And I never did. The Stroud-Pringles have always been able to hold their drink, and their bread rolls.'

There was a sullen silence, during which the Colonel buffed his monocle defiantly. 'However, Mr Wooster, you were decent enough to stump up for my meal so I should, I suppose, thank you for that.'

'It was the least we could do, Colonel.'

'It was. The very least.'

Sensing the vehicle running away from him, Lord MacAuslan attempted the handbrake. 'Gentlemen, I am so glad you are already acquainted, it will make the next step so much easier. Please, let us sit.'

As we sat, the rain clouds broke and a shaft of late-morning sunshine played over the Colonel's face. It might have been my anxious imagination, but I could have sworn I saw flecks of vichyssoise still lurking in his luxurious walrus. I beamed Jeeves a telepathic SOS, and toyed nervously with my cufflinks.

'Mr Wooster,' Lord MacAuslan continued, 'Colonel Stroud-Pringle is our Cabinet Office liaison. His boys assess all communications passed to them by the Junior Ganymede, grade them for urgency, and channel them to the appropriate department.'

The Colonel harrumphed, a noise I had hitherto encountered only in novels. 'In the normal course of things, Wooster, you and I would never meet. In fact, I don't think the Junior Ganymede has ever worked directly with employers. I've known Jeeves for years, of course, but all this ...' he flapped his hand as if dismissing the entire *mise en scène* '... is decidedly irregular.'

It's a rum sort of feeling to be invited to a dance only to have the host instruct the orchestra to stand and blow you the raspberry. But the old boy had been through a lot recently, and so I offered him my most engaging smile.

'Are you ill, man?' he barked.

'No, no, just smiling.'

'Well, don't. It's damned disturbing.'

'Right-ho!'

'Dash it all, MacAuslan,' the Colonel snarled. 'Are we entirely sure about laughing boy here? The man's a member of the Drones! If that wasn't grounds enough for summary court martial, he appears to be a blithering nincompoop.'

'I say!' I protested. 'I am still here. I can hear you.'

'Don't care!'

'Gentlemen,' Lord MacAuslan soothed, 'let us not set off on the wrong foot. Colonel, please be assured that in regards to our plans for Lord Sidcup, Mr Wooster is of paramount importance.'

'Is he?'

'He is.'

'Am I?'

'You are.'

The Colonel and I looked at each other. 'How?'

'Mr Wooster, as I explained on Wednesday night, the government is concerned that Lord Sidcup is more than a bad joke. We know that he receives funds from foreign sources, and is in regular contact with an Italian diplomatist whose politics are firmly out of court. The two men communicate in code, using a book cipher. Up until now, they have used the King James Bible – not an especially imaginative choice.'

'Spode's not an especially imaginative man,' I chipped in.

'Quite so. However, they are scheduled to switch texts very soon, and we are keen to learn at the earliest opportunity which new book they will adopt.'

'Surely,' objected Colonel Stroud-Pringle, 'we have people who can unscramble a simple book code?'

'Of course. But it takes multiple communications to decode a new cipher, and events are moving at a pace. Since we happen to know precisely when and where Lord Sidcup will be given his new text, we thought the decoding might be accelerated by a little light espionage. It was Jeeves's idea, actually.'

Jeeves remained stonily impassive. As well he might.

'And I suppose *I* am to be the espier?' I sighed, with the weariness of one who has been the stooge in many of Jeeves's burglarious brainwaves.

'Yes, and no,' said MacAuslan. 'You are to be the red herring, drawing Spode off the scent. Jeeves will be executing the interception.'

'And where, pray, will this interception take place?' Colonel Stroud-Pringle asked, with scepticism bordering on incredulity.

'At the Gaiety Theatre, next Tuesday evening. It is the open-ing of *Flotsam*, the new play by Lady Florence Craye. Lord Sidcup is one of the investing angels, and he presumably thought the *mêlée* of a theatrical first night would provide the ideal distrac-tion for his nefarious commission.'

I assumed I had misheard. 'I'm sorry, but did you say Florence Craye?'

'Yes – why? I gathered you and she were old friends.'

'Old something, certainly. In fact, I am due to take lunch with her this very afternoon, not that she knows it.'

'Oh, that is excellent,' Lord MacAuslan said.

'Is it?'

'It dovetails perfectly! We have already acquired a private box for the first night, and now we will not need to contrive an excuse for you to be there. You can just mention over lunch how much you are looking forward to seeing her new play.'

'What if I'm not? And I promise you I'm not.'

Lord MacAuslan sat back in his chair and smiled. 'Lie.'

'Look here,' said Colonel Stroud-Pringle. 'Why are we paying for chummy here to see a play? Let alone a play called *Flotsam*? What's all this about?'

'It's quite simple, Colonel. Mr Wooster will attend the opening night in order to distract Lord Sidcup during the first half. It is during this period that the new book title will be concealed for Lord Sidcup to collect – and for Jeeves to intercept.'

'Concealed? Concealed where?'

'That is where we turn to Jeeves.'

'What do you say, Jeeves?' Colonel Stroud-Pringle asked, with a tone of respect singularly absent from his exchanges with me. 'Can this nonsensical plan possibly bear the rub?'

'I foresee no significant obstacles, Colonel. Having previously reconnoitred the Gaiety Theatre, and taking into account various other lines of intelligence, I anticipate that the code will be transferred on a slip of paper concealed under Lord Sidcup's interval drinks.'

'Good God!' Colonel Stroud-Pringle gasped, his disbelief finally getting the better of him. 'Under the interval drinks? Is *nothing* sacred?'

*   *   *

The day had transformed itself into one of those tired-of-London-tired-of-life affairs. The rain-washed streets were illuminated by a dazzling silvery sunshine and everything, from telephone boxes to tour parties, gleamed as if freshly licked with varnish.

Back on the slick, wet pavement, I turned to my newly unmasked co-conspirator.

'Spying, Jeeves?'

'We prefer "reconnaissance", sir.'

'I bet you do. And all this has been going on since ...?'

'Eighteen seventy-eight, sir.'

'That's not *quite* what I meant, as well you know. Is there anything else you've neglected to mention? A wife and kiddies in the fleshpots of Bognor Regis? A secret life in the circus?'

'No, sir. You are now fully apprised of the facts.'

'I see. And you *would* have told me earlier, had it not been for the Official Secret thingamajig?'

'Of course, sir.' Jeeves nodded, gravely. 'Without a doubt.'

Despite the hairpin turn of events, there seemed little more to say. Jeeves was as insouciant as ever, perhaps even a little *more* insouciant than usual, and it occurred to me that if the Code of the Woosters extended to bunging Monty a grand, and helping Madeline buy snuff-boxes, then it should jolly well extend to assisting His Majesty thwart so hostile a barnacle as Spode.

'Well, then.'

'Precisely, sir.'

Our interview over, Jeeves biffed off to Fortnum's to forage provender for the Wooster larder, leaving me with time to kill before doing Monty's bidding, once again, and surprising Florence at lunch.

I pretended to be meandering aimlessly in the north-northwesterly direction of Quaglino's, but in reality my feet had a very specific destination in mind – and my gentleman's personal gentleman was unlikely to approve.

I stood outside the shop for quite some time, marshalling my courage, before opening the door and entering.

'Good afternoon, sir. How may I be of service?'

'Am I dreaming or did you have a pair of slippers in the window a couple of days back? Wednesday, it must have been.'

'Indeed we did, sir. From our "Gretna Green" line. Would sir care to try them on?'

'Sir very much would. Sir takes a slim nine and a half.'

A minute later the assistant returned with the slippers, which snuggled my feet like pigs in their blankets.

'Very smart, sir,' he observed. 'Very, dare I say, *jazzy*?'

I should, at this point, explain a little about this purchase – in case the reader is thinking: Wooster's given up! He's gone to seed and settled into a sluggish dotage in front of the fire. For when a chap mentions slippers, the image that springs to mind is of soft, fluffy rug-shufflers intended for nothing more vigorous than padding between the teapot and the daybed. I would, however, direct the jury to disregard all such prejudicial sentiments, for *these* slippers were not *those* slippers. These slippers were of the 'lounge' or 'smoking' variety – with hand-lasted velvet uppers, leather linings, leather soles, and hard wooden heels. They were elegant and resilient, and as suited to country-house carpets as Rugger boots are to the mud. You may possibly have seen such items embroidered with family crests or fleurs-de-lis? Well, mine were patterned in tartan.

I studied myself in a long mirror, and was not unpleased with the overall fix. 'Does this particular plaid have a name?'

'Oh, indeed, sir: Wallace Dress.'

'Wallace, eh? Well, the dark red is awfully elegant, and nicely offset by the yellow stripe. Sort of goes with everything and nothing, what?'

'Sir is an aficionado. A few of my sirs like to wear them with a dinner jacket.'

'Do they? That seems a touch immoderate. But, they will come in handy for the country, where one is forever unlacing indoor shoes for outdoor boots. I'll take them.'

'Very good, sir. Shall I have them delivered?'

I had a disturbing vision of Jeeves unwrapping the package before I had time to lay the groundwork and soften him up.

'It's probably safer if I take them with me.'

'*Safer*, sir?'

'Don't ask.'

By then, the hour of lunch was upon us, and I toddled round the corner to Quag's.

Florence Craye was sitting alone at a table for two, her elegant nose deep in a no-doubt forbidding work of German philosophy.

'You can't sit there,' she drawled, not caring to look up at my approach. 'I'm waiting for someone.'

'You're waiting for me.'

She raised her eyes. 'Bertie Wooster. What are you doing here? You're not Montague Montgomery.'

'You speak nothing but the truth, Florence. I am here in his stead.'

'Why?' she asked warily. 'Is he dead? Did he fall under a bus? It's just the sort of stupid thing he'd do.'

'Shall we have a drink?' I suggested, hoping to pour o. over troubled w.

'Order what you like, if you must.'

This wasn't sailing as smoothly as I had hoped. A lesser man might have buckled under the onslaught of her indifference, but the Woosters did not buckle at the Battle of Agincourt, and we were jolly well not going to buckle now.

'Good read?' I asked, pointing to the book she'd reluctantly set down. 'More of your chum Friedrich Nietzsche?'

'Friedrich Engels, actually. *Dialectics of Nature*. Have you read much Engels?'

'I should say so! About as much as the libraries can shelve. Good old Engels. One of the best. Top marks in my book.'

'I say, do you think so? That he tops Marx? Well, it's certainly a theory, given how closely the two men collaborated.'

Florence beamed at me with a warmth that seemed to say, 'Perhaps I have misjudged Bertie. Perhaps he is not a pea-brained gadabout after all, but a man of depth and self-improvement.' And then her beam rapidly faded as she realised I had absolutely no idea what she was on about.

'What exactly do you want, Bertie? I have a play opening in less than a week and can hardly afford to squander my time on wastrels like you.'

'Well, seeing as it's lunchtime, what I really want is lunch.'

She tapped an impatient fingernail against her glass.

'And, of course, to have a quiet word with you.'

'About?'

'I really think we should don the nosebag. I'm much more convincing on a full stomach.'

'Very well. But you are paying, and I am ordering pink champagne and oysters. Perhaps I'll find a pearl.'

I laughed. 'Has anyone ever found a pearl in a restaurant oyster?'

'It happens all the time at Quaglino's. My friend Barbara discovered one while dining at that table over there.'

Once we had dispensed with the menus, I got down to brass tacks.

'May I be blunt, Florence?'

'Are you ever subtle?'

'Do you like Monty?'

'He has a certain inconspicuous charm, I suppose.'

'He's barmy for you-hoo, you know.'

She fixed me with a look. 'Many people are – including, over the years, I seem to recall, one Bertram Wooster.'

'But Monty is *in love*, Florence. Love divine, all loves excelling.'

'So he insists on reminding me. But love is hardly sufficient.' She turned on the full headmistress act. 'Does he *think*? Does he *create*? Does he *read*? ... *Can* he, in fact, read?'

This was a tad unfair on my dear old pal who had, after all, managed to cram himself into Oxford – even if he'd lasted just two terms. Nevertheless, her scornful intellectual critique gave me an opportunity to deploy the scheme Jeeves had earlier outlined.

'Might I suggest, Florence, that you're looking at Monty through the wrong end of the telescope.'

'I find that hard to believe. Or even understand. What does it mean?'

'It means, think of the books he *hasn't* read, the music he *hasn't* heard, the operas he *hasn't* ... er, sat through.'

Florence tilted her head, like a cat puzzling a human meow. I described how the sunlit uplands of education and enlightenment awaited Monty, with her as his guide, philosopher, and friend – and could see by the softening of her face that her armour had been chinked ever so slightly.

'It's possible,' she conceded, 'that Monty might be a *tabula rasa.*'

'I'm sure he'd shave more often if you asked him.'

She twirled a strand of hair in thought. 'Let me consider it. Lord knows I see him often enough. The man trails me like a bloodhound, and he's been infesting the theatre ever since he heard about my new play.'

'Thank you, Florence. You won't regret it.'

'That remains to be seen. In return, however, you can do me a favour.'

'I am yours to command.'

'*Flotsam* opens on Tuesday.'

'I know. I have a box for that very night.'

'You do?' she smiled. 'That's awfully loyal. However, you might recall that my first play did not exactly rewrite box-office records.'

'I seem to remember that *Spindrift* had a brief-but-punchy run at the Duke of York.'

'It closed after three nights.'

'Ah.' I had forgotten just how brief-but-punchy.

'It was the reviews, Bertie. They were, without exception, howlers. I'm not one to yell "conspiracy", but there was something patently suspect about every single reviewer using the phrase "unmoored epistemological musings".'

'*Every* review said that?'

'Even the *Daily Sketch*, which has a standing moratorium on any word longer than nine letters.'

'It's like at school when we all had to get into our essays the phrase, *The blue dome of the mosque was said by some to be most beautiful.*'

'Except this is important, Bertie. This is about me.'

'I don't see how I can help, Florence. I am not a newspaper critic, nor do I know any newspaper critics.'

'You know Percy Gorringe.'

'This is true. But Gorringe writes modern verse and old-fashioned detective stories, not theatrical notices.'

'Percy is reviewing *Flotsam* for the *Evening News*.'

'Is he?' I was amazed, since not only had Gorringe once been engaged to Florence, he had also dramatised her first novel, *Spindrift*. 'Is such a thing even allowed? Are there not questions of propriety? Conflicted loyalties?'

'He's not reviewing it under his real name, of course, but under his pseudonym, Rex West.'

'And that apple-pies the situation, does it?'

Apparently, for Florence, it did. The *Evening News* was the most important paper in theatrical circles, she explained, and Rex West's first-night review would make or break *Flotsam*'s fortunes, and hers.

'Why don't you ask Gorringe yourself?' I suggested. 'You were, after all, engaged to him.'

'Exactly. I can't possibly ask him.'

'But you're asking me, Florence! And we were engaged on four separate and highly memorable occasions.'

'That's completely different. And anyway, Percy's wounds from the whole *Spindrift* fiasco are bound to be as raw as mine.'

'What do you suggest I do? Phone him up and say: "Gorringe, old bean, Wooster here. How about giving your ex-fiancée, who is also, hilariously, my ex-fiancée, a good write-up for her new play, which, hilariously, neither of us has seen?"'

'I think you might be a touch more elliptical than that, Bertie.' She plucked at her bread roll. 'Also, you have something he wants.'

'Do I? Can't think what, unless it's a competent barber.'

'Percy longs to join the Drones. Always has. He doesn't have a club, a good club I mean, and he's always felt the lack.'

'Let me get this straight. You will consent to be courted by Monty if I persuade Gorringe to write a favourable review of *Flotsam* by promising him membership of the Drones.'

'Yes. You're on the membership committee, aren't you?'

'How ever did you know that?'

'I know things, Bertie,' she menaced, like an aunt in a dark alley. 'You would do well to remember that.'

'Look here, Florence, I hate to appear mercenary, but what do I get out of this transaction?'

'My undying gratitude?'

'What of *value*, I mean.'

'Well, I promise to give Monty a fair shake, romantically speaking. He has his faults, heaven knows, but you've made me see how those faults might – with the proper sunlight and water – blossom. Also, he's rather dishy.'

I was far from persuaded, and she noticed.

'*And* I will pay for lunch. *And* I will buy you a drink on Tuesday.' She glanced around for inspiration. '*And* I will give you this.' She plucked a pink carnation out of the vase in front of us and threaded it neatly through my buttonhole. 'You can't say fairer than that, Bertie. Really, you can't.'

Her request was not entirely outrageous. Gorringe is a good enough chap and, despite his mania for short side-whiskers, I could see him sliding happily into the Drones Club deck. His poetry is, admittedly, atrocious – indeed, I still flinch at the memory of 'Caliban at Sunset', which he once read to me without any form of cautionary klaxon. But the detective novels he slings out as Rex West are goose-fleshers of the first water, and are rightly popular with those Dronesmen whose reading habits extend beyond the wine list. It wasn't likely anyone would blackball the author of *Inspector Biffen Views the Body*, let alone *The Mystery of the Pink Crayfish*. On a more self-interested note, I reasoned that a positive review of *Flotsam* would go some way to reuniting me with my long-lost and much-missed thousand quid.

'We have a deal, Florence. I cannot absolutely guarantee that Gorringe will be elected, but I will bring to bear what influence I have on my fellow committee members.'

'Excellent. When will you nobble him? You realise it needs to be before Tuesday night?'

'I'll invite him to the Drones for some snooker. I seem to recall he plays the game, and it will give me an opportunity to sound him out within the precincts of the club he hopes to join.'

'Well now, lunch hasn't been entirely pointless.'

'How kind of you to say so. By the way, are you afraid of "first-night wreckers" for *Flotsam*'s debut?'

'Ordinarily I would be, especially after the *Spindrift* debacle. But the Gaiety has an ingenious policy of "papering" the front rows with free tickets for the first few nights, so we're pretty confident that everyone who attends will be a friend. Except, of course, for the press – but they are now your pigeon.'

'I endeavour to give satisfaction, miss.'

'Oh! How is Jeeves?'

'Fighting fit, I'd say, after his annual Herne Bay shrimp massacre.'

'I *am* pleased. Do send him my love.'

'I will, of course. In return, I'm sure he'd want me to tell you that your pal Nietzsche is fundamentally unsound.'

'Ha! He may have a point there. Changing the subject, are you single at the moment, Bertie? I mean, not engaged or otherwise romantically entangled?'

'I might be ...' I hedged, like an innocent man before a sceptical jury who wonders whether a guilty plea might secure him a lighter sentence. 'Why?'

'There's someone I want you to meet.'

'Is she excessively jolly?' Most of Florence's friends were excessively jolly, and excessive jollity is just about bearable up to a point – and that point is usually breakfast.

'We play hockey together and—'

'I say, is that the time? I really must be shooting off.'

'So soon?'

'I have an appointment with my tailor.'

Florence laughed. 'That, Bertie, should be the title of your autobiography.'

*   *   *

The golden rule of tailoring is loyalty.

You need not be a frequent customer, a famed customer, or even a wealthy customer. You need not settle your account on time or indeed, as one or two Dronesmen will confirm, ever. But tailors do expect fidelity, and they police it with elephantine memories that outlast even college porters. Tailors recall with chilling precision every button they've sewn, every trouser they've cuffed, every seam they've pressed, every mark they've chalked. And so the gravest error a gentleman can make is to visit his tailor in a suit cut by another hand: no wife has been so betrayed.

For as long as I can remember my suits have been cut by Hubbard & Legg (Military and Civilian Outfitters, Tailors and Breeches Makers, Est. 1818), who perch on the corner of Old Burlington Street, and are known affectionately within the free-masonry of Savile Row as 'Inside Legg'.

I inherited the firm from my Uncle Willoughby, who in his youth would scandalise the cutters by bespeaking three-piece suits in Madras ginghams that would shock even Lord MacAuslan.

Some of Uncle Willoughby's get-ups were so eccentric that Hubbard & Legg declined to sew in the traditional maker's label for fear of ever being fingered as accomplices.

I rang the bell and was welcomed by my man. 'Mr Wooster, punctual as ever.'

'Pippety-pip, Armstrong.'

'I see we've lost weight, sir.'

'Really? I'd be surprised after a fortnight of French gastronomy.'

He studied me intently with what cutters call the 'rock of eye' – a visual self-possession, accrued over a lifetime, that allows them to measure freehand and scissor by instinct. 'I'd guess a pound, sir, possibly more. We might want to have a look at that coat if we maintain this form. Now, how may we be of assistance?'

'I'd like to order a dinner jacket.'

He looked askance. 'I hope there's nothing wrong with our new dinner jacket, sir?'

The 'new' dinner jacket to which Armstrong referred was at least seven years old, but, as with dogs, tailoring time passes at its own peculiar tock. Any item of clothing younger than a decade or so is regarded as 'new', and an 'old' suit usually refers to one bequeathed by a long-dead kinsman. Properly cared for, a Savile Row suit can be handed down the generations – like gout.

'No, no, nothing wrong,' I reassured. 'The soup-and-fish is still wowing the crowds. But I was intrigued by the idea of something double-breasted.'

'I see, sir. Very contemporary. In which case, I think we might take some new measurements, if we have time?'

'Time I have.'

'Kindly step through.'

We ascended to the second floor where a series of fitting-rooms branched off a long corridor; Armstrong's room, number six, overlooked Clifford Street. I followed him in, and slipped out of my jacket, tie, shoes, and trousers.

'Now, Mr Wooster, silk, velvet, or barathea?'

'Barathea.'

'At the same weight as before?'

'Yes.'

'Black, white, or midnight blue?'

'Black.'

'For the coat, were we thinking four buttons or six?'

The appropriate answer was strongly implied by his inflection. 'Four.'

'Excellent, sir, and if we will just take a stand.'

I stepped up onto the wooden plinth and Armstrong got to work with the tape, memorialising the Wooster physique in a good two-dozen measurements, which he jotted down in an ancient order book with a thick stub of pencil.

'As I suspected, sir, we have lost about a third of an inch around the waist, and a little less around the chest. Now, for the particulars.'

What followed was a list of stylistic mantraps artfully disguised as innocent questions. A secular catechism that offered many diabolical temptations but only one canonically orthodox sartorial truth.

'Three or four at the sleeve?'

'Four.'

'Silk-covered, bone, horn, or barathea?'

'Silk.'

'Turn-back cuffs?'

'No.'

'As to the lapels, sir, we advise a wide peak rather than a notch for a DB coat.'

'I think I've spotted a few shawl collars, no?'

He looked at me as if indulging an American tourist who swears they've seen the Loch Ness monster. 'It's *possible*, sir.'

'Wide peak it is.'

'For the facings: Twill, silk, or satin?'

'Silk.'

'Bright or dull?

'Dull. And I'd like wide buttonholes on both lapels, with some pretty solid gimping.'

His eyebrows sprang into action. 'Both lapels?'

The tranquillity of our confessional was shattered by a barbarous roar – 'No! No! No! *Above* the knee, you fool!' – which exploded from the fitting-room next door in a voice I'd be prepared to swear belonged to Roderick Spode. Aunt Dahlia was right, I thought: London really is a little village, and that blasted gorilla was everywhere.

I rolled my eyes. 'Lord Sidcup, I presume?'

Armstrong moved not a muscle – for the silver rule of tailoring is discretion, and what tailors demand in loyalty they repay, in spades, with silence. Your average doctor, lawyer, or parish priest is a veritable town crier of scandal in comparison to the sphinx-like tailor, who takes the myriad confidences he acquires in the course of his career to the cutting-rooms of the next world.

Such diplomacy is not to be sneezed at, for the suit is a window to the soul: lightweight cotton when cash is tight, Italian cashmere when an inheritance lands; waistlines drawn in during illness or anxiety, and let out at times of excess. Weddings, funerals, christenings, and court appearances – all of life's landmarks are sanctified, quietly and confidentially, by one's tailor.

The next vocal outburst obviated any need for independent confirmation: 'No, you imbecile! The armband is worn on the left! The left, man! I salute with the right. Like this: *Heil, Spode!* You see? *Heil, Spode! Heil, Spode!*' There was a brief intermission before Lord Sidcup thundered out of his fitting room. 'And it had better be ready by next week,' he shouted. 'All of it!'

Armstrong carried on as if such ferocious outbursts were par for the course – which, for all I knew, they were.

'Now, sir, trousers. A single braid or double?'

'Double.'

He flinched.

'Single, then. But what would you say to a zip fastening instead of buttons?'

'I'd say very little, sir. Fully lined, or half?'

'To the knee, I think.'

'As for inside coat pockets, sir, we suggest a single left-hand breast pocket, but we can add a second ticket pocket for a cigarette case, if we'd like?'

'Do that.'

'And a pen pocket?'

'Hmm.'

He shrugged. 'Some do, sir, some don't.' This was clearly no shibboleth.

'I will then,' I said, thinking of my new Junior Ganymede commission. 'You never know when something will need to be taken down in evidence.'

'Quite so. And will we be dancing or just dining?'

'Both, but likely not in that order.'

'And the usual silk lining?'

'Naturally. Wooster navy is essential.'

'Right then, sir, is that everything?'

'I think so.'

'Very good. I shall see you downstairs.'

I re-togged myself in a quick few minutes and was heading for the stairs when an underhand thought snuck up on me. I turned back and found the door of fitting-room five wide open. Inside, upon a desk strewn with fabric swatches and button samplers, was a Hubbard & Legg order book, open at a page inscribed: *Sidcup, seventh Earl; Full Dress Uniform.*

I skimmed down the inventory of Spode's gargantuan dimensions until I came to *Shorts, Black, Ceremonial*, against which various measurements were pencilled, including an inside leg of fourteen inches, and a waist of forty-seven.

It was the work of seconds to locate a piece of India rubber and gently erase the top bar of the seven, instantly shrinking Spode's gluttonous girth by six inches without the poor man having to endure the indignities of exercise or diet. That should cramp his salute, I said to myself, returning back down to the shop.

'Will there be anything else, sir?' Armstrong enquired.

'I don't think so. When do you expect the first fitting?'

'In about three weeks, if that is convenient?'

'Splendid. I'm in no hurry. Give me a call.'

'New shoes, sir?' he asked, observing my purchase.

'Indeed so, and something fairly corking.' I opened the box and handed him a slipper.

'Ah, Wallace Dress. A very distinguished tartan. Does Mr Jeeves approve?'

'Unclear. Jeeves is not yet aware of their existence.'

'We *are* living dangerously, sir!'

And then it dawned on me that the real victim of my practical joke would not be Spode, but the fine craftsmen of Hubbard & Legg, whose lives would be made miserable by the irrepressible wrath and inevitable writs of a petty tyrant.

'You know, Armstrong, I think I may have left my wallet upstairs.'

'Shall I fetch it, sir?'

'No, I'll go.'

I returned to fitting-room five, located a stub of pencil, and regretfully reinstated Spode's coastline to its monstrous reality. It was rather crestfalling to discover that setting right my wrong-doing felt far less virtuous than I'd hoped. And then, catching sight of myself in one of the room's numerous mirrors, Machiavellian whimsy struck.

Stealing over to where Spode's unfinished tunic hung limply on a dummy, I plucked some petals from my pink carnation buttonhole and tucked them into the half-stitched canvas of his breast pocket. There, I fancied, they might, just possibly, soften Lord Sidcup's hard and treasonous heart.

I exited Hubbard & Legg and began sauntering in a homeward direction when who should I meet but my old mucker, the fifth Baron Chuffnell – known to his pals as Chuffy, and to his wife, who is a stickler for birth certificates, as Marmaduke.

'Shabash, Bertie!'

'Shabash to you, Chuffy. Where are you off to at such a pace?'

'The club.'

'Your club is my club, old horse, and that club reopens next Tuesday.'

'Not the Drones, my other club.'

He accented 'other' with an impish sort of smirk that immediately goosed my beezer. 'What club is this, Chuffy? Something disreputable?'

'If you consider gambling disreputable.'

'Crockfords?'

'Oh no, nothing so hidebound. It's the Nomadical. Care to tag along?'

I dithered. 'By rights I should be heading home to prepare for the drive to Brinkley Court.'

'Listen, why don't you leave the tribulations to Jeeves, come with me to the Nomadical, and he can scoop you up later in the motor?'

'I could ... though I don't have much in the way of coin.' And then I remembered my Monte Carlo envelope. 'Unless they accept francs?'

'The Nomadical takes pretty much anything – from bars of gold to an IOU.'

'Capital. I will telephone Jeeves from the club – which is where, by the way?'

'It's currently on Curzon Street.'

'Currently?'

'I'll fill you in as we walk.'

The Nomadical, so Chuffy explained, is a club without a home. Or rather, its homes are legion, but they belong to other people. The club's proprietors, a shady gang that Chuffy declined to name, rent grand houses on short-term leases that rarely extend beyond three or four months. Once they are in possession of the keys, the Nomadical moves with haste to transform a new property into a den of illiquidity. A large private house is, it seems, tailor-made for such an enterprise: public rooms for gaming, kitchens for cooking, a dining-room for drinking, and bedrooms for offices and to store unneeded furniture. Within twenty-four hours of acquiring a new home, the Nomadical is up, running, and taking money off its members.

'If the club keeps moving,' I asked Chuffy, 'how do you know where to go?'

'There's a secret telephone number. You call it up, sing them your song, and they give you the latest address and its special knock.'

'Sorry, you sing them a *song*?'

'Every member is given a song to identify them. You don't actually have to sing it, you can whistle the tune if you're shy.'

'What's yours? "Tulip Time in Sing Sing"?'

'None of your beeswax!'

'And the knock?'

'Each new house is given a Morse code knock, so the doormen know you're a member.'

'Is it – how to put this delicately – *legal*?'

'I can't think of a single aspect of the Nomadical Club that falls within the law.'

'Surely, then, the property owners object and summon the cops?'

'The owners don't know, and seldom find out. Their homes are always returned in the mintiest of conditions – usually far smarter than when they were let. I think once, or possibly twice, someone has smelled a rat, or been tipped off by neighbours, but in these cases the Nomadical has a pretty unbeatable trump.'

'Which is?'

'They always overpay.'

'I don't get it.'

'Should the owners be tempted to call in the law, the Nomadical will show that the rent they paid for the property was far in excess of the market rate.'

'I still don't get it.'

'Who would pay such a fabulous rent, but a criminal enterprise? And who would accept it, but a willing accomplice?'

'Aiding and betting!'

'Very witty, Bertie. And here we are.'

We had arrived at an imposing double-height front door, which, I was amused to see, lay diagonally opposite the Junior Ganymede's lair. I wondered if the country's finest butlers knew what infamy ran riot in easy range of a gently lofted niblick.

Chuffy knocked with a deliberate RAP-tap-tap-RAP pattern – '"X" in Morse code,' he divulged with a grin – and the door was opened by a thuggish bruiser who was fooling no one in his tailcoat and gloves. He waved us into a white marble hallway with an insinuating leer: 'Cards, gents? Step right up.'

'This is the life, Chuffy. About as elegant as Monte Carlo without the agony of mangling French.'

'And there's the added benefit of nosing around a new house every once in a while. Most intriguing.'

'How does one apply for membership?'

'One doesn't. One has to be invited. So behave yourself, Bertie.'

Baccarat was being played on three tables in the library. We found a couple of empty seats, and I handed over a sheaf of notes.

Moments later a steward returned with a tray of pastel-coloured betting plaques.

'Either I have come into money, Chuffy, or these chips are denominated in something eccentric.'

'Lira. They're from the Casinò Montefiorello. Just lop off a couple of noughts and all will be golden.'

Play proceeded at a steady clip, and my winnings and losses kept an approximate pace so that, after an hour or so, I was roughly at par – assuming, that is, I had got the hang of the franc–lira–sterling conversions. I was preparing to take a breather and elongate the limbs when a fellow I recognised entered the room.

'Who's that?' asked Chuffy, following my gaze.

'My bank manager.'

'Oh, God!' he cried, stuffing our chips into his pockets.

'At ease, old man, he's just been defrocked. And even when he had the keys and combinations, Buffty was an inveterate punter. Which, I suppose, explains his presence here.'

'Mr Wooster, what a gladness!' said Henry Buffton-Acton, approaching our table with a Pickwickian swagger. He was four parts chalk-stripe, three parts whiskers, and two parts gin.

'I think we can dispense with the bank-hall formalities, Buffty, now that you have dispensed with Trollope's.'

'Ah, so you heard about that?'

'It's the end of an era. I'm more sorry than I can say.'

'Thank you, dear boy, your sympathies are appreciated. But, what did you make of Sir Gilbert Skinner?'

'He's no Buffty, that's a cert. Something about him curdles the milk – if you know what I mean. He's decidedly *ethical*, I'm told.'

'So he insists, but I'd not be so certain.' He lowered his voice. 'Before he sacked me as manager, I was also *his* manager. And, while I'd never violate the seal of the banking hall, let's just say his personal accounts had some deuced unorthodox debits and credits.'

'That figures. Self-styled paragons like Sir Gilbert are just itching to fail you in some unpardonable way. Give me a clubman any day of the week. You can always rely on a clubman to do the right thing.'

'Eventually,' added Chuffy.

I made the requisite introductions, and invited Buffty to sit and chance his chips with us.

'I won't, thank you, baccarat's never been lucky for me. But why don't you join me upstairs where we're playing something special.'

'Special?'

'Ever heard of a game called EO?'

We hadn't.

'Even-Odd – it's an early form of roulette. Quite amusing and very rare. Heaven knows where they contrived to locate an original table. I think EO was last played in anger sometime late in the reign of William IV.'

Chuffy was intrigued. 'How does it work?'

'Come see.'

The Even-Odd table is a fiendish contrivance, circular in design and about five feet across. Set in its centre is a roulette wheel, of sorts, whose forty slots are alternately marked 'E' and 'O'. Around the circumference are a dozen playing positions, where punters place their chips on which of these two letters they predict the ball will land. You'd think there'd be a fifty-fifty chance of doubling your money or losing the lot, except for one diabolical wrinkle: the house reserves an 'E' and an 'O' for itself, and whenever the pill halts in one of these slots – which it does with taxing frequency – the losing bets are raked away and the winning bets ignored.

As each spin lasts no more than a couple of minutes, it rapidly became clear that Even-Odd was simply the gaming equivalent of a threshing machine, ruthlessly designed to separate the wheat (my money) from the chaff (me).

'This is unbearable, Buffty. A nightmare! I will soon be undone.'

'They used to say that "E" and "O" were the most expensive letters in the alphabet.'

'You might have mentioned that earlier.'

Just then a commotion erupted in the hall downstairs – the crash of furniture, the bang of doors, and the wallop of one, possibly two, bodies – and a blood-icing caterwaul rang out.

'*Marm*-a-DUKE!'

'It's the police,' gasped one of the members.

'Worse,' sighed Chuffy. 'It's my wife.'

Lady Chuffnell is a spirited customer and a manifest beauty with whom, when she was plain Miss Pauline Stoker, I had fallen head-over-heels – and to whom I had become very briefly engaged. (Putting 'briefly' into context: if the Orient Express takes ninety-six hours to clickety-clack between Paris and

Constantinople, Pauline and I could have been engaged twice over during that quixotic voyage, or four times if we'd had the foresight to book a return.)

Much like Florence Craye, Pauline had graduated with distinction from the school of romantic hard knocks, and she gave the shortest of shrift to any man who, having been drawn into her orbit, failed to meet her unreachable mark.

Chuffy's panic was, therefore, not without cause.

'How did she find me here? She can't find me here. I can't be here! You can't be here, either, Bertie. Because if she sees you here, she might guess that I'm here ... and I can't be here.'

'So you said.'

'Well, I can't! She made me solemnly promise to quit the cards, and you know how I hate to default on a solemn promise.'

'You hate to get caught.'

'Borus-snorus, Bertie. Are you going to help me evade my wife, or not?'

Of course I was, and not just because I had little desire to reacquaint myself with the fair Pauline when she was in such vixenish humour. There was also the question of Lady Luck, who had, it seemed, abandoned me entirely in favour of the impenetrable charms of Henry Buffton-Acton.

'Is there an inconspicuous way out of this place?' I asked the croupier.

My question offended him to the roots. 'This is the Nomadical! We have a back-door exit, a basement exit, and a rooftop exit – as well as several well-tested hiding places, and a hamper of quick-change costumes. In the blink of an eye you could, sir, become a postman, a fireman, or even a nun. All have proved highly effective in the past.'

'I think the rooftop, please, given our antagonist is in the hall and most likely on her way up here.'

'Very good, sir. Follow me.'

'Will you be joining us, Buffty?'

'Not likely,' he pointed to a mountain of chips, 'I'm on a blue blazer of a streak. And, anyway, by the sound of it, it might be quite a hoot to encounter Lady Chuffnell.'

Our egress from the Nomadical Club was far less perilous than I had feared. The garden-facing bedrooms on the top floor were equipped with large sash windows which opened onto a generous parapet gutter that ran along the back of the house. Chuffy and I cautiously auto-defenestrated, crab-walked along this channel, and stepped over a low partition onto the wide stone roof-terrace of the house next door.

Here, in the late-afternoon sunshine, an elderly couple were taking tea and playing canasta.

'Sorry to intrude, sir, madam,' said Chuffy, mimicking the flat, bureaucratic tones of a police detective. 'But have two criminal-looking types come this way?'

'What!' the old boy gasped. 'On the fifth floor?'

'They're cat-burglars,' I explained. 'One is known as Alpine Joe, the other—'

'Devious Felix,' said Chuffy, with the impeccable timing of a cross-talk comedian.

'Heavens! Are they dangerous, Officer?'

'Not unless provoked, sir. They're pretty furtive, you see, being as they are cat-burglars.'

Chuffy proceeded to give our nonplussed friends a detailed description of the two of us, down to our ties, cufflinks, and the shoebox I was holding.

'Oh, no. We've seen no one like that, Officer. And I'm sure we'd remember if we had. We've got an eye for the uncommon, haven't we, Mabs?'

Mabs nodded, surreptitiously sliding one of her husband's red threes over to her side of the table.

'Well, if you do observe anything out of the ordinary, I'd ask you to telephone Scotland Yard and ask for Inspector—'

'Witherspoon,' I supplied. 'Chief Inspector Witherspoon.'

'Straight away, Officer. And thank you for your vigilance. We feel safer already, don't we, Mabs?'

Mabs nodded, stealthily pinching an extra card from the top of the deck.

'I'm glad, sir,' said Chuffy. 'This is a safe neighbourhood, by and large, though you can't be too careful. Now, might we avail ourselves of your stairs?'

As we left the house I spotted Jeeves parked at the wheel of the trusty Widgeon Seven outside the Nomadical's front door.

'Thank you, Chuffy, that was an amusing, if impoverishing, afternoon. I suppose I'll see you at the Drones on Tuesday?'

'Probably not. I have a feeling Pauline will curtail my clubbing for a week or two.'

'Well then, I'll be saying Abyssinia.'

'Abyssinia!'

I strolled over to the motor, concealed my shoebox in one of the cases lashed to the boot, and jumped into the passenger seat. 'Brinkley Court, Jeeves! And spare neither whip nor spur.'

'Very good, sir.'

We pulled away.

'I say, did you know you were sat outside an illicit gambling den?'

'The Nomadical, sir? Yes, sir.'

'Don't tell me the Junior Ganymede has eyes within that hedgerow as well?'

'One of the chefs, sir, and two of the croupiers. However, given the club's intrinsically peripatetic nature, very few foreign individuals are members, so the intelligence we glean has hitherto been of limited utility.'

'I see. Well, I'm going to doze for a spell. Wake me in the unlikely event anything interesting occurs *en route*.'

An hour or so later there was an occurrence, though it would be stretching your credulity to call it interesting. On the road to Kingston Bagpuize, something towards the business end of the vehicle clumped dramatically. It carried on clumping at irregular intervals for about fifteen miles, before eventually clumping off altogether.

As luck would have it, we ground to a halt directly outside a public house, where we were able to dine unexpectedly well while a mechanic was found to locate the missing part and reattach it with heavy twine and hope. It still clumped, mind you, for the remainder of our now laboriously sluggish journey, and we limped clumping up the gravel drive of Aunt Dahlia's lair sometime after one in the morning.

It is a truth universally acknowledged that Brinkley Court, Brinkley-cum-Snodsfield-in-the-Marsh, is quite the crumpet-dropper.

Were you to pluck from the shelf an illustrated dictionary, and flick idly to the entry for *Home, stately*, I am confident that the hand-coloured engraving accompanying the text would match this dominion down to its buttercream stone and peerless green lawns.

I'm no authority on matters architectural, but there's something in the general blueprint of windows, doors, chimney pots, and gargoyles that elevates the spirit and gladdens the soul. According to Jeeves, a good building should demonstrate 'commodity, firmness, and delight' – all of which Brinkley Court knocks into a cocked hat, even in the dead of night.

The only blot on this otherwise harmonious landscape is the presence of my much-loved, though frequently vexatious, Aunt Dahlia – just as every bridge in Norway is bedevilled by a troll.

While Jeeves hauled the luggage up to our usual quarters, I went in search of a tincture.

Previous midnight quests for refreshment had taught me that the drawing-room would be bereft of cocktail paraphernalia at this dark hour. But I knew from rumour that Uncle Tom kept hidden in the library a cache of strong drink for moments of extreme unction – which usually congregate in early April as the deadline for Income Tax looms.

I browsed the shelves behind his desk until I came across a handsome set of bound editions of the *Temperance Monthly Visitor 1859–1862*. Concealed within the hollowed-out volume for 1860 was, as I had earnestly hoped, a bottle of vintage Armagnac and a small glass tumbler. I poured myself an unstinting measure, raised a toast to the Inland Revenue, and was gazing out across the moonlit croquet lawn when I heard the tell-tale uproar of someone straining every sinew not to make a sound.

As the library door inched cautiously open, I dived behind the sofa.

Looking back on my life, I seem to have spent a goodish slice of it hiding behind various items of furniture. As a result, I consider myself something of an expert in the hazards arising from squeaky floorboards, tripsome rugs, and the sleeping habits of misanthropic Pekinese.

I am regularly asked for advice on country-house concealment by my fellow Dronesmen, indeed it has been suggested that

I pen a slim monograph on the subject under the *nom de plume* 'Ottoman'.

There are, of course, three ways to hide behind a sofa.

First, the Crocodile, where you lie flat on the ground, parallel to the pelmet, so as to minimise any reflection in the French windows behind you.

Second, the Panther, where you crouch on all fours, ready to pounce for freedom straight through the French windows behind you.

And, finally, for seasoned hands only, the Mongoose, where you balance on tiptoe, fingertips on cushion tops, and bob up and down to sneak glances at the goings-on.

Reluctant to abandon my drink, I adopted a Panther-Mongoose hybrid, and began devising an alibi concerning lost collar-studs for the moment the lights were lit and all was discovered. But illumination came there none. Instead, I heard the lifting of the telephone and the dialling of a number. So silent was the night that the ringing tone was clearly audible, as was the Germanic voice that answered.

Jeeves, naturally, devours Goethe in the original black letter, but to me the language is an impossibility of consonants that, once in a while, collide to form the only German I know – the word for 'house of cards'. Fortunately my nameless companion communicated in English, so I was able to grasp one half of the eavesdropped dialogue:

— *Kartenhaus?*

— It's me.

— *Kartenhaus! Kartenhaus, Kartenhaus. Kartenhaus.*

— Yes, perfect reproductions. Impossible to detect.

— *Kartenhaus Kartenhaus?*

— All of the banknotes.

— *Kar! Ten! Haus! ... Kartenhaus?*

— About a fortnight.

— *Kartenhaus?*

— Within reason, as much as we need.

— *Kartenhaus, Kar-tenhaus. Kartenhaus!*

— *Kartenhaus!*

An unseen hand returned the receiver to its cradle, and unseen feet made swiftly for the door.

From the safety of the sofa's dorsal region, I attempted to identify the owner of the voice I had just overheard. It certainly wasn't Uncle Tom, nor was it Seppings, Brinkley Court's venerable butler and the most upright pillar of society one could imagine. I wasn't sure who else was down for the weekend, but one of the guests had an oddly familiar manner of speech.

It was only after I had finished my nightcap, and tiptoed gingerly towards the door, that I detected the lingering odour of Turkish cologne.

SATURDAY

Saturday was as oojah-cum-spiff as a summer's day could be. Not only was the lark on the wing and the snail on the thorn – *comme par ordinaire* – but as far as the eye could see every other member of the animal kingdom was suitably conjoined with its appropriate poetical appurtenance.

I breakfasted in bed, as is my wont in the country, and was smoking an early-morning stinker when Jeeves swam in with a jug of hot water and approached me with the cut-throat.

'Any idea who's down this weekend?' I asked, as he got to work with the foaming brush. 'I've seen not a soul since we arrived.'

'The remaining guests are due later this afternoon, sir. I gather they include Mr Graydon Hogg, who will be accompanied by his wife, and Lord MacAuslan.'

'MacAuslan's coming? Did you know about this?'

'No, sir. Although he and Mr Travers have long been friends.'

'Well, well, well. He's a dark horse. Unlike Hogg, who's just an ass. I wonder why *he* was invited.'

I've known Graydon Hogg MP on and off for decades. He was decent enough at school and when he first joined the Drones, but soon after became preoccupied with self-enrichment, self-promotion, and many other pernicious 'selfs-' beside. Although he affects the courtly pose of an Elizabethan parliamentarian – the words 'whither' and 'methinks' are never far from his lips – money is his true master and politics merely a means of soaping palms and greasing poles.

On the rare occasions Hogg attends the House of Commons, his ambitions are confined to wrecking proceedings with obscure points of order. (His fellow MPs call him 'Whiner the Poo'.) And, infamously, his maiden speech failed even once to mention his East Looe constituency, consisting instead of a litany of slanders against his mother.

All in all, it was odd that Hogg was at Brinkley Court, and odder still that he'd snared himself a wife.

'Who in heaven did Hogg induce to marry him?'

'Miss Tabitha Spode, sir.'

'Tibby? Tibby Spode? Tibby the niece of Roderick Spode? *That* Tibby?'

'Yes, sir. The ceremony was a fortnight ago. Mr and Mrs Hogg are presently touring Worcestershire on honeymoon.'

'And they say romance is dead.'

Tibby is rather a poppet. True, she is related to the abominable Spodeman, but it never does to judge a niece by her uncle; I would certainly object to being judged by my aunts. And, to be fair, Tibby seems always to recoil from Spode's more despotic tendencies while remaining fond of the brute in a 'love-the-sinner-hate-the-sin' sort of way. Which made it all the more inexplicable that she had cast her radiant pearls before a swine like Hogg, who was, if not *echt*-Spodean, certainly far from Spode-sceptic.

The cast list descending on Brinkley Court was undoubtedly intriguing, but it failed to throw any light on last night's *Kartenhaus* oddity in the library. And so I asked Jeeves if he knew of any other visitors who might be lurking in the brushwood.

'I could not say, sir, although several additional guest-rooms have been prepared.' By this time he had dispensed with the blade and was besieging my pores with a hot towel. 'Will there be anything else, sir?'

I was on the verge of disclosing the particulars of my moonlit eavesdropping encounter when caution held my tongue. Having only yesterday been initiated into the Junior Ganymede conspiracy, I resolved to see if I could unravel, single-handed, the curious incident of the dialogue in the night-time.

'I think not, thanks. I plan to take the latest Rex West for a spin in the sunshine, so perhaps just a splash of cologne?'

An hour or so later I was lying doggo in the tall grass, checking the eyelids for holes, when Aunt Dahlia poked me with a croquet mallet.

'Bertie, Bertie, Bertie, idle as ever. Follow me!'

'To the end of the earth,' I yawned, clambering to my feet, and plucking burrs from my trousers.

'Not necessary,' she squawked over her shoulder, 'just to the potting sheds.'

After wending our way through the kitchen garden and past the greenhouses, we arrived at a small, low, red-brick building all set about with apple trees. Aunt Dahlia sprung the heavy rusty padlock with a heavy rusty key, and shoved me unceremoniously inside.

I was immediately engulfed by a miasma of spices, and my instant reaction was to sneeze. And sneeze. And sneeze again.

'Do stop that, Bertie. It's unnecessary and unhygienic.'

'But,' I sneezed, my eyes streaming, 'the air is poisoned!'

'Fiddlesticks! Just a little tamarind, perhaps. Garlic, possibly. Cloves.'

I sneezed again. 'You should sound the gas gong and provide smoke hoods.'

'Don't be so melodramatic. I've been working in here for weeks, and look at me.'

'You're acclimatised.' I sneezed. 'Either that, or you have gills.'

My sneezes continued, much to Aunt Dahlia's annoyance, and it took some time before my eyes had dried sufficiently to take in our surroundings. The dim, airless space in which we stood resembled nothing less than the cell of a bygone apothecary. The shelves were stacked with jars, vials, casks, and flagons, and the benches were crowded with scales, flasks, and funnels, and a rat's nest of clamps, retorts, and tubes. The only anachronism was a jaunty wall calendar promoting motorised lawnmowers. (*The Atco needs but one attendant – an intelligent lad will do!*)

'Been busy, Dr Crippen?'

'As a child at play, Bertie. Don't touch that pestle! In fact, hands in pockets, if you please.'

Aunt Dahlia gripped my shoulders and rotated me clockwise until I was facing a shelf on which she'd arrayed a procession of brightly labelled bottles.

'You recall our conversation about Worcestershire sauce?'

'It clangs a distant clapper.'

'Good. Now, what do you see before you?'

I knew this to be a trick question, but only the obvious was forthcoming: 'Bottles?'

'No, jingle-brains. What you see is *history*.'

'Good-o.'

She picked up a long-handled spoon and, pointing to each product in turn, reeled off their names like a pathologist anatomising a cadaver: 'Coratch Sauce, Halford Sauce, Harvey Sauce, John Bull Sauce, King of Oude Sauce, Quin Sauce, Reading Sauce, Royal Osborne Sauce, Soho Sauce, and Soyer's Sultana Sauce.'

'And that one?' I asked, pointing with my nose to the last in line, since my hands remained confined to my trousers.

She peered at the label. 'Rowland's Macassar Hair Oil ... I can't think how that got there.'

'It's probably delicious.'

'Anyway, *history*. Each of these sauces once challenged the mighty Lea and Perrins, and each of them failed. We, irksome nephew, shall not fail!'

She gripped my shoulders once again, and rotated me counter-clockwise until I was facing a small desk shrouded by a panel of white linen.

'Now, pay attention.' Gently she drew back the cloth to expose a neat row of glass-stoppered jars, elegantly numbered from one to six. 'You see before you, Brinkley Sauce.'

'All of them?'

'One of them.'

'Eh?'

'Each is a different formulation.'

I perked up. 'Oh, is it a game? Like three-card monte?'

'Three-what *what*?' she yapped.

I outlined the elements of 'find the lady' – tracking a card-sharp's legerdemain to pick the queen from betwixt two knaves – and was about to demonstrate the con with three beakers and a walnut shell when Aunt Dahlia rapped my knuckles with her long-handled spoon.

'It's *nothing* like that,' she scolded. 'Well, possibly a little. It's certainly a question of selection, but not selection by chance. Tonight, the recipe for Brinkley Sauce will be chosen by no less an authority than Mr Harold Redmane.'

'Who?'

'Harold Redmane has, for the past twenty-three years, been Lea and Perrins' chief taster.'

'Why on earth would Harold Redmane help the competition?'

Aunt Dahlia sighed. 'He won't know he's helping the competition, you poltroon. He won't even know we *are* the competition. He'll just be a guest tonight for supper—' She stopped abruptly, screwed shut her eyes, and went puce in the dial.

'I say, are you all right?'

She held up a hand and turned to the wall. After an excruciating interval, she sneezed explosively and repeatedly.

'Aha!' I crowed. 'Just a little tamarind, perhaps? Garlic, possibly? Cloves?'

'I don't know what you're talking about, Bertie,' she sniffed, mascara streaming down her cheeks. 'Merely the mildest effects of hay fever. Now, where was I?'

'Supper. *Ce soir.*'

'Ah, yes. Now, listen carefully. Six courses will be served tonight, and each course will make liberal use of one of these versions of Brinkley Sauce. Are you clear?'

'As the cloudless hour.'

'You shall sit next to Mr Redmane and interrogate him closely – but casually, mind – on which of the sauces he likes best, and why.'

'I was wondering when the shoe would drop.'

'The Americans call it "industrial espionage". I read about it in the *Church Times.*'

'And how does the epicurean Anatole feel about all this? Come to think of it, why isn't this vain and deceitful alchemy taking place in his kitchen?'

Aunt Dahlia studied her fingernails, the personification of guilt. 'Anatole is on holiday.'

'Hang on a sec, old fruit. You lured me down here on the distinct promise that Anatole was returned from Grenoble and, quote, "stood ready to give my gluttony free rein".'

'Return-*ing* from Grenoble, I said. Not return-*ed*. If you had worked harder at your English grammar you would grasp the nuance.'

Nuance, my eye! We both knew that Anatole would never tolerate such Frankensteinian meddling in his culinary *sanctum sanctorum.* He very nearly chucked it in when Aunt Dahlia had the audacity to bring home a packet of margarine.

'I thought it prudent to wait until Anatole was safely across the Channel,' she paused, 'before devising these sauces, and tonight's meal.'

'Good God!' This was such a terrifying revelation, I hardly dared seek confirmation. 'You ... *cook?*'

Aunt Dahlia assumed a regal air. 'I supervise, which amounts to much the same thing. The trifling details of chopping and boiling I left to Giovanni.'

'Giovanni? Who he?'

'A temporary chef sent by the agency. Giovanni's been tremendously helpful, if a little bemused. I'm not sure the Italians really *get* Worcestershire sauce. Can't think why. Something to do with the spice route, perhaps? Anyway, Anatole returns tomorrow and will cook for you an especially sybaritic Sunday lunch. In the meantime, tonight's supper needs planning.'

'And why is Giovanni not planning supper?'

'Giovanni left early this morning for a new position in London. But he has assembled all of the sauces, and the staff are presently busy with tonight's menu.'

'So why am I here?'

'To learn about Brinkley Sauce, and prepare yourself for Mr Redmane! Really, Bertie, do you peeve me for sport?'

*　*　*

I left Aunt Dahlia's dark satanic mill in something of a daze, the victim of oxygen starvation, capsicum poisoning, and what I believe sea-divers call the staggers. Rubbing spice into these culinary wounds, I had been press-ganged into a scheme so lame-brained I was almost too ashamed to seek counsel from the Mycroft of Mayfair.

International relations had been strained since late last night, when Jeeves, unpacking the Wooster impedimenta, came upon my new tartan slippers. He said nothing, naturally – that is not his way – but I was not altogether surprised to wake this morning and spy my shoes neatly arranged in the waste-paper basket. The safest place for such disputatious footwear was evidently on my feet.

Indeed, I was wearing the *casus belli* as I entered my room and found my man giving the summer worsteds a good going-over with a stiff brush.

I resolved to give no quarter.

'What-ho, Jeeves. Hard at it?'

'Moderately, sir. The kitchen is under a certain strain with Mr Anatole away, so I assisted Mr Seppings in the cellar with the wine for tonight's supper. I also supervised the mechanic who arrived to repair the motor car.'

'Was it the flywheel?' I guessed the only engine part I know.

Jeeves set about my country brogues with the brown-on-brown-off.

'No, sir.'

'Has anyone else arrived? MacAuslan? Hogg?'

'No, sir.'

He wasn't in the mood for idle banter, that was abundantly clear. Nevertheless, I persisted.

'Jeeves, you won't guess the insanity of Aunt Dahlia's latest half-pie scheme!'

'I fear you may be correct, sir.'

'She's creating a Worcestershire sauce to rival Lea and Perrins.'

'Very good, sir.' The man could be as incurious as a cobblestone.

'She's cooked up six versions, and plans to serve them tonight to the Lea and Perrins chief taster.'

This piqued his interest, and he looked up from his polishing. 'I'm surprised, sir, that any employee of so esteemed a company would be willing to assist Mrs Travers in such an endeavour.'

'That's exactly what I said! But she has lured him here under false whatnots, and he has no idea he's about to commit industrious espionage.'

'I see, sir. How novel.'

'She's all of a flutter, you know. Expects to make her fortune.'

'While I admire Mrs Travers' enthusiasm, sir, I do not foresee Lea and Perrins being unduly perturbed by the competition.'

'Neither do I. But – here's the biscuit – what if she has, in fact, scenarioed the perfect Worcestershire sauce. What then?'

There's a moment when you know you've disappointed Jeeves. He conceals it, of course, like the hardy perennial he is, but I can always tell when the pressure gauge drops a millibar or two.

'Assuming, sir, that Mrs Travers has indeed created a Worcestershire sauce to equal or surpass Lea and Perrins ...' he paused to let the absurdity of the idea marinade '... there are other significant hurdles.'

'Such as?'

'It would require some time to research the subject in detail, sir, but offhand, I might suggest: sourcing and importing raw ingredients, industrial manufacture, bottling, labelling, ware-housing, distribution, advertising, domestic sales, foreign sales, defending inevitable legal challenges, obtaining a Royal Warrant, and finally, sir, naming the product.'

'Oh, she's got the name! She's going to call it Brinkley Sauce.'

'In which case, sir, her success is assured.'

'I know, I know. It's completely doolally. What's worse, I am to be the ventriloquist's dummy in her cockeyed venture – unless you can think of a way to unpuppet me?'

He glanced down at my slippers. 'Nothing springs immedi-ately to mind, sir, but I shall give the matter my full attention.'

'Right-ho. Well, as aunts bid, nephews serve.'

'So I have observed, sir.'

We were interrupted by a terrific hammering on the door, as if a raid by the Keystone Kops had been set to the music of Wagner.

'Who is it?' I trilled.

'It's me, you simpleton.'

'Do you have a warrant?'

'I'm coming in, and so help me God, you had better be decent.'

The handle turned, and in flew an aunt.

'It's a calamity,' Dahlia blurted, before seeing we were not alone. 'Oh, hullo, Jeeves, I didn't know you were here, although I'm frightfully glad you are.'

'Good morning, Mrs Travers.'

'The calamity?' I asked. 'That justifies this deplorable violation of sanctuary?'

'He's back!' she yawped.

'Who?'

'Anatole!'

'I thought he was returning tomorrow?'

'Well, that's what I thought he said, but with that accent ...'

'If you had worked harder at your French vocabulary you would have grasped the nuance.'

'This is not the time for asinine quips, Bertie. Anatole has just telephoned from the station because there was no car to collect him and, heavens, is he upset! What's more, he says he's looking forward to meeting Giovanni. It seems they've been corresponding.'

'But you said Giovanni left this morning.'

'Just after breakfast. And that's not the worst of it. When Anatole discovers tonight's little supper, he will walk out never to return, quite possibly followed by your uncle.'

'What would you have us do?'

'Something. Anything. I've dispatched Waterbury to collect him in the Rolls, which gives us about twenty minutes to come up with some kind of plan.'

'Well—'

'Not you, buttinski – Jeeves! Any thoughts, Jeeves? I assume dunderhead here has snitched my plans for Brinkley Sauce?'

'Mr Wooster was kind enough to share some of the particulars concerning your most intriguing venture, madam.'

I deflected Aunt Dahlia's tut-mouthed disapproval with the merest of shrugs. I mean to say, if Jeeves can't be trusted with the family silver then life would indeed be nasty, brutish, and short.

'If I grasp the matter correctly, madam, it seems there are three intersecting objectives. The first, to keep concealed both Brinkley Sauce and the preparations for tonight's meal. The second, to engineer some kind of encounter with the now-departed Mr Giovanni. And the third, to ensure Mr Anatole remains effectively absent until tomorrow morning.'

Aunt Dahlia groaned like a sat-upon accordion. 'It sounds even more hopeless when you list it like that.'

Jeeves gave a contemplative frown. 'I wonder, madam, did Mr Anatole ever meet Mr Giovanni?'

'Is this really relevant?' I asked. 'Time ticks by.'

'It is axiomatic, sir.'

'No,' said Aunt Dahlia, 'they never met. Everything was arranged through the agency, and Anatole left for France the day before Giovanni arrived.'

'That is providential, madam. And would I be correct in assuming that Mr Giovanni is an Italian gentleman?'

'He could hardly be more Italian. He's from Venice and never stopped singing about gondolas, at least that's what it sounded like to me. His accent is thicker than Anatole's.'

Jeeves turned to me with a speculative look, and the fog suddenly cleared.

'Oh, no. Categorically not. It's entirely absurd, unreasonably humiliating, and it couldn't possibly work.'

'What couldn't work, Bertie?'

'Jeeves wants me to pretend to be Giovanni.'

'Brilliant!' Aunt Dahlia declared. 'Why didn't I think of that?'

'Because it's not brilliant, it's complete and utter lunacy. An absolute no go. Anatole has known me for years and he won't be fooled for a second.'

'If I may be permitted to disagree, sir, there are several points in our favour. First, Mr Anatole does not expect you to be at Brinkley Court, and so the comparison will not suggest itself. Second, Mr Giovanni's strong Venetian accent will add a useful element of what stage magicians call "misdirection". And third, given the undeviating and encompassing nature of a chef's uniform, we will need only to disguise your face.'

'Jeeves, if you say the word "moustache" I will not be held responsible for my actions.'

'No, sir. Even if I thought a counterfeit mystacinous hairpiece would be expedient, I am far from confident we could locate such an item in the time presently before us.'

'So, what do you suggest?'

'A pair of spectacles, sir.'

'That's it? That's the alpha and omega of your proposed disguise?'

'Yes, sir, assuming they are of a sufficiently unusual and distracting design.'

'*Hoick halloo!*' yawped Aunt Dahlia, with the wild euphoria of one who, while galloping destructively across a tenant farmer's potato field, has sighted, in the far distance, Reynard tucking into a spot of tiffin in the henhouse. 'The new under-gardener has a very peculiar pair of glasses. He lost an eye, you see, so one of the discs is completely black.'

'That sounds ideal, madam. When did he enter your employment?'

'Last week, why?'

'In which case, madam, Mr Anatole will not have met him. Do you know if he is working today?'

'He was knee-deep in the rhubarb a little earlier.'

Someone brainy once observed that war is first impossible and then inevitable – and something depressingly similar was coming to a head in my bedroom. The speed and certainty with which Jeeves's preposterous scheme had unfolded meant that my participation was all but inescapable – but I'd be dashed if I was facing the enemy alone.

'And how will *you* be helping, aunt o' mine? This is, after all, a calamity entirely of your construction.'

'How kind of you to remind me, Bertie. What *will* I be doing, Jeeves?'

'Your role, madam, will be to direct the kitchen staff in concealing all traces of tonight's meal.'

'Concealing them where? The kitchen is preparing six courses in quantities sufficient to deluge a small village. This is hardly something we can kick under the rug.'

'Might I suggest the stable blocks, madam, which afford ample space and provide little incentive for Mr Anatole to visit?'

I began to object, when Aunt Dahlia reached out and placed her hand over my mouth. 'We haven't time for your not-at-all-ing, Bertie. A maniacal Frenchman is approaching at speed, and if you want to taste his *Nonnettes de poulet Agnès Sorel* ever again, I suggest you shut up and jump to it.'

We divided to conquer. Aunt Dahlia descended to the kitchens to orchestrate the exodus; Jeeves went in search of the monocular under-gardener; and I hastened to the laundry room to get my hands on some chef's whites and one of those amusingly towering hats.

The kitchen of Brinkley Court is a cavernous, cream-tiled room, with a majestic iron range and more pots, pans, spoons, and tongs than you can imagine anyone using in a lifetime. There are three entrances. To the south, double doors give out to the kitchen garden. To the north, a green-baize swing door leads to the main house. And to the west, a frosted-glass door opens into a labyrinth of pantries, storerooms, cold rooms, and offices.

The first to arrive, I found the place empty and spotless, although with a forbidding stench of curried fish. Soon after, Aunt Dahlia entered from the kitchen garden, vermilion-faced and puffing, and Jeeves swung in through the green-baize door holding a pair of spectacles.

'Are those the gig-lamps?'

'Yes, sir. I'm afraid Herbert is considerably incommoded without them.'

I saw why as soon as I put them on. The left eye was completely opaque, and the right had a lens so thick that it reduced my sight to a series of dizzying, coloured blurs. Only by blinking for extended periods could I hope to remain vertical.

'I told Waterbury to signal when he was at the gates,' said Aunt Dahlia and, as if in reply, a stately honk announced itself and we were soon treated to the luxurious percussion of Silver Ghost crunching across gravel.

'You and I should be leaving now, madam,' said Jeeves. 'And don't forget, sir, that because Mr Giovanni hails from northern Italy, you should be careful not to overstress the double consonants in phrases like *un piatto di risotto* or *un cucchiaio di zucchero*.'

'Wait, *what*? You speak Italian? Why aren't *you* playing Giovanni?'

But Jeeves had already swung Aunt Dahlia out through the green-baize door, and I found myself standing alone.

Seconds later, Anatole stormed in from the kitchen garden. If he'd been waxy at the train station, he was positively incandescent now. '*Where* is my staff?' he shouted. '*What* is that disgusting *odeur*? And *who*, monsieur, are *you*?'

I took a deep breath, and launched in.

'*I am Giovanni!*' I ululated in the most Italian accent I could conceive, throwing my hands into the air for good measure.

Anatole stopped in his tracks. His face broke into a wide smile of welcome and his soup-strainer moustache visibly quivered

with joy. We embraced. By which I mean he embraced me –
though the effect was similarly engulfing.

'Ah, *mon brave!*' he boomed. 'Please, *je m'excuse*, Monsieur
Giovanni! I am so late, and there was no car, and so ... *bof!*'

'It is an honour to meet the *famoso* Signor Anatole.'

'Monsieur, you are *trop gentil*. Anatole, like you, is a humble
seeker of the culinary knowledge.'

Unable to think of anything in Italian or English that would
serve as a reply, I bowed deeply – an act, I instantly discovered,
that did little to improve my vertigo.

Anatole put his arm around my shoulder. 'Please to tell me,
Monsieur Giovanni, is there anything I can taste? I am thinking
you have many specialities of the Veneto?'

'Oh, er, *sì, sì.*'

'*Baccalà mantecato? Seppie al nero? Sarde in saor?* And *bien sûr*,
the famous *Fegato alla veneziana?* I must savour all things! Give
please to me *every* dish.'

I had been wrong to doubt Jeeves. His artfully simple disguise had hoodwinked Anatole completely, although it was
making me decidedly seasick. I started to mumble something
about macaroni, gesticulating wildly and aimlessly, when, like
a guardian angel, Seppings emerged through the swing door.

'Welcome back, Mr Anatole,' he said gravely. 'There is an
urgent telephone call for you on the house line.'

Anatole stamped his foot like a thwarted child. '*Mon dieu*,
Monsieur Seppings! We cannot be intruded. We are at working.
Who dares to dislocate Anatole?'

'It's Mr Bertram Wooster, he's calling from London.'

This was unforeseen.

'Monsieur Bertie?' Anatole threw up his hands in Gallic indignation. '*Sacrebleu!* You will *excusez-moi*, Monsieur Giovanni. There is no resting the wicked. *Absolument* no resting!'

As soon as Seppings had guided Anatole into the house, Jeeves entered from the garden. I whipped off my glasses, and steadied myself against a table.

'What the devil is going on, Jeeves?'

'I will be happy to elucidate matters to your complete satisfaction at a more opportune moment, sir. However it is imperative that you speak to Mr Anatole without delay.'

He led me through the pantry door, past various larders and linen rooms, into Anatole's office where a telephone sat in the centre of a cluttered desk. Jeeves fiddled with a switch and handed me the receiver.

'What am I supposed to be calling about?' I hissed, but before Jeeves could reply, Anatole came on the line.

'Hullo there, Anatole! ... Yes, that's right, Bertie here, *bonjour* ... Yes ... No ... Well, you know, I burn the occasional slice of toast! ... That's right ... What do I need? Well ...'

Jeeves mimed the act of eating while dancing on the spot.

'A dinner party ... Yes, I'm hosting ...'

Jeeves shook his head vigorously and mimed stirring a pot.

'Not hosting, actually, so much as cooking ... I know! ... Yes ... Well, not *that* funny, surely? ... I see, yes ... Ha, ha, ha ... Tonight? ... Er ...'

Jeeves nodded.

'Tonight ... How many for ...?'

Jeeves held up six fingers.

'Six ... Yes, nothing elaborate, but important to get things right ... Now my question is – *my question is?*'

Jeeves mimed breaking eggs.

'Eggs? ... It's about eggs ...'

Jeeves shivered dramatically.

'Should they be chilled, or ...'

Jeeves gestured airily around us.

'... room temperature? ... Yes, room temperature! ... For what dish? ... Good question ... For ...?'

Jeeves wobbled his hand equivocally.

'May ...?'

He placed a hand on his head and pointed at his face.

'On? ... Nose? ... May-on-nose ... Oh, yes, *mayonnaise*! Should the eggs be chilled or room temperature for mayonnaise? ... Ah, I see ... Yes ... Very good ... And the oil? ... Excellent ... Very slowly ... Right ... From a height ... Good ... Is there anything else, you ask ... Let me think ...'

Jeeves shook his head.

'No, that's everything ... Yes ... Thank you, Anatole. Sorry to disturb.'

Jeeves waved his hand and pointed urgently to the wall calendar.

'Oh, hang on ... I'm coming down tomorrow ... Brinkley Court, that's right ... Sunday lunch ... Yes, splendid ... Toodle-pip ... No, thank *you*.'

I put down the phone.

'Very cunning, Jeeves. Very cunning indeed.'

'I considered it a useful insurance, sir. In case he recognised you, or had cause to question your identity later.'

'Later?'

'At some point in the future, sir.'

We returned to the kitchen to find a strange little rotund man, dressed like a gamekeeper, glancing about the room with a perplexed look.

'Hullo?' I ventured, slipping back on my glasses. 'Can I help?'

He scrutinised me quizzically. 'You are Anatole?'

Before I'd fathomed who I was supposed to be, he flung his arms into the air and shrieked, '*I am Giovanni!*'

I glanced at Jeeves, who looked as thoroughly punch-drunk as I felt, and realised there was nothing to be done but muster my French and press on.

'*Oui*, Monsieur Giovanni, *je suis Anatole!* It is *mon plaisir* to meet you *finalement*. But why have you *retourné* so soon?'

'*Mi scusi*, Signor Anatole! *Sono pazzo!* I am forgetting my recipe books. I drive almost to London, and then *mi ricordo!* I leave them *in ufficio*. And they are so precious to me, *come i bambini* – like the little babies.'

'I say, Jee—'

'Jefferies,' corrected Jeeves, firmly, 'and Mr Seppings is upstairs.'

'Er, *oui*, Jefferies, could you *aider* Monsieur Giovanni *avec* his recipes in *le bureau*?'

'Certainly, Mr Anatole. Mr Giovanni, would you care to follow me?'

Jeeves escorted Giovanni into the pantry, giving me just enough time to take a breath before Anatole roared back through the baize.

'The English *milords!*' He tapped his head, furiously. 'Always the craziness. *Always!*'

'Er, *oui*, no, I mean, *sì*.'

'Monsieur Bertie, he cannot even boil the water! And tonight he prepares the supper meal for six! *Incroyable!*'

This was, I felt, a little unkind. 'But he is a good man, no, Signor Bertie?'

'*Bien sûr!* Monsieur Bertie is *très gentil*. But a chef? No! Anatole must say: NEVER!'

I heard footsteps and feared Jeeves might be returning with the genuine Giovanni. Instead, Seppings emerged through the swing door, bearing a silver tray with two flutes of champagne.

'Mrs Travers sent these down to welcome you back, Mr Anatole, and to thank Mr Giovanni for his help this past fortnight.'

'Ahhh, Madame Travers!' sighed Anatole, tenderly. 'She is so much the English *milady*, no?'

'Oh, absolutely, I mean, er, *certo*.'

Anatole took a glass and raised it towards me in a toast. '*À votre santé*, Monsieur Giovanni.'

Seppings glared at me with intense alarm, and I somehow guessed his meaning.

'Wait! Signor Anatole, it is the Italian *tradizione* to swap glasses for *salute*.'

'*Est-ce vrai?* I did not know of this!'

'Oh, *sì*, it is, er ... a sign of trust.'

'Ah, *oui*, the trust. So important *dans la cuisine*, I think.'

We swapped glasses.

'*Cin-cin*, Signor Anatole.'

'*Santé*, Monsieur Giovanni.'

I glanced at Seppings, who tilted back his head like a turtle coming up for air. This time his insinuation was obvious, and I depleted my glass in a gulp. Anatole, politely, followed my lead and shortly thereafter slid unconscious to the floor.

'Is he dead, Seppings? Have you killed him? This seems a little excessive, even for an aunt. And it rather renders her libretto null and void.'

'He's resting, sir. Mrs Travers fortified his champagne with a triple dose of her sleeping draught.'

'Ah, the old Mickey Finn! It's a good thing we swapped glasses. I suppose it would have spoiled the effect to label one of them "Drink Me".'

'Indeed, sir. We estimate he will sleep for about fourteen hours.'

An emphatic clearing of a throat warned us that Jeeves was approaching from the office, but there was nothing Seppings or I could do to conceal Anatole's shallow-breathing carcass.

Giovanni entered first, clutching his recipe books with paternal pride. He took one look at the crumpled corpse, and emitted a high-pitched scream.

'But who is this, Seppings? Is he *morto*?'

Seppings is a sound chap, and a first-rate butler, but not exactly nimble in the art of dissembling. So when it comes to jinks of almost any height, he's rather prone to stare like an owl and bray like a mule.

'He's er ... er ... er—'

'Drunk,' intercepted Jeeves. 'Exceedingly drunk. It's Mrs Travers' nephew, Mr Bertram Wooster. A sad case, Mr Giovanni. Tragic, really.'

How sharper than a serpent's tooth, I thought, to have a treasonous servant.

'Mr Wooster drinks.' Jeeves mimed the act of imbibing. 'And he dresses up. Periodically, as you can see, he drinks *and* dresses up.'

'Ah, *sì*, I have heard of Signor Bertie.' Giovanni turned to me, rotating his index finger against his temple. 'The *inglesi*, Signor Anatole. All of them *sono veramente pazzi*.'

'Well, absolutely, *oui*!' I replied, frantically searching for any remaining scraps of my prep-school French. '*La plume de ma tante*, and all that.'

Clearly deciding that enough was as good as a feast, Jeeves stepped forward and took control. 'Mr Anatole, would you help me carry Mr Wooster to his room? And Mr Seppings, will you show Mr Giovanni to his car?'

I stood waiting for something to happen before remembering that, in Act IV of this ridiculous panto, I was playing the part of Anatole.

'Ah! *Oui*, Monsieur Jefferies, a *bonne idée*. Monsieur Giovanni, it was a *grand plaisir* to meet you. I bid you *au revoir*.'

'And it was *un grande piacere* for me, Signor Anatole. *Arrivederci!*'

Seppings escorted Giovanni out into the kitchen garden and closed the door firmly behind him.

'I drink, Jeeves? I dress up? *Et tu*, valet?'

'I am sorry about that, sir. I considered identifying Mr Anatole as your cousin, Mr Bonzo Travers, but could not be sure that Mr Giovanni had not made his acquaintance. Since I was certain he had never met you, I considered it expedient to avail myself of such a liberty.'

'Dash it, Jeeves! Why didn't you just invent a name? Is that not what "Smith" is for?'

'Possibly, sir. However, I am of the opinion that verisimilitude cannot be overestimated in ventures such as this. Furthermore, as it was possible that Mr Giovanni had heard your name during the course of his employment, I judged he might be reassured.'

'Reassured? By an unconscious inebriate collapsed in the middle of his kitchen?'

I was on the brink of furnishing Jeeves with a brief but meaningful discourse on biting the hand that feeds when Aunt Dahlia's head popped round the garden door.

'Is the coast clear?'

'Yes, madam.'

'And Anatole's out for the count?'

'Soundly, madam.'

'*Tally-ho!*' And in she marched followed by the massed ranks of kitchen and garden staff, all of whom, except for her, were burdened like beasts with the doings for supper.

Jeeves and I hoisted Anatole to his feet, and were manhandling him towards the green-baize door, when into the room swung a haze of Turkish cologne.

'Good God!' exclaimed Sir Gilbert Skinner. 'Is he dead?'

'No, sir,' said Jeeves serenely, as if lugging a cadaver was all in a day's toil – which, come to think of it, for him it rather was. 'Merely very tired.'

Sir Gilbert could not have cared less. 'I've been pressing the button for what seems like days. I assume the bells actually work in this place?'

'May I be of assistance, sir?'

'Did you plan to serve lunch today?'

'Lunch!' squawked Aunt Dahlia, emerging from the midst of the assembled confusion. 'I'd completely forgotten about lunch. Please forgive me. As you can see, things here are a little confused. A cold collation will be laid out in the Blue Room in about half an hour. I do hope that's not too informal for you? But I assure you that supper tonight will be a banquet of Tudor proportions!'

'It will have to do, won't it?' Sir Gilbert pouted. 'And, *if* it is not too much to ask, and *if* everyone's had a good night's sleep, might I possibly have a brandy and soda in the drawing-room?' And before anyone could reply, he left.

I turned to Aunt Dahlia. 'What, pray tell, is *he* doing here?'

'Sir Gilbert? He's here to see your uncle about some silver. Why?'

'I think the least you could do is warn a chap he's spending the weekend with his bank manager. Thank God he didn't recognise me.'

It took Jeeves and me quite some effort to haul Anatole up to his room, and we were on the brink of success when Uncle Tom ambled upon us.

'Heavens, Jeeves! Is he dead?'

'No, sir. Mr Anatole is simply exhausted.'

Uncle Tom nodded sympathetically. 'France can be a strain.' He turned to me with a friendly smile. 'I'm sorry, I don't think we've met.'

This was yet another vote of confidence in Jeeves's spectacular disguise, but once again I was left swimming for a reply. I obviously wasn't Anatole, and I couldn't be Giovanni, whom Uncle Tom was bound to have met, but who else might I be, dressed in whites and heaving about a comatose chef?

Fortunately, Uncle Tom noticed my eyewear and put two and two together. 'Forgive me, it's Herbert, isn't it? Kind of you to step out of the garden and pitch in with supper.'

With no idea of how Herbert spoke, I reached for my trusty West Country accent, which, quibbling ears have complained, sometimes contains the faintest traces of pirate.

'Arrr, that be so, m'lord. I be 'Erbert, at ye service. Always a tacket to come in from them roobarbs to coddle in the skunner-room.'

'Good, good. Glad to hear it,' said Uncle Tom, hiding his bafflement commendably. 'Any danger of lunch in the not-too-distant?'

* * *

The guests for supper crowded around at seven for drinks in the drawing-room. I stole in at a quarter past, and was hunting around for the cocktail caboodle when Seppings stepped up with a tray.

'Sherry, sir?'

'Just sherry?'

'Yes, sir.'

'Nothing a drop more *spiritual*?'

'I'm sorry, sir. Not tonight.'

I took a sip and was instantly entranced. 'I say, Seppings, are you quite sure this ambrosia is sherry?'

'Yes, sir. A 1775 Frontera.'

'Lawks! 1775? Nearly as prehistoric as Uncle Tom, what!'

'Sir is very droll.'

Equipped with my schooner of sunbeams, and spying a full decanter recklessly unattended on a side-table, the evening began to brighten. And then someone kicked me.

'Do stand up straight, Bertie. You slouch like a weeping willow.'

'And good evening to you, most heartless of aunts.'

'Are you ready for the off?'

'Champing at the bit.'

She eyed my almost empty glass like a Borgia calculating dosage. 'Not drinking too much, I hope. I require from you a clear head and a legible hand. Where is your pen?'

I took out my silver pencil and Excalibured it aloft. 'The brave man with a sword.'

'Really, Bertie, I wish you wouldn't quote Oscar Wilde. In case you haven't noticed, there's a clergyman present and The Reverend Prebendary David Miller does not take kindly to anti-scriptural innuendo.'

'I spied the gospel-grinder. But where is my dinner companion, Archbishop Lea and Perrins?'

Aunt Dahlia gestured towards a diminutive man in a rumpled, mismatched suit conversing with Uncle Tom.

'He doesn't look like a chief taster,' I observed.

'Oh, really? And how, in your superior judgement, ought a chief taster to look?'

'I was expecting a hungry, lean-faced villain. This chap resembles the traveller from an antique land.'

'Where you see antiques, Bertie, I see experience. And a palette refined by decades of sniffs, sips, and swirls. You mustn't be so superficial, it will lead you astray.' She peered at him through her pince-nez. 'That said, I did expect him to be wearing a dinner jacket.'

'Who's being superficial now?'

She gave me a contemptuous look. 'Dressing for dinner is far from superficial, Bertie. It is the bedrock of civilised society.'

'... As Oscar Wilde might have said. Where on earth did you meet this taster crumb?'

'At the Bull and Bush public house, opposite the Lea and Perrins factory.'

'*You*, Queen of Sheba, went drinking in a workmen's boozer?'

'I did, for that is where the workmen are. He was in the public bar, naturally, but I struck up a conversation, lured him into the saloon, and invited him to dine.'

'How did you know who "he" was?'

'I set Seppings on his trail. You'd be amazed how good butlers are at ferreting out intelligence.'

A quick scan of her features reassured me that her observation was utterly absent of guile – nevertheless, I deemed it prudent to change the subject at speed. 'Shall I go and make nice with this sipper extraordinaire? Set the wheels in motion, and all that?'

'No, not yet. You'll exhaust your meagre ration of small talk before the meal has begun. Why don't you go and introduce yourself to Lord MacAuslan. He's over there, in the kilt.'

'I know MacAuslan,' I said. 'He used to employ Jeeves. But who's that with him? His daughter?'

'Niece, actually. Smart girl. Too smart for you, anyway. Off you pop, and go easy with the sherry. I have my beady eye on you.'

I set off to reacquaint myself with his lordship when I was waylaid by Graydon Hogg.

'Bertie! Well met. I was told you might be here.'

'What-ho, Graydon. I gather congratters are in order?'

'They are indeed, permit me to introduce the little lady—'

Tibby interrupted him. 'Oh, Bertie and I go way back!'

'Do you?' He was put out.

'Into the dim-and-distant,' I tormented, pecking Tibby's cheek with modest affection. 'So, Graydon, is the Commons keeping you busy?'

'Well, Parliament is still in recess, but there's always constituency work to be catching up on.'

I resisted the temptation to guffaw.

'Although,' he continued, 'strictly *entre nous*, I'm thinking of resigning the Whip and sitting as an independent Black Short.'

I was shocked. 'Aren't they a little *repugnant*?'

'Oh, no, not in the slightest. The Black Shorts are much misunderstood, methinks. They're not as "dangerous" or "threatening" as the newspapers pretend – they just have common-sense policies for what's great for Great Britain. You should hear Lord Sidcup orate – he's uncommonly persuasive.'

I glanced at Tibby, whose social smile was melting from Mona Lisa ambiguity into what Jeeves once informed me was the 'existential anguish of Edvard Munch's *Scream*'.

Thankfully, Hogg brought these grim proceedings to a halt.

'I hate to be rude, sirrah, but I must just seek a private audience with your uncle. Can I leave you alone for a sec?'

And, without condescending to acknowledge his wife, he departed.

'So, then, Tibby. Wedded bliss. How is the first flush of married life?'

'You know. Joyous.'

She sounded not at all convinced, and the Wooster soul ached a little with fellow-feeling.

'But how did it happen? The last time we met you were engaged to that lovely Irish poet. The one who insisted on rhyming "Siobhan" with "hand-spun yarn".'

'Ruaidhrí? He *was* lovely, wasn't he? I even got used to his verse. But you know how these things unfold: Graydon was mad keen, Uncle Roderick was mad keen, I was keen enough. And then, almost before I knew it, the "Wedding March" was ringing out, and I was doing the "I do's".'

'Is he serious about this Black Short stuff?'

'Graydon? I don't know. He seems to be. He's surprisingly close to Uncle Roderick, closer than I've ever been, at least on the subject of politics.' She enunciated this final word with something approaching a shiver.

'Doesn't this *Heil, Spode*-ing distress you?'

'You have no idea. But, look, if I can dilute Graydon, and Graydon can dilute Uncle Roderick, then maybe things will calm down a little.'

'Does that seem likely?'

'I'm not sure.' She looked apprehensive. 'What else is to be done?'

From across the room Graydon snapped his fingers, like an oik summoning a sommelier.

Tibby sighed. 'I have to go, Bertie. Perhaps we can have a chat sometime? Just the two of us?'

'But of course. You have only to holler.'

Lord MacAuslan was quite a sight. His interpretation of evening clothes suitable for a country supper was dramatically more ceremonial than anyone else's, including Seppings'. He had on a green velvet doublet with silver buttons, a long dress kilt (presumably in MacAuslan tartan), a lace jabot, a silver-chained sporran, and silk garters with knee-length hose, into which a lethal-looking staghorn *sgian-dubh* was tucked. It was as if he'd just stepped off a bottle of single malt, something I would have gladly dived into after my mournful encounter with Graydon and Tibby.

'Good evening, Mr Wooster,' Lord MacAuslan said, extending his hand in welcome. 'What a pleasant surprise to see you again after so many years.'

'Oh, yes, absolutely. Such a long time.'

'Permit me to introduce my niece, Iona MacAuslan.'

'How do you do, Mr Wooster,' she said, in an accent as charmingly Scottish as her uncle's.

'Oh, please, call me Bertie, Miss MacAuslan. Almost everybody does.'

'Then you must call me Iona.'

Iona, it must be said, was a deep breath of Highland air. Tall, dark, and constructed along the aerodynamic lines of a sports car, she had the no-nonsense look of one who, when the mood took her, was prepared to indulge a certain amount of nonsense.

In contrast to her uncle, she was dressed with beguiling simplicity in a floor-length gown stitched from a silver fabric that managed simultaneously to reflect and absorb the light – not unlike her sparkling, soft grey eyes.

'Do you live at Brinkley Court, Bertie?' Iona asked.

'Heavens no! I am merely an occasional inmate, jailed by my aunt for crimes unknown.'

'I am similarly persecuted by uncles,' she frowned.

Lord MacAuslan nodded emphatically.

'Surely,' I protested, 'aunts are a terror far greater than uncles? I seem to have dozens of both, and have repeatedly found that—'

She finished my thought: '—the female of the species is more meddling than the male?'

'Precisely!'

'You could be right, I suppose, but having only uncles …' She shrugged.

'Might I be permitted to defend myself, and the noble cause of uncledom?' asked Lord MacAuslan.

'Certainly not,' Iona smiled. 'That would take all the fun out of it.'

'Kewcee is very cruel to her uncle,' Lord MacAuslan explained. 'She's quite like an aunt, in that respect.'

'Kewcee?' I asked.

'It's because I'm in silk,' Iona said.

'You're a barrister?' I was getting confused.

'She's teasing you, Mr Wooster. She's a photographer. Kewcee is no more than a family nickname.'

Iona blushed, charmingly. I changed the subject, gallantly.

'So what brings you to Brinkley Court?' I asked. 'Photography?'

'Sport, actually.'

'Huntin', shootin', fishin'?'

'Flyin'.'

'Flyin'?'

'Aeroplanes.' She pointed to the ceiling. 'Big metal birds. In the sky. Surely you've seen them, Bertie. They're extremely hard to miss.'

'You *flew* to Brinkley Court? How magnificent. For how long have you been dodging the clouds?'

'Some years now. Whenever the chance arises and the weather permits.'

'I suppose it's devilishly complicated?'

'Can you drive a car?'

'I can. Is it much like driving a car?'

'Not really, now I think about it. But it's a start. I could take you up one day, if you'd like?'

'That would be capital.'

'We could hop over the silver streak for lunch in Le Touquet?'

'Include me in.'

My attention was diverted by Sir Gilbert Skinner, who had just entered the room wearing a billowing velvet cape over his dinner jacket.

'Do you know that man?' I asked Lord MacAuslan.

'Of course! That Vandyke of his follows you round the room like the eyes in an oil painting.'

He was referring to Sir Gilbert's pointed beard – the kind of face-fuzz that the owner assumes looks racy and devil-may-care, but which everyone else knows requires hours of daily topiary. In Sir Gilbert's case, the snow-white goatee served only to draw one's gaze to the extraordinary divot atop his head, which was an optimistically youthful shade of treacle.

I was about to divulge my misgivings about Sir Gilbert, when Seppings cudgelled the dinner gong and conversation ceased.

'I'm looking forward to supper,' Iona whispered into my ear. 'I hear the chef is something of a virtuoso.'

Before I could disclose the awful truth, Aunt Dahlia barged in. She grabbed Lord MacAuslan, pushed Uncle Tom towards Iona, and led the procession into the dining-room. The rest of us crocodiled along behind, and stalked round the six-yard-long table to locate our place cards.

We were thirteen at dinner, which should have been an omen.

Aunt Dahlia had deliberately invited an odd number of guests so that I could be inconspicuously sat next to Mr Redmane without upsetting the conventional interleaving of the sexes.

Before each setting stood a menu that, in a break with Brinkley Court tradition, had been typed out in English.

I have rarely seen a more threatening document.

Mock Turtle Soup Madras
Devilled Lobster Rissoles
Stewed Tench
Broiled Sheep's Kidneys Ceylon
Curried Fowl with Calcutta Artichokes
Burmese Rarebit

An unease descended on the room as the assembled company read of its fate, and Uncle Tom, who had evidently forgotten his secret briefing, captured the prevailing despair: 'Good heavens, darling, this is strong stuff! Is it Lent?'

Aunt Dahlia forced a smile, and signalled urgently to the footmen for our wine glasses to be filled right up to the brim and, if necessary, beyond.

When Prebendary Miller appointed himself to say grace, he unconsciously spoke for us all: 'For what we are about to receive, may the good Lord save our souls.'

Despite the torrent of wine that poured, the meal refused to flow. The ferocious heat of the sauces in which every dish was drowned rendered conventional conversation almost impossible. Graydon Hogg, accustomed as he was to dominating proceedings, dominated proceedings – and the rest of us were happy to sit back and let him drone on. All except for Aunt Dahlia, that is, who sent up a barrage of discursive balloons, each of which floated limply away on eddies of embarrassed silence.

Spirits buoyed during the brief inter-course ceasefires, when our plates were cleared and endless jugs of iced water delivered. But the mercury quickly plunged whenever a fresh dish appeared, smothered in a different but equally vindictive sauce. There was an almost continuous shuffling of knives and forks as mounds of inedible food were concealed under the cutlery, and the less-inhibited guests fanned themselves with menus, as if waving white flags of surrender.

Adding oenological insult to culinary injury, the wines that Uncle Tom had been coaxed into unlocking from the inner cellar might as well have been spiked with gall. So caustic were Aunt Dahlia's creations that some of France's most historic vintages were reduced to little more than ruinously expensive vinegar: a 1914 Bollinger, an 1864 Lafite, and an 1811 d'Yquem. Poor Tom, for whom each bottle was a beloved child, was visibly bereft.

The only person to enjoy himself was Mr Redmane, who ate every mouthful of every dish and, to the genuine horror of everyone present, asked for second helpings of the stewed tench.

I was seated at the far end of the table, well below where the salt would have been had the cruet not been banished to safeguard the innocence of our palates. Aunt Dahlia's motive for this *placement* was presumably to draw from her any suspicion my interrogations might arouse in Mr Redmane. Of course, it also meant that she was well out of conversational earshot, and obliged, therefore, to rely on our facial expressions to gauge the progress of her scheme.

At increasingly frequent intervals she craned her head round the candelabra to beam me enquiring stares, raised eyebrows, and urgent pencilling gestures. But, separated as we were down a two-putt of mahogany, there was little I could do to satisfy her curiosity, which became ever more insatiable as the funeral dragged on.

My strict instructions had been to monopolise Mr Redmane, ascertain his views on every dish, and discreetly jot down any pearls of wisdom he chanced to drop. And so, after each course, I peppered him with the questions Aunt Dahlia had prepared: *Too salty? Too sour? Too sweet? Too bitter? Insufficient paprika? Excess anchovy? A pinch more asafoetida? A touch less garam masala?*

To each enquiry, Mr Redmane furrowed his brow, thought for a moment, and replied: 'Toothsome.'

The soup was 'toothsome'.

The rissoles were 'toothsome'.

The stewed tench was 'particularly toothsome'.

Perhaps, I thought, Mr Redmane had tumbled our game. Or perhaps he was just a man of crippling professional modesty. In any event, after the broiled sheep's kidneys, I gave up writing 'toothsome' on my cuff.

Had any of the other guests been asked for an opinion, I feel sure they'd have been neither so reticent nor so kind. *Curdled, acrid, corrosive, repellent* – this was the meal's true thesaurus. At one stage I overheard Tibby Spode describe the soup as 'rather like eating electricity with a rusty knife'.

The solitary glimmer of joy throughout the accursed feast was Iona MacAuslan – who sat diagonally opposite me, between taciturn Uncle Tom and verbose Sir Gilbert, twinkling hypnotically in the candlelight. My gaze was continually drawn to her, like an eager beagle to aniseed, and once in a while, when our eyes chanced to meet, she shared thrillingly conspiratorial grimaces of outrage.

By the time the Burmese rarebit had been cleared away, uneaten by all but one, the atmosphere was as bilious as it was rebellious. Like me, my fellow guests had reasonably assumed that the legendary Anatole would be at the meal's helm, navigating them skilfully through the tranquil seas of culinary bliss. No one could have been prepared for this foul and violent squall.

When Aunt Dahlia rose tremulously to lead the ladies away, Mr Redmane rose to depart with her.

'You'll stay for some port with the men?' she asked, confused by this breach of protocol.

'It would be a pleasure,' Mr Redmane bowed, 'after such a very *toothsome* meal. Sadly, though, I must take my leave.'

'So soon?'

'Indeed. Elsewise I shall be late for work.'

'On a Saturday night?'

'Oh yes. I clock in at eleven fifteen sharp, not a minute later.'

'Ah,' Aunt Dahlia smiled, knowingly. 'So you do your tasting after dark. How fascinating. Something to do with the full moon, I expect?'

'Tasting? Dear me, no. I don't *taste*.'

'But Mr Redmane, you're the Lea and Perrins chief taster!'

'Oh, no. I'm Mr Redmayne, the Lea and Perrins night-watchman.'

'Forgive me, I don't see the ...?'

'Redmayne with a "y". Happens quite a bit, actually. One week, I got his wages and he got mine. I can't say who was more surprised.'

Surprise was *le mot juste*. I have never in all my puff seen an aunt so utterly taxidermised. Her clandestine chemistry, this gruesome banquet, the poisoning that surely awaited us – all had been for naught.

With nothing left to say, and insurgency stirring in the ranks, Aunt Dahlia gathered her womenfolk and withdrew – but not before directing a hard and inquisitorial glare at Seppings, who had clearly steered her to the wrong pub.

I escorted Mr Redmayne-with-a-y to the front door, and bade him good night. He hovered on the threshold like the cat in the adage, and spoke in a voice charged with emotion.

'May I just say this ...'

'What?'

'You're a lucky man.'

'Eh?'

'She's a fine woman. Very fine indeed.'

I realised then he was completely pontooned. 'Whom did you have in mind, Mr Redmayne?'

'Your wife, of course!'

'My *wife*?'

'Mrs Travers! Dahlia, if I may be so bold? She is a very fine woman and you, Mr Travers ... *you* are a very lucky man.'

'Ah, yes, I expect I am.'

'Listen, d'you think she'd ever come back to the Bull and Bush for another little drinkie?'

'It's possible, I suppose.'

'You could come too, of course. Naturally. You're her husband. Only right and proper.' He nodded his head in agreement with himself. 'But do you think *she'd* ever come back? For another little drinkie? With me?'

I began to wonder if he'd ever actually leave.

'I'll keep an eye out for her.' He pointed to his eye, in case his meaning was unclear. 'Will you tell her I'll keep an eye out for her? Will you do that for me?'

'I will, Mr Redmayne, of course.'

'A very fine woman … No!' He corrected himself, angrily. 'Very *toothsome*.'

I watched him wig-wag down the gravel drive in the approximate direction of the gates, before scooting back to see if anything could be salvaged from the Cockburn '68.

The dining room was denuded of women by the time I returned, and the men had clustered themselves around a decanter at the top of the table. I took a seat between Uncle Tom and Lord MacAuslan, and spectated a progressively tense argle-bargle between Sir Gilbert and Graydon Hogg.

'What are they spatting about?' I asked Uncle Tom discreetly.

'Beats me. Something to do with passports, I think.'

'Passports?' I said, loud enough, apparently, for Lord MacAuslan to apologise and slide over the decanter.

I turned my attention to the debate.

'And d'ye know *why* they're blue?' Graydon Hogg slurred – the man was palpably drunker than Redmayne. Either no one knew, or no one cared to answer, which suited Hogg's rhetorical style down to the ground. 'Because Britannia rules the waves! *Rules* them! And what colour are the waves? Blue! Blue waves. Britannia rules the blue waves, with blue passports.'

This had an intoxicated sort of logic, but the whiffled Hogg was far from done.

'Ana-nother-thing … *Stamps!* You know what's special about our great British postage stamps? Do you? *Do you?* Anyone?'

This time Sir Gilbert elected to answer – he chaired one of England's oldest banks, dash it, and it had been minutes since he had enjoyed the sound of his own voice. 'Of course. Ours are the only postal stamps in the world which do not feature the name of the issuing country.'

'Thassright! And d'you know *why*? I'll tell you why. Because we *invented* the postal service, thasswhy. Invented it! Just like we invented the passport.' Hogg slugged back his port and slammed his glass upside down on the table, as if at a cricket-club dinner. 'So if you ask me, the blue British passport should just say "passport", with the royal crest and nothing else besides. No country name needed, because we are Great Britain. And we are great. And we are blue.'

At this juncture Seppings entered with a fresh decanter of port and a box of cigars. I helped myself to a sip of one and a Havana from the other.

Hogg leaned drunkenly over the table. 'How d'you do that, Bertie?'

'Do what?'

'Blow smoke rings. Never had the knack.'

'It's easier done than said,' I explained. 'The trick is to imitate a goldfish ... like so ... while exhaling in the manner of a puffer-fish ... like so ...'

As my perfectly orbicular rings floated up to the ceiling, Hogg took a deep drag on his cigar, formed his lips into a moue, and choked himself half to death.

'It takes practice, mind. You need to keep your mouth almost completely shut, which not everyone finds easy.'

The conversation returned to politics and continued in an increasingly inebriate and combative vein. After about twenty minutes, Uncle Tom could take no more. He stood, gently tapped the table, and spoke.

'Shall we join the ladies?'

5

SUNDAY

Sunday breakfast at Brinkley Court begins early in the summer, giving churchgoers plenty of time to stroll across the meadows at a leisurely pace. But after a fitful night dreaming of ice cream and fire hoses, I entered the dining-room on the lateish side.

As per, the sideboard groaned under a cornucopia of eggs, bacon, kippers, and kedgeree. In stark contrast, my fellow guests sat before nakedly empty plates sipping black coffee and shooting fearful glances at the buffet. Bitten hard by supper, they were twice shy at breakfast.

As a blood relative of the noticeably absent hosts, I felt duty-bound to jolly things up a little. 'Good morning, good morning,' I beamed. 'Nobody hungry?'

Lord MacAuslan gave me a pained glance, Iona snickered, and Sir Gilbert sat silently reading the *Sunday Times*.

'I think maybe some black pudding ...'

'Please, Mr Wooster,' MacAuslan groaned.

'Or maybe just some bicarb. Is it just us?'

'Mr and Mrs Hogg were here briefly, but have since left for St Mary's. And I've not yet seen your uncle or aunt.'

I attempted to include Sir Gilbert in our conversation. 'I didn't know they got the papers here this early.'

'They don't.'

'And yet ...'

He peered at me with irritation. 'I had them driven up from London.'

'Anything of interest?'

'To you? Doubtful.'

This was a charmless conversational dead-end.

Iona caught my eye, and walked her fingers across the table by way of suggesting a perambulation. As I nodded my assent, Uncle Tom popped his head round the door.

'Morning all,' he said cheerfully, 'I trust you slept well. Gilbert, is now a convenient time?'

Sir Gilbert rose, tucked the papers under his arm, and left without a word.

'What was all that about?' asked Iona.

'Antique silver – it usually is with Uncle Tom.'

'So, shall we stroll? It's a perfect morning.'

'I'm game. Care to join us, MacAuslan?'

'Would that I could, but there are some documents I must read before tomorrow.'

'Do you mind if I pop upstairs and get my camera?' Iona asked.

'Not at all. Let us reconvene in the boot room in ten minutes.'

Having exchanged my slippers for some outdoor shoes, I sat in the sunshine on the boot-room steps, tickling Augustus behind his ears. When Iona joined us, he gave a yowl of salutation and rolled on to his back in playful submission. Cats are, of course, excellent judges of character. After briefly paying tribute to the ancient bond between egocentric feline and sycophantic human, we left him to his dust-bath, and strolled off across the sward.

'I say, Iona, I'm sorry you suffered so much Sir Gilbert last night. Was he a terrible grind?'

'He was. Almost beyond belief. But I amused myself by playing The Game.'

'Game? You have a game? What game is this?'

'It's something I invented to pass the time when trapped in conversational corners by blatherskites like Sir Gilbert.'

'And the rules?'

'Oh, there's only one rule: You have to ask *them* as many questions as you can before *they* ask one of you. To make it more challenging, your questions should become more and more implausible until, finally, your interlocutor is forced by the laws of common decency to articulate the final, fatal winning words.'

'Which are?'

'*But enough about me ...*'

'How far did you get with Sir Gilbert?'

Iona laughed. 'Oh, he won! Hands down. We had six courses of Sir Gilbert and nothing but Sir Gilbert. It was a command performance. The man is a natural. I regret not selling tickets.'

'Did you learn anything of interest?'

'Interest is not a word I would use. However, I can tell you the names of his tailor, his barber, and his shoemaker, where he garages his car, where he goes on holiday, about his first marriage, his current marriage, the state of his blood pressure (high), the state of his digestion (poor), his intermittent insomnia,' she took a breath, 'and that's just for starters.'

'You poor thing.'

'No, really – all that came during the starter. I was then lectured on interest rates, tax rates, monetary policy, and the Gold Standard – which got him on to politics, politicians, the ignorance of the electorate, the ignorance of Parliament, the ignorance of pretty much everyone, in fact, except for Sir Gilbert. He has, you see, an unshakeable faith in all things Sir Gilbert.' She shuddered with the memory. 'I have nothing but sympathy for the first Mrs Sir Gilbert, and can only assume the current Mrs Sir Gilbert is deaf.'

'Did you find out why she's not with him?'

'Of course! She – and her name is Priscilla, by-the-by – is taking a hydrotherapy cure in Bad Nauheim, which I assume is simply an excuse to evade her halitotic husband. Unless she's having an affair. And I rather hope she is.'

Our meanderings had taken us over a wooden bridge that spanned a small stream, and into a copse of silver birch. Iona halted and pointed to something moving in the dappled shadows roughly a half-swing chip shot away.

'Isn't that Graydon Hogg?'

It was. And he was entwined around a woman who was most certainly not his newly-wedded wife.

'Would you call that canoodling?' whispered Iona.

'It's certainly a species of oodling. So much for church!'

'So much for marriage! Stand over there and let me take your photograph.'

'Eh?'

'Over there, quick. The light is perfect.'

She snapped a couple of frames, and tucked her camera back into her jacket. By the time I had turned round, Hogg and his mystery woman had vanished.

'Cripes,' I said. 'Do we tell Tibby?'

'I don't think so. I mean, there *might* be an innocent explanation. Actually, I don't know why I said that – he's clearly a toad. That poor lassie.'

'Lunch is going to be joyful.'

'Speaking of lunch, Bertie, reminds me of supper …' She let the word hang in the air like a threat.

'Ah, yes. Supper.'

'Is it true what people were saying last night? That she's inventing a new kind of condiment?'

I decided that, having suffered the consequences of Aunt Dahlia's sorcery, Iona deserved at least to know its genesis. And so I gave her the full story – from the furtive garden-shed alchemy to Redmayne's erroneous entrapment in the Bull and Bush.

Iona listened intently, before summarising the situation with commendable pith. 'She's mad!'

'I've said so for years.'

'I mean, even if she could create an edible Brinkley Sauce – and I have my doubts – then what of finding ingredients, large-scale manufacture—'

I cut in. 'Jeeves is of the same mind. You should compare notes.'

'Do you think last night will have deterred her at all?'

'If I know aunts, and my scars suggest I do, then I would have to say: No. I predict she will bide her time, lick her wounds, regroup, re-arm, and then rain down fire from out of the sun, like the Red Baron.'

'She is quite ... *purposeful*,' Iona said.

'She is. But, deep within her thuds a heart of gold – especially when compared to my Aunt Agatha, who wears barbed wire close to the skin and assassinates tradesmen with a well-aimed sneer.'

Iona thought for a while as we strolled back towards the house. 'If all you say about aunts is true, then why is there no adjective for aunts as "avuncular" describes uncles?'

'Oh, but there is: *Materteral*.'

She laughed. 'Is that one of Jeeves's?'

'Not at all! I went to the library and looked it up especially.'

We concluded our tour of the Brinkley Court domain and returned, via the boot room, to the hall, where Aunt Dahlia was doing something ghastly with hollyhocks and an ornate china vase.

She greeted Iona affectionately, before turning a peevish oyster on me. 'There you are, ugly. Why do you insist on vanishing when you are most required?'

'And good morning to you, timeworn relic.'

'Hush, child, and open your ears. I want you to go and chivvy your uncle. He's fretting in the library and could do with a pre-luncheon bucking-up.'

'I will biff forthwith.'

'Not so fast! First, tell me both what you think of my flowers.'

It was the hesitation that killed us. Had we answered immediately almost anything we said would have been better than the haunting silence that ensued. In truth, Aunt Dahlia's floral melange resembled nothing less than a crayon scrawl of a scarecrow's funeral drawn by an insolent child. But I wasn't entirely convinced such a mordant critique would find an appreciative ear.

'Gosh,' I began confidently, hoping the words would somehow emerge as I spoke.

'May I?' asked Iona, plucking the secateurs from Aunt Dahlia's mystified hand and setting about the stems with the rapacious thrust and parry of a fencing mistress. 'The aim,' she said, rotating the vase as she slashed away, 'is to create symmetry, volume, and depth from every angle. Especially if the arrangement is to be positioned in front of a mirror.'

Aunt Dahlia isn't often impressed. No, scratch that: I've *never* seen Aunt Dahlia impressed. But this bravura display of horticultural savagery had the old bird well and truly gripped.

Iona stepped back to assess the full effect of her composition. 'What do you think, Mrs Travers?'

Gone from Aunt Dahlia's face was her customary expression of high and indignant dudgeon. Instead she looked – and it staggers me to write this – happy.

'Iona, my dear, this is quite divine. How green your fingers must be. Now, might you assist me in my study, where I am at war with some really quite frightful hydrangeas?'

'It would be my pleasure, Mrs Travers.'

I found Uncle Tom perched on the edge of his chair, peering through jeweller's spectacles at a silver and glass contraption.

'What-ho, Unc.'

'Bertram, me boy,' he replied with slow deliberation, not looking up from his delicate endeavours with a tuft of cotton wool.

'What's all this then? Polishing your decanters?'

'It's a tantalus.'

'A what-a-lus?'

He set down his tuft, and sat back with a sigh. Normally pretty tight-lipped, Thomas Portarlington Travers is roused to loquacity whenever the subject of silver comes up. And, in his company, it comes up with Swiss regularity.

'Did your extensive schooling ever teach you the Greek legend of Tantalus?'

'Er, remind me.'

'Son of Zeus? Banished to Hades for stealing ambrosia? Ring any bells?'

'Is he the chap who had to push a boulder up a hill?'

'No, Bertie, that was Sisyphus. Tantalus' punishment was eternally to suffer insatiable hunger and unquenchable thirst. Grapes withdrew from his grasp and water receded from his lips.'

'Sounds nasty. But what has that to do with these decanters?'

'This *tantalus*,' Uncle Tom corrected, 'mimics that ordeal by preventing dipsomaniacs, like you, from purloining my divine nectars.'

'Aha! So they can *see* the whisky, but they can't drink it?'

'Correct.'

'Tantalising! How does it work?'

'This silver cage locks the decanters in place, and these silver brackets prevent the stoppers from being removed.' He flourished

a tiny silver key. 'With this, however, one can unlock the mechanism ... like so ... deploy this catch ... like so ... and, presto!'

'How infernally clever. Is it worth a bundle?'

'It is. This piece is by Fabergé, circa 1890. Regard the filigree
scrollwork, the decorative foliage, the gadroon borders, the acorn
finial.'

'Consider them regarded. Very choice.'

'Sadly, it's up for auction tomorrow.'

'Has it come to that?'

'I'm afraid so.'

'The usual, I suppose?'

'You know, I simply can't imagine what they do up there all
day.' He glowered heavenwards. 'I think they must be slating that
roof with gold leaf.'

'My commiserations, Uncle Tom. It's a topping contraption
and I can see why you'd be mouldy to hammer it out.'

'And that dreadful Sir Gilbert just offered me a pre-emptive
bid of eight thousand pounds.'

'Which you didn't accept?'

'I sent him packing!'

'Isn't eight large a good price?'

'It's an excellent price. But, you know, it's not about the money.'

This is exactly the sort of bombshell remark that, in drawing-room comedies, causes young ladies to faint into young men's
arms, and butlers to let slip entire tureens of soup. To say that
money was close to Uncle Tom's heart was to misapprehend how
much the old chap valued blood. I have often thought that a stage
manager, struggling to provide suitably dramatic sound effects for

the eye-gouging scene in *King Lear*, need do nothing more than whisper 'supertax' into Uncle Tom's lughole, and stand well back.

It's true that when I was at school, Uncle Tom could always be relied upon for a ten-bob postal order with no questions asked. But any sum greater than an o' goblin or two required the immediate deployment of smelling salts, for the man had a one-way wallet.

'I say, are you quite yourself? Shall I summon doctors?'

'I know, me boy, I know. Something about Sir Gilbert Skinner simply makes me sick.'

'I couldn't agree more. He's just become my bank manager. But how do you know him?'

'We have the same club.'

This was news. 'I had no idea you belonged anywhere. I thought you avoided clubs like the cholera.'

'I do. Almost never go. Nothing but boring wine and blah-blah-blah.'

'But why, if you dislike him so much, is Sir Gilbert at Brinkley Court?'

'He invited himself down to look over my collection. But I see now that his motive all along was to bag the tantalus before the sale.'

'Clearly he's not short of the stuff.'

'He's richer than Croesus.'

'So you declined to sell the tantalus?'

'I did, and he was livid. Accused me of dragging him down here on false pretences.'

'But he dragged himself!'

'A point I put to him in no uncertain terms.'

'So presumably he'll just bid for it at tomorrow's auction.'

'And there's nothing I can do to stop him.'

'Can't you pull it from the sale? Say you've had a change of heart.'

'Not without pain. They've put the blasted thing on the cover of the catalogue, and would fine me a fortune if I withdrew at this late stage.'

'So the only way to ensure that Sir Gilbert doesn't get his hands on it is—'

'I do hope you're not going to say "bid for the tantalus yourself"?'

'Why not? You'd be giving the money with one hand and taking it back with the other. Case closed. Next defendant, please.'

'Except for one niggling snag. Not only would I have to pay the auctioneers a seller's commission, I would also have to pay them a buyer's premium.'

'So you'd actually lose money?'

'Twice.'

It was a wrench to see the old boy torn between his two passions of fine silver and saving money, and I tried hard to puzzle a solution.

'Could you destroy it?' I asked. 'Elbow it off a high shelf while dusting?'

Tom gave me a baleful look.

'Of course. Yes. Sorry.'

'We've been slow!' cried Tom, abruptly. 'We should ask Jeeves to cook up a plan.'

'We could,' I wavered. 'The thing is, I'm not sure how amenable Jeeves is at the moment, plan-wise.'

'Why? Have you fallen out?'

'Not as such. But he has taken umbrage at my new slippers, and this time I've declined to come to heel.'

Uncle Tom leaned over and peered down at my footwear. 'Oh, I'm sure Jeeves will come round. I think they're glorious. What's the word people use these days? *Jazzy?*'

This was far from music to my ears. Tom's appreciation of silver may be *nonpareil*, but his taste in clothing means that, unless dragooned by Aunt Dahlia into semi-decent attire, he would be safe from detection in an identity parade of dustmen. It was impossible, therefore, to take unalloyed pride in any sartorial statement that came with Uncle Tom's heartfelt endorsement.

'It might be better if you asked Jeeves yourself,' I suggested. 'I'm sure he'd cluster round if you explained the state of play.'

'Good idea!' Uncle Tom sprang to his feet with an uncharacteristic surge of pep. 'I shall go and beard him now.'

I followed Uncle Tom into the hall, where Seppings was collecting the withered remains of Iona's floral slaughter.

'Ahoy there, Seppings.'

'Good afternoon, sir.'

I lowered my voice. 'Is Anatole alive?'

'Yes, sir.'

'Is he ambulant? *Compos mentis*? Oriented to time and place?'

'He is preparing luncheon at this very moment, sir.'

'Do we have any idea of what, from yesterday, he remembers?'

'He recalls meeting "Mr Giovanni" briefly, sir, but nothing after that. He seems to have put the incident down to one of his sporadic attacks of *mal au foie*.'

'That's a bit of luck. Although it does seem unusually cruel for one who cooks liver so perfectly to suffer from such an affliction. Reminds me of that Greek blighter who was chained to a rock and had his liver pecked out once a day by an eagle. What was his name?'

'I couldn't say, sir.'

It's always a jolt to be reminded that not every senior servant is as encyclopaedically learned as Jeeves. Just because a chap is attired in the black coat and wing collar, it does not follow that he is *au fait* with Greek mythology, metaphysical poetry, *Debrett's Peerage*, or the disposition of individual dogs at Battersea Greyhound Track. I've often wondered whether Jeeves is wasting himself at my side when he could be answering a calling more suited to his talents – like ruling benevolently over Imperial Rome.

'Well, I'm relieved Anatole survived his sedation, but I might still give the kitchens a widish berth.'

'That does seem prudent, sir.'

'V.g. Now, do you happen to know the whereabouts of Lord MacAuslan?'

'He is in the drawing-room, sir, reading.'

Seppings is seldom mistaken about such matters, and I discovered Lord MacAuslan, as prophesied, perusing a sheaf of papers with his feet up. He greeted me warmly, while artfully slipping the documents back into his briefcase.

'Mr Wooster! What time do you have?'

I checked. 'A little after noon.'

'Well, then!'

I opened the door, called to Seppings, and pointed at my wristwatch.

'Very good, sir.'

He returned half a minute later with the necessary. 'Shall I, sir?'

'I'll mother.' As the door closed, I turned to Lord MacAuslan. 'What will it be? Whisky and water? Brandy and soda? Gin and quinine?'

'What's the whisky? If you'll forgive my presumption.'

'It's a Bruichladdich, if you'll forgive my pronunciation.'

'A dram of *Bruichladdich*,' he gently corrected, 'with the smallest of splashes would be grand.'

I prepared the drinks, and took a seat. 'What do you make of Sir Gilbert?'

Lord MacAuslan answered my q. with a q. 'What do *you* make of Sir Gilbert?'

'That's the thing – I'm not at all sure. Something dashed peculiar took place late on Friday, and it's still pulling at the frayed ends. I hoped to confide in you last night, but there was never a good moment.'

'Go on.'

I recounted my late-night library eavesdropping encounter, complete with the accents as best as I could manage.

'And you're certain it was Sir Gilbert Skinner?' asked Lord MacAuslan.

'Witnessing the clouds of his Turkish cologne, I should say it was definitely him. And now I've had more opportunities to hear Sir Gilbert speak, the voice fits too.'

'It's a shame you don't speak German.'

'I admit *Kartenhaus* is limiting.'

'It's all very odd,' he said, staring out of the French windows.

'Not that odd! After all, Sir Gilbert is the chairman of Trollope's. Surely he was discussing banknotes? And forgeries of same?'

'I wouldn't be so sure.'

'I thought there was a new batch of dodgy slush we all had to be guarding against?'

'Who told you that?'

'Sir Gilbert himself!'

'Actually, we think this may be something else. Do you know the St Luke's Printing Works on Old Street?'

'If you hum it, I'll sing along.'

'It's where the Bank of England prints our banknotes.'

'I thought you said this wasn't about banknotes.'

'St Luke's also produces strictly controlled quantities of *this*.' He leaned over and produced from his briefcase a small bottle of slick black fluid.

'They've struck oil? In Clerkenwell? That puts a very different perspective on things.'

'Not oil,' said Lord MacAuslan, gently. 'Ink.'

'Oh, well, cancel the parade.'

He passed me the bottle. 'Do you notice anything unusual?'

I examined the ink as I imagined an authority on ink would examine some ink. I shook the bottle to test its viscosity, held it up to the light to inspect its hue, and unscrewed the cap to obtain a delicate honk.

'Nope,' I concluded. 'Looks like ink to me.'

'The bottle you are holding contains Bank Black – a unique formula of ink produced exclusively, and secretly, for the Bank of England. It was invented in 1842 by Mr Alfred Smee and it is, you will agree, most unusually and exceptionally black?'

I re-examined the bottle. 'None more black.'

'But once on paper, Mr Wooster, Bank Black actually *darkens* over time.'

'Crafty old Mr Smee. And this is the ink they use to print banknotes?'

'Banknotes, bearer bonds, dividend warrants, and passports.'

By now I knew Lord MacAuslan well enough to grasp that the last item on any of his beloved lists was the one to bet the house on. 'Sir Gilbert is forging passports!'

'Someone is. And excellent forgeries they are too. Until recently, the only way we could detect the counterfeits was by the ink they used, which faded rather than intensified over time. However, if the forgers start using the correct ink – Bank Black, that is – the country will face serious peril.'

'Worse than being flooded with dodgy fivers?'

'Not worse, necessarily, but the risk is equally grave. Counterfeit currency will have a devastating effect on an economy, if introduced in sufficient quantities. But a nation's security can be put in jeopardy with just one expertly forged passport.'

'And you suspect Sir G's involved?'

'We didn't – but now I'm not so sure. The Junior Ganymede has for a while been interested in Sir Gilbert, whose expensive tastes appear incompatible with his income or assets. What you overheard on Friday gives us a promising angle of enquiry into him, and the forgeries.'

'Time for another?' I asked, strolling to the tray. 'I think I need one.'

'Absolutely.'

'So what do we do now? Dog Sir Gilbert's footsteps? Listen at his keyhole? Steam open his letters with a kettle?'

Lord MacAuslan was about to answer when the hall gong echoed, and so we oiled out to the dining-room with our glasses in hand.

Lunch, as promised, was a properly Anatolian affair, and the menu card, back once again in French, read like a condemned prisoner's letter of reprieve:

Velouté d'Asperges aux Quenelles
Petits Soufflés au Foie Gras
Darne de Saumon à la Chambord
Chapon de Pintade, sauce Périgueux
Crème de Fraises à la Chartreuse

Although an ice shelf of etiquette ensured that no one mentioned last night's misadventure, the general praise of lunch was so effusive that a sensitive soul might have detected the faintest undertow of irony. Purely by way of experiment, I asked Iona to pass the pepper; she obliged with a smirk, but Aunt Dahlia's countenance registered nothing untoward, apart from her usual irascibility towards me. The mood may have been helped by Uncle Tom insisting we give the previous night's wines a second chance. Released from the torture of the spice rack they revealed themselves in all their supernacular glory.

Glancing round the table, I noticed we were a much diminished crowd. 'What happened to everyone?'

'The Hoggs had a luncheon engagement in Market Snodsbury,' said Aunt Dahlia. 'And Sir Gilbert has driven home.'

'In his two-seater huff,' added Uncle Tom. 'Which I hope he crashes into stinging nettles.'

'It's a little indecorous to clishmaclaver about a fellow guest,' said Lord MacAuslan, 'but I once heard a moderately amusing tale about Sir Gilbert.'

'You'll find no objection to speaking ill of the dread here,' encouraged Uncle Tom. 'Pray continue.'

'Well, some decades ago, Sir Gilbert joined a gentlemen's club just off Whitehall called the Associated Civil Service. It wasn't a large club, but its membership was notably distinguished. It was joked that if a porter announced "Taxi for Sir Charles" half the smoking-room would stand up and make for the door.'

'Similar things happen at the Drones,' I added, 'whenever the *gendarmes* arrive.'

'Sir Gilbert's election to the Associated Civil Service was immediately regretted. He was preening, pedantic, and a thundering bore. But, he was also a stickler for the club's rules. So, while he was often ragged and widely ostracised, no legitimate reason could be found for ejecting him.'

'No trumped-up charges of pinching the spoons?' asked Iona.

'Indeed not. But Sir Gilbert's presence became so unappealing that many members stopped using the club on days they feared he might appear. After a deluge of complaints, the general committee devised a plan and put it to a postal ballot.'

'What was this plan?' I asked, eager to know if it might come in handy at the Drones.

'Have you ever heard of the Associated Civil Service?'

'Actually, no,' I said, 'and I thought I knew most of the London haunts.'

'*That* was the plan. After an almost unanimous vote, the general committee forfeited the clubhouse lease and dissolved the Associated Civil Service entirely. Then, after a six-month interval, they opened a brand-new club just around the corner. It had a different name, but an identical membership – save for one member.'

I gasped. 'You don't mean the Northcote-Trevelyan Club on Canon Row?'

'The very same.'

'Well, stap me vitals! That was sneaky.'

'You see, Bertie me boy,' said Uncle Tom, 'this is precisely why I couldn't sell Sir Gilbert the tantalus. Wiser heads than mine concluded many years ago that the man is a fat-headed ass.'

'Does it not seem,' asked Iona, 'a remarkably expensive and convoluted undertaking simply to eject a single member?'

'Perhaps,' said Lord MacAuslan, 'but let us not forget, they were civil servants.'

'What puzzles me,' remarked Aunt Dahlia, forking food from my plate, as is her whim when important guests are absent, 'is how such a blistering hellhound ever came to be chairman of a bank as exalted as Trollope's.'

Just then Jeeves entered with a telegram for Uncle Tom, who read it with a brow of deepening furrow.

'What gives?' I asked. 'You have a face like Wednesday's child.'

Uncle Tom screwed up the missive and threw it testily into the fireplace. 'Roderick Spode is holding another of his absurd rallies in Market Snodsbury this afternoon.'

'On a Sunday?' said Iona, shocked.

'It's too bad. He's received permission from the mayor and, despite being on the town council, it seems there's nothing I can do to stop it.'

'It won't be a large gathering, will it?' Lord MacAuslan asked.

'I shouldn't think so; they seldom are. But it's the principle. Apparently he's going to speak from Snodsbury Bridge at three thirty.'

'We should attend and hurl vegetables,' I suggested, unfondly remembering last night's artichokes, which might have been cooked for the express purpose of electioneering.

'I'm not sure I can face seeing that tin-pot crackpot strutting about,' grumbled Uncle Tom, 'even if I thought a volley of compost would help.'

Jeeves coughed very slightly. 'Excuse me, sir, but will there be a reply?'

'Oh, er, no. Thank you, Jeeves.'

'Very good, sir,' he replied, before leaning down beside Lord MacAuslan and murmuring something into his ear.

Lord MacAuslan listened, nodded, consulted his watch, and smiled. 'There may be something we can do after all, Mr Travers. Would you mind if I made a telephone call?'

'Call away, old boy. Use the blower in the hall.'

The meal marched on, and after ten or so minutes Lord MacAuslan returned, with a distinct spring to his step. 'I suggest, Mr Wooster, we make a small detour on our return to London. Seeing Lord Sidcup speak may yet prove worth our while.'

We left Brinkley Court in two cars – Jeeves drove me, Iona drove her uncle – and arrived in Market Snodsbury at about a quarter to four. We strolled along the western bank of the River Severn until we found a bench with an unobstructed, though well-concealed, view of Snodsbury Bridge.

Bang in the middle of this graceful stone structure, surrounded by thirty or so black-shorted acolytes, was Lord Sidcup – standing on a soap-box, and dressed in a bizarre military regalia seemingly cobbled together from the uniforms of the Scouts, the fire brigade, and the Royal Bavarian Army. No wonder he'd been visiting Hubbard & Legg for a decent bit of tailoring.

'What's all that on his chest?' asked Iona, indicating Spode's ludicrous collection of badges and ribbons which feebly approximated military decorations.

'Prizes from a Christmas cracker?' I suggested.

Spode himself was in full flow, gesticulating clownishly with what he must have imagined were intensely rhetorical gestures: the clenched fist, the ironic shrug, the sweeping palm, the slicing chop, the beckoning finger, the hand on hip. Every so often, he attempted a Roman salute, which his acolytes returned with a risible cry of '*Heil, Spode!*'

If his mannerisms were histrionic, his message was gibberish. 'We must be ceaseless in our fight to Keep Great Britain Great,' he kept on repeating. 'The British way of life, the British sense of fair play, the British love of Britishness.'

'It's as if he has a vocabulary of thirty words,' observed Lord MacAuslan, 'and just throws them together indiscriminately.'

'How does he do that with his hair?' asked Iona.

'A better question would be: Why?'

The crowd shifted slightly and we were afforded a glimpse of two people standing by Spode's side and not dressed in any sort of uniform: Graydon and Tibby.

'Spy the Hoggs?' I asked MacAuslan.

'I do indeed. That explains their absence at lunch.'

Iona discreetly raised her camera and snapped a few pictures.

'I wonder why Madeline Bassett's not here,' I said.

The Guildhall clock struck the hour, and Lord MacAuslan glanced about expectantly. 'Any time now, I should say.'

As if on cue, the unmistakable strains of 'Rule, Britannia!' floated out over the warm summer air. Quiet at first, the music grew steadily in volume, and then became blaringly present as, across the river, the full band of the Worcestershire Regiment marched into view.

Spode was momentarily shocked, then puzzled, then thrilled. Clearly he had not been expecting a military salute, but since one had suddenly materialised, and since it was obviously no less than he deserved, he was more than happy to assume the credit and incorporate it into his peroration.

'And here, good burghers of Market Snodsbury, are the brave men of the British Army.' He gestured grandly at the musicians trooping towards him. 'These heroic men fought at Waterloo, at Lexington, at Blenheim.'

'Is he mad?' said Lord MacAuslan. 'They were centuries ago.'

'In 1815, 1775, and 1704, m'lord,' Jeeves murmured, almost to himself.

Spode banged on. 'These valiant British soldiers know from good old-fashioned British experience that we must fight for the British inch, the British mile, the British furlong, the British firkin.'

And then, from behind us, emerged an unlikely crescendo of what can only be described as oinking. We turned to see a handful of men with long wooden staves driving towards the western approach of Snodsbury Bridge several hundred pigs.

Spode turned too, and blinked in dismay as he attempted to make sense of the looming pastoral scene. 'Furthermore,' he roared over the swelling cacophony, 'we must fight for the British farmer, the British field, the British pig, the British chop.'

As the Worcestershire Regiment stepped on to the east side of the bridge they seamlessly segued into 'The British Grenadiers', and those onlookers who had not already departed stepped back to let them pass. I noticed that Hogg and Tibby were nowhere to be seen – they had clearly bolted at the first sign of trumpets.

Spode's initial delight slid quickly into alarm, and his eyes narrowed as band and pigs marched ever closer, corralling the Saviours of Britain into an anxious, cowardly knot.

'Valiant men!' he bellowed over the din. 'So many men! Such valiance!'

Finally, when it became clear that no one could hear him over the 'tow, row, row' of 'The British Grenadiers', Spode produced from his pocket a tiny Union Jack and waved it patriotically to the bass drum's rhythmic boom.

The life of an acolyte, I reflected from the comfort of my bench, isn't up to much. Presumably these men had risen early, excited for a day of saluting, and had assembled on this pictur-esque bridge to bask in the greater glory of Spode. And now, through no real fault of their own, save perhaps for a biddable naivety and a love of dressing up, they were trapped between a drove of grunting pigs and a phalanx of glissandoing trombones.

These acolytes were faced with a question: To flee or not to flee? To suffer the slings and arrows of a military brass section, or jump off a bridge into the rushing waters of the Severn? As yards gave way to feet, and feet gave way to inches, the question became increasingly moot. They jumped.

Spode stood alone, waving his tiny little flag in a bathetic attempt to eke out the final moments of self-appointed bravado. Beads of sweat broke out over his porcine face, and his hatchet eyes flashed left and right in a frenzy of alarm. The soap-box on which he stood was displaying similar signs of distress – unused, as it was, to bearing such a mammoth weight. Its wooden joints began to splinter as it tottered in time to the unsympathetic resonance of marching boots, and then its fragile structure sud-denly gave way, toppling Spode backwards over the balustrade and into the drink.

Betwixt fall and splash, the Worcestershire Regiment struck up 'God Save the King', and I could swear I saw the seventh Earl of Sidcup attempt a salute as he plummeted.

Soon he was backstroking to shore along with the rest of his gang, serenaded by slow, mocking applause from the good burghers of Market Snodsbury, who recognised a drowned rat when they saw one.

'That was decidedly satisfactory,' said Lord MacAuslan, rising to his feet. 'And the pigs, Jeeves, were a lovely touch.'

'Thank you, m'lord. I thought they might add something to the occasion.'

'Mr Wooster, we shall reconvene in London on Tuesday.'

'Absolutely, although we could follow you back?'

'Except we are driving to the airfield.'

'Ah, yes, flyin'. I completely forgot.' I turned to Iona. 'Will I see you any time soon?'

'I don't think so. I return to Edinburgh on Tuesday. Unless you happen to be free for lunch tomorrow?'

'As a nightingale.'

'Wonderful. Shall we say Berkeley Square at one?'

'We shall. Until then.'

'That had all the bells and whistles of a Reginald Jeeves production,' I said, as we headed back to the Smoke in the delightfully unclumping jalopy. 'How ever did you think it up?'

'I was inspired by Mr Seppings, sir, who speaks approvingly of the band of the Worcestershire Regiment, in which his cousin plays the tuba.'

'How marvellous. I've always rather admired the tuba.'

'When I learned of Lord Sidcup's plans, sir, it occurred to me that the Worcestershire Regiment might enjoy exercising its ancient Freedom of Snodsbury Bridge.'

'They have such a freedom?'

'Indeed, sir. It dates back to 1791 when, as the 29th Regiment of Foot, they rescued a family from a burning building in the middle of Market Snodsbury. Since that time, they have been entitled to march across Snodsbury Bridge with "drums beating, colours flying, and bayonets fixed".'

'And you just happened to know this, did you?'

'I take a passing interest in local history, sir. And because Mr Travers served with the East Worcestershire Volunteers, the library at Brinkley Court is admirably stocked with volumes on the subject. I merely mentioned this freedom to Lord MacAuslan, and suggested he telephone Colonel Stroud-Pringle to see if something might be arranged.'

'Good old Col. S.-P. I didn't think he was the sort of chap to have a funny bone. What about the pigs?'

'That was simply good fortune, sir. The new under-gardener, Herbert—'

'Him with the daffy goggles?'

'Yes, sir. Herbert used to keep pigs as a younger man, and his family still maintains a sizeable drift not far from here.'

'And you somehow convinced Herbert and his kin to take their pigs for a stroll through the centre of Market Snodsbury?'

'Yes, sir. And some of his neighbours.'

'I realise you have significant powers of persuasion, Jeeves, but even so!'

'There was a small financial incentive, sir. The Junior Ganymede allocates funds for such *ad hoc* disbursements.'

'Spare me the details. I wish to remain blissful.'

'Very good, sir. I might just finally add that I also drew inspiration from the pontifical incident some years ago at Ditteridge Hall.'

'Ah yes, when I pushed the ankle-biter Oswald off the bridge into the brackish lake below?'

'Just so, sir.'

'Jeeves, you never fail to astonish me.'

'Thank you, sir. I endeavour to give satisfaction.'

'And you've fixed the clump!'

He corrected me. 'The *clank*, sir.'

'I don't think so, it was definitely a *clumping* that serenaded Friday's journey.'

'It pains me to contradict you, sir, but metal does not *clump*.'

'What rot! Anything can *clump* or *clank*. The words are interwhatsitable.'

'Sadly, sir, I must respectfully disagree. *Clump* is a sound made by non-metallic articles – heavy boots, perhaps, or boxing gloves. Metals *clink, clank*, or, periodically, *clunk*. I would draw your attention to the sound of silver coins, prison shackles, and padlocks, respectively. Wordsworth, you will recall, described "clanking chains" as "perfect liberty", and Tennyson penned "unlifted was the clinking latch". Glassware also *clinks*, sir, but only when suitably thin and hollow; you may have noticed that full bottles *clunk*. *Thudding* is noteworthy since, like *clumping*, it is cognate with ametallous collisions, such as horses' hooves impacting on turf. Metals only *thud* when striking softer surfaces – an anvil, for instance, dropped onto a Persian carpet. When heavy metals like church bells percuss they *ring* or *clang*. Smaller bells *tinkle* or *chime*, especially when observed by poets, sir, who often concern themselves with the subject of tintinnabulation.'

We drove in silence for a mile or so.

'Finished, Jeeves?'

'Yes, sir.'

'Good. Now, on a more profitable subject, did Uncle Tom tell you about his tantalus dilemma?'

'He did, sir.'

'Have you had a chance to exert the cranium? Is there anything we can do to snooter the pernicious Sir Gilbert?'

'I am giving the matter my full attention, sir, but would caution against optimism. One of the defining characteristics of a public auction is that anyone is entitled to attend and, with satisfactory *bona fides*, bid.'

'So, short of kidnapping Sir Gilbert ...'

'Precisely, sir. And abducting the chairman of Trollope and Sons is not a course of action that I could, in good conscience, commend.'

'Fairy-snuff. But it does mean that Uncle Tom is over a barrel. He can't afford to withdraw the tantalus, and if the auction proceeds then Sir Gilbert is sure to nab it.'

'A succinct *précis* of the impasse, sir.'

'It's like that chess position where however you move you are pickled.'

'*Zugzwang*, sir.'

'*Zugzwang?*'

'It's German, sir.'

'Doesn't sound right. Then again, nothing in German sounds completely right.'

'The word is a portmanteau, sir. *Zug* means move, and *Zwang* is an obligation.'

'So Uncle Tom is *Zwanged* to *Zug* unless you can think of a nifty *zolution*.'

'I will do my very best, sir.'

And, despite our recent frictions over tartan slippers and the nomenclature of onomatopoeia, I knew for a fact that he would.

6

MONDAY

I woke with the disconcerting feeling that – with all due respect to Jeeves's chum Pangloss – all might jolly well *not* be for the best in the best of all possible worlds.

Staring up at the plasterwork I scanned the horizon for thunderclouds before stubbing my mental toe on the name Madeline Bassett. The memory of Thursday night at the Hot Spot flooded back. Why, I kicked myself, had I right-hoed to help purchase a snuff-box for Spode? Gallantry, presumably, and the solemn obligation of a *preux chevalier*. But I couldn't help feeling like a signalman in front of a bank of levers, ensuring the correct points were switched on the correct lines: Madeline towards Spode; Florence towards Monty; Gorringe towards a Drones Club membership, via a *Flotsam*-review branch-line.

My gloomy Mondayitis was interrupted by Jeeves, who shimmered in with the cup that cheers.

'Good morning, sir.'

'Is it? I have grave doubts.'

He drew back the curtains and the sun cascaded in.

'I'm sorry to hear that, sir.'

'What's the *thing* to *thing*, Jeeves, that's *thinged* with those *thingummies*?'

He closed one eye and tapped out the syllables, like a pianist practising scales.

'The road to hell, sir? That is paved with good intentions?'

'That's the one. Though my good intentions have merely paved the road to Bond Street, and a shopping binge with Madeline Bassett.'

'Is Miss Bassett still engaged to Lord Sidcup, sir?' he asked, stooping to collect various items of clothing I'd hung up on the floor last night.

'She was still engaged on Thursday, if that counts for any-thing? And I'm doing my level best to ensure she remains in such a condition until wedding rings are exchanged and St James's is safe once again for bachelors.'

'A noble calling, sir.'

I collapsed onto the pillows. 'I don't know, Jeeves. Perhaps we should sell the farm and go to sea.'

'Might a kipper ameliorate your disposition, sir?'

'We can but roll the dice.'

I'm pleased to report that the kipper did the trick. As did the eggs and bacon, the tea and toast, and a leisurely half-hour with the *Sporting Times*. After which, I was feeling pretty bobbish and much myself.

'Jeeves, might you have time this morning to place a bet?'

'Certainly, sir. Which horse do you favour?'

'I'd like a score on Privateer.'

'In the two o'clock at Kempton Park?' He gave me an uneasy look. 'I could not confidently endorse such a proposition, sir.'

'Iggsplane.'

'First, sir, I remain of the view that the stable is far from sanguine. And second, due to the recent spell of clement weather, the ground at Kempton Park is harder even than usual. Such fast going, I suggest, favours another of the runners.'

'Oh, really? Which?'

'Treadgold, sir.'

There's no doubting that Jeeves is well up on his bloodstock, and I would usually take a horse from him without a second thought. However, I happened to know that this particular tip was copper-bottomed bunkum.

'Treadgold? Oh no. Dear me, no. No, no, no. You see, Bingo Little is pals with a bookie's tout called Fred, and the hush-hush word on the rail is that Treadgold is as slow as molasses.'

'If I may, sir—'

'Might as well bet on a steamroller.'

'Except, sir—'

I'm afraid to say I rather gave Jeeves the high hat. 'You may stake your weekly envelope as you see fit, but I would like a double sawbuck on Privateer. To win.'

'Very good, sir. I shall leave directly after breakfast.'

It was a little awkward to change the subject after this minor equine *contretemps*, but the man who is on the right side of a kipper knows no fear.

'I say, Jeeves, have you been able to conjure anything to help Uncle Tom best Sir Gilbert at the auction?'

'I'm sorry to say, sir, that I have not.'

'This is out of form. Are you ailing?'

'No, sir.'

'Perhaps you need even more fish in your diet? I can heartily recommend the kippers.'

'Thank you, sir, but no. It disquiets me considerably not to be able to assist Mr Travers in this particular enterprise.'

I knew there was little point dogging the question, for when Jeeves has made up his mind, gravity can go whistle.

'Well, I'm sure you gave it the sweat. Uncle Tom will have to fend off Sir Gilbert as best he can. Do you happen to know when battle commences?'

'The auction begins at one thirty, sir. But since Mr Travers's tantalus is listed as lot 108, I estimate you need not arrive at Shipley's much before three.'

'Care to join us? Watch the cut and thrust?'

'That is kind of you, sir, but unfortunately I have a prior engagement.'

'Righty-ho.' I stood up and stretched. 'I shall retire to the sitting-room and smoke a condemned man's last gasper before this morning's ill-advised tryst with the Mad Bat.'

*   *   *

I encountered Madeline in the sunshine outside Brown's Hotel. She was dressed like an Easter bunny, with a wide floppy bonnet and bright yellow parasol, and was diligently studying an oversize reference book.

'Top of the morning, Madeline. Swotting for an exam?'

'Hullo, Bertie! Actually, I'm learning the most fascinating things. Do you know this book?'

She held up *Fortune-Telling with Flowers* by Lionel Dennis Freeman – the cover of which featured a distressingly ugly man (presumably L. D. F. himself) winking lecherously at the reader, while his schnozzle protruded deep inside the voluptuous mauve petals of some hideous floral mutation.

'No, but it looks ... mesmerising.'

'It is! When's your birthday?'

'The fifteenth of October. Every year.'

She consulted the index. 'How too utterly too! You are *Aster amellus*, otherwise known as the Michaelmas daisy.'

'I always felt as much. Does this botanic accolade signify anything in particular?'

'Oh, absolutely! Every flower has its own unique "qualities and dispositions", you see.' She consulted the book. 'Yours are: Spirited. Desire to please. Hermitage. Pluck.'

'What does "hermitage" mean?'

'I'm not altogether sure, but it's bound to be something lovely!'

'Bound to be. What flower are you?'

'Can't you guess?'

Oddly enough, I couldn't.

'Lily of the valley, of course! *Convallaria majalis*. Which signifies: Harmony. Warmth of feeling. Dedication. Constancy.'

'Jolly good.'

'Now, let's see if you and I are *preordained*.' She turned to an appendix and scanned a table. 'Michaelmas daisy ... and ... lily of the valley.' She looked semi-combobulated. 'Well, the Flower Bed of Affinity says we are an *imaginable match*, but not an *envisaged match*.'

This was a relief. 'Hey-ho. Star-cross'd once more.'

'Don't you believe in floromancy, Bertie?'

'I like daffodils, if that butters the cabbage?'

'You really ought to believe. Floromancy is why I'm certain that Roderick is my true love. It's written in the soil. He's *Digitalis purpurea*, you see, so we are made for each other.'

'His digits are purple?'

'*Digitalis purpurea*! The foxglove. Isn't that divine?'

'Aren't foxgloves, you know, poisonous?'

'Don't be a noodle! Of course they aren't.'

She was bound to find out sooner or later, I thought, and then I remembered the pink petals I had snuck into Spode's new uniform.

'Tell me, Madeline, what does Lionel Dennis Freeman have to say about the preordination of foxgloves and carnations? Are they envisaged?'

'Why do you want to know?' she enquired, suspiciously.

'No reason. Merely an enquiring mind.'

She turned to the appendix, puzzled at the table, and smiled contentedly. 'Oh, I *am* sorry, Bertie. The Flower Bed of Affinity advises *shun* – and that's about the worst possible affinity there is.'

'Shun, eh? Perhaps there's something to this divination what-have-you after all. Now, Madeline, shall we be about our snuff-box-buying business?'

Lambert Lyall is one of those curious old shops even Dickens would have called Dickensian. No matter the date, or the weather outside, once you are ensconced within its dark, oak panelling it's perpetually Christmas Eve and you have trudged through drifting snow to locate the perfect gift for a brutally exacting aunt.

The door jingled as I guided Madeline inside.

'Mr Wooster,' welcomed the proprietor, resembling in every dimension an actor playing the part of a Bond Street jeweller. 'What pure gratification to see you again.'

'Madeline, may I introduce Lambert Lyall, from whom I have been buying snuff-boxes for centuries.'

'How do you do?'

'Lambert, this is Miss Madeline Bassett.'

'Charmed, Miss Bassett,' Lyall genuflected. 'Utterly charmed.'

'We've come—'

Lyall silenced me with a raised hand. 'Speak not another word, Mr Wooster. I've been saving something *very* special for you.'

He disappeared into a back room, leaving us to mooch around the shop observing its ordered chaos of trinkets, bibelots, and bric-à-brac. A considerable amount of banging and thudding emanated from behind the curtain, and Madeline gave me a questioning look.

'He mentioned some mother-of-pearl last time I was here,' I reassured. 'I expect that's what he's hunting out.'

After a good deal more crashing, Lyall returned and beckoned us to the counter, on which he'd placed a small tray draped with a panel of silk. I had a terrible premonition that under this shroud would be six fresh bottles of Brinkley Sauce.

The reality was far, far worse.

Lyall drew back the silk with fastidious care to reveal a dazzling array of diamond engagement rings.

I think my heart actually stopped.

'I knew the day would come, Mr Wooster,' Lyall croaked with pride, tears rolling down his cheek. 'I said to Mrs Lyall, I said, "It can't be long now for Mr Wooster." And here you are, you two — truly, love's young dream.'

I opened my mouth to speak when Madeline touched my arm.

'Shall we, Bertie?' she whispered. 'Finally? After all these years? Is it a sign? Is it in the stars? Is it *destined*?'

The speed of this conjugal *volte-face* was breathtaking, and I vowed to write a stiff letter to Mr Freeman of Freeman's *Fortune-Telling with Flowers* demanding a comprehensive rewrite for lily of the valley: 'Dedication' and 'Constancy' my foot!

'No, Madeline,' I whispered back, 'it's not destined, just completely deranged. Remember "Lady Sidcup". Never forget "Lady Sidcup".'

I turned to the counter. 'Lambert, old bean, I think you might have the wrong impression. Miss Bassett is indeed engaged, but tragically not to me. Her future husband is no less than the seventh Earl of Sidcup.'

To substantiate my claim I pointed to Madeline's plover's egg, which glinted threateningly in the shop's eternal twilight.

Lambert Lyall crumpled in abject mortification — like one who has mistaken a paunch for pregnancy and launched in with heartfelt congratulations and suggestions for suitable names and capable nannies.

'Mr Wooster, Miss Bassett, I am most profoundly sorry.' He took a handkerchief to his moistened eyes. 'Really, I don't know what to say.'

'Think nothing of it, Lambert. A perfectly innocent mistake and, of course, terribly flattering for yours truly. Less flattering for Miss Bassett, but she has the seventh Earl to console her.'

Lambert pulled himself together. 'May I ask how I *can* be of assistance, Mr Wooster?'

'Snuff-boxes, Lambert. Boxes for snuff.'

'But of course, sir. For you or,' he was taking no chances, 'Miss Bassett?'

'Do women really take snuff?' asked Madeline sceptically.

'A few do, miss. The "old guard", one might call them. And the "fast set". Both indulge from time to time.'

'How very strange. What do they see in it?'

'It's not so much a question of *seeing*, miss, but of *feeling*. Let me show you.'

He held out his left hand, splayed open his fingers as wide as he could, and rotated his wrist so his thumb pointed upwards. 'See that, miss? The little dimple there?' He indicated a small triangular indentation, about the size of a pea, formed by the flexed tendons where his thumb merged into his wrist. 'That little dimple is what we call the "anatomical snuff-box".'

Madeline splayed wide her hand and discovered she too possessed such a dimple. 'How peculiar. I never knew I had one of those.'

'You've got two, miss. One on each hand. Now, watch this.' He took a large pinch of snuff from a box on the counter, and packed it into his anatomical indentation. 'Care to partake, miss?'

'I don't think so.'

'Mr Wooster?'

'Never before lunch.'

Lambert Lyall raised his wrist and lowered his nose. At the precise juncture where nostril met tobacco he took a mighty sniff and tossed back his head in ecstasy. 'Ah! ... Cock of the North. You can't beat it, miss, not for flavour.' He sneezed explosively into his handkerchief. 'Nor for kick.'

Madeline turned to me, appalled. 'Is *this* what Roderick does for pleasure?'

'Once in a while, you know, when the old barometer plummets.'

'It seems a thoroughly beastly thing to do. If I had my doubts before, Bertie, I am now quite certain this is not a pastime to be encouraged.'

Snuff, I recognised, had been a major miscalculation, and I struggled to reframe the undertaking in language closer to Madeline's heart.

'Well,' I extemporised, 'you don't *have* to keep snuff in a snuff-box.'

She regarded me doubtingly.

'Spode might use it to store ... er ... dandelion feathers ... or eyelashes ... or ... dewdrops?'

'Oh, he could, couldn't he!' Madeline squeaked with excitement. 'You are marvellous, Bertie. All his beastly friends at his beastly club would be thinking: *There's Lord Sidcup with his snuff-box full of snuff.* But he – and I – and you – would know it was really just bursting with daisy chains and kisses.'

Lambert Lyall's face was a picture of stoic bewilderment. 'Shall I show you our selection, miss?'

He steered us to a glass cabinet in which were displayed scores of snuff-boxes in every conceivable shape, design, and material. My taste gravitates to the simple and unadorned. A polished tortoiseshell oval, or elegant silver pyxis does for the Wooster collection. Madeline, however, was drawn to the wildly garish and ostentatious.

'Oh look, Bertie, what about this one?' She pointed to a perfectly repulsive gold specimen on which the Union Jack had been picked out in diamonds, rubies, and lapis lazuli.

'Is it new?' she asked.

'It's antique, miss … this is an antiques shop.'

'Does it have a happy story?'

'*All* of our pieces have happy stories, miss.'

This struck me as manifestly laughable, since the surrender of jewellery is only ever prompted by divorce, bankruptcy, or death – or some tragic combination of said apocalyptic jockeys. Madeline, however, was lapping it up.

'How romantic! Roderick will simply adore it. He loves a happy story. And this box is just so terribly *him*. Don't you agree, Bertie?'

I examined the vulgar, jingoistic knick-knack with a jaded eye. 'I would go so far as to say, Madeline, that this snuff-box captures the very essence of Roderick Spode.'

She clapped her hands and skipped up and down, like a penguin put in charge of the krill. 'I'll take it! Can you engrave a message inside?'

'Certainly, miss, what would you like? His lordship's initials, perhaps? Or the date of your upcoming nuptials?'

Madeline thought for a moment. 'Could you put: "To R from M with Ooooooooooooooooooodles of Love"?'

Lyall took this in his stride. 'Of course, miss. How many "O"s would you say there were in "oodles"?'

Madeline giggled. 'As many as you can fit, silly!'

Once the formalities of purchase and collection had been completed, we said our goodbyes. As he and I shook hands, Lyall leaned in confidentially. 'Once again, sir, I'm most dreadfully sorry.'

'Water under. Give it not another thought.'

He pulled me closer still. 'And, if I may presume, sir, a lucky escape.'

We had just exited the shop when SMYTH'S FOR SNUFF came barrelling down the street towards us.

'Bertie! M'old china,' he gorblimied in his widest Cockney vowels.

'Ahoy there, Monty. I thought we were meeting at the Gaiety Theatre?'

'We are! The dress rehearsal starts at five. I'm just clocking up some hours in the sandwich beforehand.'

'Do you know this gentleman?' asked Madeline, with the disdainful hauteur she imagined the future Lady Sidcup should deploy.

'I can hardly deny it,' I said. 'Miss Madeline Bassett, I have the inestimable honour of presenting to you Mr Montague Montgomery.'

'How d'ye do?' he drawled, abandoning his working persona and bowing as best he could from within his wooden frame.

'Oh, hullo,' Madeline replied, charmingly disarmed. 'Are you anything to do with the Widcombe Montgomeries?'

'Indeed I am. Widcombe through and through.'

'I think I know your cousin Millicent.'

'Milly? How marvellous.'

This was getting dreadfully spoony. 'I take it, Montague, that Bond Street is the ritzy new stomping ground you mentioned on the phone?'

'Indeed it jolly well is. Bond Street, Mount Street, the Royal Arcade. And I'm getting a lot of enquiring stares, I can tell you.'

'I can see why,' admired Madeline.

Monty gave me the side-eye. 'But what are you two doing here, together?'

'Somewhat coincidentally, now that you've arrived, I've been helping Madeline acquire a snuff-box.'

'Perfect timing!' Monty beamed. 'Half a mo.'

He fumbled about in his trousers for an uncomfortably long time before eventually unearthing two small packages, which he bestowed extravagantly upon Madeline.

'What's this?' she asked, warily.

'Snuff, Miss Bassett. The finest money can buy. This one is here is Wall Flower, it's especially fragrant. And this one is Otterburn, which I would classify as very definitely stimulating.'

Madeline took the daintiest possible sniff of Wall Flower, from a distance of about three feet. 'Oh my, it smells just like summer! You *are* clever, Mr Montgomery.'

Something about the way they held each other's gaze set alarm bells ringing. It was imperative that Monty remained focused on Florence, and Madeline remained focused on Spode. A fly in the ointment of love's status quo would be ruinous to every shareholder, and that included me.

It was time to take the cosh to Cupid.

'I say, Madeline, did you know Monty is stepping out with Florence Craye?' I turned to Monty. 'And Madeline is engaged to Roderick Spode?'

The effect was immediate, dramatic, and fatal – like salting a snail. Both parties took a step back and straightened themselves up: Madeline suddenly remembered the prize of becoming Lady Sidcup, and Monty suddenly remembered that loitering inside the sandwich was a two-quid offence.

After a cordial exchange of farewells, Monty clunked off to inconvenience people down the Burlington Arcade, and I escorted Madeline towards the greenery of Berkeley Square.

'What a fascinating man,' said Madeline.

'That's one school of thought,' I said, 'though not a very well-attended school.'

We were standing in the centre of Berkeley Square Gardens when Spode approached us from a northerly direction, stomping down the gravel like a clockwork soldier.

I opted for a strategy of defensive pre-emption. 'Before you get any outlandish ideas, Spode, Madeline and I have only just met.'

Spode snorted incredulously and slapped his gloves against his tall leather boots. 'Twice in a week, Wooster? Do you take me for some kind of dim-wit?'

I was fairly sure this was a question best left unanswered, but Madeline stepped up to the crease.

'It's true, Roderick. I was admiring the trees, and the flowers, and the birds, and then I saw Bertie, and I thought: *Hullo! There's Bertie. All alone. Looking so sad. I must go and comfort him.*'

'All alone, eh? Like a snake in the grass.'

'In point of fact, Spode, I am here to meet someone else.'

'I don't think so, Wooster. Who on earth would want to meet you?'

I was composing a crushing riposte to this cheap shot of slander when, with timing as impeccable as her apparel, Iona strolled upon us.

'Hullo, Bertie,' she said, kissing me decorously on the cheek.

'Iona, may I present Lord Sidcup and the soon-to-be Lady Sidcup, Miss Madeline Bassett.'

'A pleasure,' said Iona. 'And felicitations to you both.'

'Soon-to-be Sidcups, may I present Miss Iona MacAuslan.'

Spode bowed with absurd formality. 'Delighted, miss, I'm sure.'

Madeline was less sure and not at all delighted. 'How long have you known Mr Wooster?' she enquired, twisting the plover's egg resentfully round her finger.

Iona took my arm. 'Oh, not long, but it feels like years, wouldn't you say, Bertie?'

'A lifetime.'

Madeline gave a simpering sort of smile.

Iona turned to Spode. 'Would you be anything to do with the Black Short movement at all, Lord Sidcup?'

He snapped to attention like a surgical truss. 'I have the honour, Miss MacAuslan, to be the founder of the Black Shorts, and their leader.'

'I must say, I think what you are doing is remarkable. Very remarkable indeed.'

Spode is disgustingly puffed up at the best of times, and I feared Iona's remark, devilishly ambiguous though it was, might actually pop his waistcoat buttons.

'I am flattered you think so. We must be ceaseless in our British fight to Keep Great Britain Great. Our fight for the British way of life, the British sense of fair play, the British—'

Madeline, for whom this speech must once have been charming, was having none of it. 'We should be going, Roderick,' she cut in. 'Else we will be late.'

'Perhaps you would care to join us for lunch?' asked Spode, somehow managing to convey that, while his invitation technically extended to both of us, it would be infinitely preferable if Iona came alone and I were to go boil my head.

'Another time, perhaps, Lord Sidcup,' Iona demurred. 'For at this moment Bertie and I must conspire gunpowder, treason, and plot.'

We exchanged handshakes of goodbye – vigorously *bonhomous* from Spode, jealously refrigerated from Madeline – and set off as couples in opposite directions. After just a few yards, Spode called my name and summoned me back to the centre of the square. He leaned in close and I could feel the bristles of his nasty little moustache against my ear. 'If I ever see you alone with Madeline again, Wooster, I will tear you limb from limb.' He patted me on the shoulder and crunched off down the gravel.

'What was that about?' asked Iona.

'Oh, just the standard-issue Spode death threat. The man hands out two a day during the Season. He really is an absolute shower.'

'He's dried off from yesterday.'

'That's true. He should be dunked in the River Severn on a daily basis.'

'What's *she* like?'

'Madeline? A good enough sort, I suppose, albeit with a tendency to soppy whimsicality. She insists, for example, that dewdrops are angels' tears.'

'But they are, aren't they?'

'It is, as Jeeves would say, a hypothesis that defies scientific validation.'

'Have you known her long?'

'Long enough to have been engaged three or four times.'

Iona laughed. 'That would explain her cold hand and green eye.'

'So where are we lunching? How about Wiltons?'

She mulled the idea. 'Let's go to my club.'

Iona's club turned out to be the Lyceum – an imposingly grand, ladies-only establishment whose monumental clubhouse on Piccadilly made the Drones premises seem rather like a cabman's shelter.

We were shown to our table by a sulky waitress who proffered two sets of leather-bound menus – one pair dark red, the other navy blue. 'Table or cart?' she said in flat tones of boredom.

I gave a Iona a quizzical look.

'*Table* or *carte*?' she translated into French. 'Are we shirkers or workers?'

'Iona, I am adrift.'

'The Lyceum isn't a club for gentlemen of indolent means, Bertie. We cater to women of toil *and* ladies of rank – two groups with very different financial means. The blue *table d'hôte* menus are for the workers, the red *à la carte* for the shirkers.'

'I see, in that case ...' I pointed to the dark-red menus, and Iona nodded her approval.

'Do you drink at lunchtime, Bertie?'

'Invariably.'

'Jolly good. Me too.' She turned to the waitress. 'May we have a bottle of the club white burgundy, please?'

After the arrival of our wine, and the dispatching of our order, I raised my glass in a toast: '... *But enough about me.*'

'Oh, very clever, Bertie,' Iona laughed. 'First class!'

'It only looks like I'm not paying attention.'

Iona placed her elbows on the table and leaned forward conspiratorially. 'My uncle tells me that you *know*.'

'Beg pardon?'

'About the Junior Ganymede!'

'Oh, yes. He told me on Friday.' I glanced around the room. 'Do *you* know?'

She gave me a look.

'Of course you know, sorry. But *how* do you know? I take it your uncle didn't let slip an Official Secret in the course of family gossip?'

'You might say I'm *involved*. Informally, occasionally, deniably. I suppose I have been since I was a bairn, when Uncle Torquil would borrow me and my pram to give a more domestic appearance to clandestine meetings in Holyrood Park.'

I'm not sure which intrigued me more: learning Iona had been steeped in espionage since birth, or discovering Lord MacAuslan's Christian name was Torquil.

'So, you're *not* a photographer?'

'Oh no, I'm *also* a photographer, in fact I'm mainly a photographer. But photography is the perfect camouflage for Junior Ganymede work, especially when abroad.'

'How so?'

'Get caught with a camera concealed in a hatbox and you're in all sorts of hot water. But, strangely, no one gives you a second glance if you stand in the middle of the street surreptitiously snapping Aunt Minnies.'

'You have an Aunt Minnie?' I thought she had nothing but uncles.

'Aunt Minnies are innocent-looking photographs with a guilty secret.'

'Such as?'

'Well, I might be taking tourist snaps of you standing on Weidendammer Bridge in Berlin. Innocuous enough, you say. But look closer. At your feet is a briefcase marked in such a way that the dimensions of the bridge can be accurately surveyed.'

'Which is useful for?'

'Armoured-vehicle movements. Or perhaps I'm taking a photograph of you waving goodbye at Centocelle airfield in Rome. Who would ever suspect that the only thing in focus through my wide-angle lens is the fuel depot behind you?'

'I say, that *is* cunning. But are we really going to *invade* these places?'

'You can never know too much too soon, Bertie. And we're not just interested in buildings. We have also to consider human frailties.'

'Naturally.'

'I might just happen to be at the Hotel Quisisana, taking pictures of Capri – snap, snap, snap – but who else is in shot? A very single woman having a very romantic drink with the very married Giacomo Feliziani.'

'Who he?'

'The Italian minister of defence.'

'Your Aunt Minnie gets about, doesn't she?'

'I also photograph babies.'

'Because they, er …' Try as I might, I couldn't think of a single clandestine reason for photographing a baby.

'Because their mothers pay me, Bertie. I have a studio in Edinburgh.'

All this explained the photographs she'd taken of Graydon and Tibby with Spode, and those of Graydon with his mystery woman in the woods. I took a sip of wine. 'How did you learn these rubber-heeled tricks? Did you acquire the secrets of espionage at Uncle Torquil's knee?'

'Only partly. The Junior Ganymede has a training camp – more of a large country house, really – on the Kent coast, near Whitstable.'

I sensed another piece of the Jeevesian jigsaw slotting into place, and it was one of those absolutely crucial corner pieces. 'Would this training camp be located, by any chance, in Herne Bay?'

Iona was startled. 'However did you know that?'

'Just a shrimp-like hunch.'

'They have all sorts of facilities there, including photography. But I also help out the Junior Ganymede in other capacities, as I believe you are about to do at the Gaiety Theatre tomorrow?'

'Well, you know, anything to oblige.'

'That's the spirit. Speaking of obliging, I have something delicate to ask you. But it should probably wait until pudding. You do eat pudding, don't you?'

'Invariably.'

'Jolly good. Me too.'

Once the dessert trolley had been wheeled squeaking away, Iona placed a full stop on our Ganymede *tête-à-tête* and began a new conversational paragraph.

'Bertie.'

'Still here.'

'You know that delicate thing I wanted to ask you?'

'Ask away. You will find me an open book.'

She took a breath and steeled herself. 'I need a man.'

'Really?' I croaked through a half-inhaled gooseberry.

'I'm old enough. I have the money. It's time.'

This called for caution, and more than a soupçon of modesty. 'Did you have ... anyone in mind?'

'Jeeves.'

'What!'

'Except that he's taken.'

'When you say "taken" ...?'

'With a job. In gainful employment. And I would never do that to a friend,' she smiled, 'albeit a very new and hardly proven friend.'

'Ah, right. Sorry. Inverse terminus, stick-wise. So, you need a gentleman's personal gentleman?'

'Not a butler?'

This was, I explained, a common confusion. Seppings is a butler; he runs Brinkley Court and the legion of staff therein. Jeeves, however, is a gentleman's personal gentleman – 'a valet with a brain', Uncle Tom once said – and he runs me. Some valets evolve into GPGs, and most GPGs can buttle with the best. But much weeping and gnashing of teeth is caused by mistaking one group for another, since the Guild is pretty hot on issues of demarcation.

'I see,' said Iona. 'So, I need a gentleman's personal gentleman, but for a gentlewoman.'

'Might I ask why you don't engage a maid or a housekeeper?'

'Oh, that's easy: housekeepers treat you like a child, and maids treat you like a mother. What I want is an equal or, ideally, a better. I saw Jeeves in action at Brinkley Court and was instantly dazzled. He has an air of, I don't know, regal authority. He's like a rare bird with unrufflable plumage.'

'I should warn you, Iona, Jeeveses are not easy to find, and harder still to hang on to. However, you've knocked at the right door, since I have made a detailed and comprehensive study of the subject.'

'Will I need a pencil?'

'Gentlemen's personal gentlemen come in four varieties: Drinkers, Cufflinkers, Thinkers, and Stinkers.'

'I definitely need a pencil.'

'Drinkers unsurreptitiously guzzle your spirits and tear through a wine cellar with no regard to vintage. They are ruinously expensive, dependably unreliable, and, far worst of all, you end up nursing *them* after a night of heavyweight revelry.'

'Right,' she said. 'No drinkers.'

'Cufflinkers are a mixed bag. Pros: they shine shoes, match socks, iron shirts, fold trousers, sponge and press suits, and arrange your wardrobe according to season and colour. Cons: they are forever raising pettifogging objections to tartan slippers and Alpine hats.'

'Alpine hats?'

'Blue, with a pink feather.'

'I see. So, Cufflinkers into the "Maybe" column. Next?'

'Thinkers are, within reason, the best. They are invaluable when extricating the young master, or mistress, from the social shipwreck. But, then again, they can't help leaving volumes of Spinoza lying around in a perpetual quest to educate and improve. So, with Thinkers it's swings and roundabouts.'

'Assuming you're not the kind of brute who prefers a roundabout,' she said with feeling. 'And that just leaves Stinkers. What of them?'

'Oh, they just stink.'

'Who, then, picks a Stinker?'

'No one *picks* a Stinker! Stinkers simply emerge, like a slug in the *soufflé*.'

Iona glanced mournfully down and pushed aside her half-eaten *Soufflé surprise*. 'So, I want a Thinker?'

'Were it so simple! As with Jekyll and Hyde, you have to combine two of the varieties. Jeeves is a "Thinker-cum-Cufflinker", which I have found to be the most harmonious double act. But there are those who swear by the "Thinker-Drinker" combination, arguing that the drinking tends to mitigate the worst effects of the thinking.'

Iona gazed at me in wonder. Or horror. Or amusement. To be honest, it was hard to tell what she was thinking.

'If I follow you, Bertie, and I'm not sure anyone should, I'm looking for a non-stinking, gently cufflinking, lightly drinking thinker?'

'Eggs-zachary!'

'Any names spring to mind?'

'Er ... no.'

'No?' Iona protested. 'After that preposterous overture, you offer me nothing but "No"?'

She was right, of course – *facta, non verba* and all that – so I tormented the old lemon to conjure a suitable candidate. Most of the butlers, GPGs, and valets I know are suckered to their employers like homesick limpets. I can't imagine Seppings ever leaving Uncle Tom, or Oakshott quitting Uncle Willoughby. As the decades pass, masters and manservants grow ever more intertwined until, like inosculated beech trees, it becomes impossible to imagine one existing independently from the other without simply keeling over.

The remaining rogues' gallery of men for hire was hardly suitable for a woman with the refined sensibility and arch irony of Iona MacAuslan. There was Merriewold (Drinker), Casey (Thinker-Drinker), Sann (Drinker-Thinker), Rathbone (Drinker-Drinker), Leith (Thinker-ex-Drinker), LaFarge (Cufflinker), Dane (Cufflinker *ad absurdum*), Begivney (Stinker), Ilag (utter Stinker), and Bingley (Stinker *extraordinaire*).

And then the name Crawshaw popped into my head.

'You know, there is a chap who might be perfect: Algernon Crawshaw. Quite a Thinker, not much of a Drinker, understated Cufflinker when the mood takes him. But sound. A safe pair of hands, and wise beyond his years. I met him briefly a couple of Christmases ago, and was dashed impressed. Let me parlay with Jeeves and see if Crawshaw comes up to his snuff.'

'Would you? I'd be awfully grateful. You might ascertain whether Mr Crawshaw would object to working for a woman. Some of the traditionalists, I gather, very much do.'

We stepped out of the cool quiet of the Lyceum into the sunlit bustle of Piccadilly.

'Well, that was very jovial, Iona. I enjoyed being a shirker.'

'I thought you might,' she smiled. 'I imagine it came easily to you.'

'I'm headed for South Audley Street to cheer on Uncle Tom at his tantalus auction, care to chum along?'

'Sadly, I have a date in the darkroom.'

'Oh, what's showing?'

'The photographic darkroom, Bertie. Developing and print-ing, dodging and burning?'

'Ah well, another time, I hope. Maybe when you are next down from Edinburgh?'

'I'd like that.'

'Wish us luck!'

'I'm quite sure you won't need it,' she smiled, walking away with a purposeful step to her well-turned ankle – the kind of ankle, I judged, that could out-Ginger the deftest of Rogers.

*   *   *

Shipley's may not be the most famous auction house in London, but there is, I'm assured, no grander or more trustworthy consignee for those who can tell their brass from their ormolu.

The 'Important Silver and Objects of Virtu' sale was in full swing by the time I slipped in and spotted Uncle Tom hovering apprehensively in an alcove.

'Any sign of Sir Gilbert?' I whispered.

By way of response, he handed me a telegram.

APOLOGIES FOR YESTERDAY TOM. BLAME SILVER FEVER.
BOWING OUT OF AUCTION. BEST OF LUCK. GILBERT

'He's not bidding?' This was a turn-up. 'So, we didn't need Jeeves after all.'

'Only if we get a good price,' observed Uncle Tom, morosely. 'Otherwise I might live to regret giving him the air.'

A round of applause signalled the sale of the latest lot – an ornate silver cow-creamer purchased by a lady so elaborately hatted she could only be some luckless bozo's aunt.

Uncle Tom nudged me. 'We're up.'

'And now, ladies and gentlemen,' boomed the auctioneer, 'we come to lot 108 – the catalogue-cover lot – a fine, solid-silver and cut-glass double-decanter tantalus by the House of Fabergé. Hallmarked in Cyrillic, 1890. In mint condition, with lock and mechanism in good working order.'

He surveyed the room.

'I'll start the bidding at one thousand pounds? Do I have a thousand?'

I saw a grey head nod.

'Thank you, sir ... One thousand one hundred? Thank you, sir ... And two hundred? ... Two hundred ... And three hundred ... With you, madam ... Four hundred? ... Thank you, sir ... Against you, madam ... Five hundred, thank you ... And six hundred? ... Six hundred, sir, thank you ... Seven? ... A new bidder, thank you, Your Reverence ... Eight hundred? ... And nine hundred, thank you ... Two thousand? ... Thank you, sir ... Two thousand two hundred ... With you, madam ... and two thousand four hundred ...'

The bidding had acquired an inexorable momentum, like a toddler's first headlong lurches towards an unattended stove. If you've ever been to an auction you'll know this is a sure sign that some poor devil is about to lose their shirt.

Uncle Tom was enthralled. His eyes darted around the room like a Wimbledon umpire, searching out the nods, winks, and ear pulls that were rapidly inflating his bank balance. As we hit five thousand pounds a brown-overalled porter appeared at my side.

'Mr Wooster?' he muttered out of the corner of his mouth. 'Got a note for you, chief.'

I instantly clocked Jeeves's copperplate on the envelope, and could hear his voice in the text:

Your urgent presence at the Junior Ganymede Club would be greatly appreciated, sir.

Secure in the knowledge that the score was decidedly 'advantage Travers', I left Uncle Tom to it, dashing out of Shipley's and running pell-mell down South Audley Street and into Curzon Street.

The door of the Junior Ganymede was opened by a youthful porter who sped me up a broad staircase to the second-floor committee room. Here, at one end of a lengthy boardroom table, sat Jeeves, flanked by a dozen or so black-suited valets. Way down at the far end of the table stood a candlestick telephone. The mouthpiece was directed back towards Jeeves, and the receiver was pressed to the very shapely ear of Miss Iona MacAuslan.

I gave her a look as if to say, 'Darkroom, eh?'

She replied with a mischievous twinkle.

Jeeves was in his element, projecting from the diaphragm with the sing-song cadence of the professional gavel-wielder.

'... I have five thousand on the telephone ... do I hear five thousand five hundred?'

He paused to accept an imaginary bid.

'Thank you, sir ... five thousand five hundred ... Any advance? ... Do I hear six thousand? ...'

All eyes swivelled down the table; Iona nodded.

'Six thousand, on the telephone, thank you, sir ... Do I hear six thousand five hundred?'

Jeeves decided to milk the moment.

'Are you quite sure, ladies and gentlemen? ... Not even for this outstanding example of Fabergé craftsmanship? ... With lock and mechanism in good working order? ... Fair warning ... I'm selling at six thousand, on the telephone ... Going once at six thousand ... Going twice ... For the final time of asking, at six thousand ...'

He banged a meerschaum pipe on the edge of the table. 'Gone! ... To the telephone bidder ... at six thousand pounds.'

Jeeves raised his hand to orchestrate a brief ripple of applause, and then read aloud from the auction catalogue. 'Our next lot, lot 109, is an "intriguing silver porringer made by Strauss and Co., hallmarked for London, 1889". I'd like to start the bidding at four hundred—'

Iona interrupted. 'He's rung off!'

The conclave of valets burst into genuine applause and, with a volley of handshakes and backslaps, dispersed laughing down to the bar.

I strode over to buttonhole the 'auctioneer' and his 'assistant'.

'Jeeves, what just happened?'

'Sir Gilbert Skinner appears to have bought a Fabergé tantalus for six thousand pounds, sir.'

'That was Sir Gilbert on the horn?'

'It was,' said Iona.

'But *this* isn't the auction – I've just come from the auction!'

'Quite so, sir.'

'So, this is … what?'

'A ruse, sir.'

'Care to enlighten me, Jeeves?'

'Certainly, sir. The seed was planted even before Mr Travers asked for my assistance, when I unavoidably overheard your uncle's meeting with Sir Gilbert yesterday morning. That negotiation, I fear, could not be described as amicable. Mr Travers's final offer was that Sir Gilbert would obtain the tantalus over his dead body. Sir Gilbert countered that he was sure such an arrangement could be made.'

'Pistols at dawn!'

'Aware that Sir Gilbert intended to leave Brinkley Court before luncheon, I contrived to encounter him prior to his departure.'

'Lurking by the garages?'

'Something like that, sir. After briefly discussing the fastest route to London, I affected hostility towards your uncle on account of some minor slight. Feigning a desire for retribution, I offered Sir Gilbert information on how to acquire the tantalus at a good price.'

'I expect he bit your hand off. What did you say?'

'I advised Sir Gilbert that your uncle was planning to "trot up" the price of the tantalus by employing a ring of shills to bid against him. I suggested he absent himself from the saleroom and participate anonymously by telephone.'

'Do they have telephone bidding at Shipley's?' I asked.

'It has recently been introduced, sir, for sales with an international audience.'

I pondered for a moment. 'Why, then, did Sir Gilbert telegram Uncle Tom this morning to say he was withdrawing from the auction?'

'*Did* he, sir?' It's quite a thing to wrong-foot Jeeves and witness the flywheels spinning behind his normally unflappable eyes. 'I hadn't foreseen such a development.'

'My guess,' said Iona, 'is that Sir Gilbert was simply icing the cake. His telegram was designed to lull Uncle Tom into a false sense of security and ensure he didn't inflate the bidding anyway.'

Jeeves nodded sagely. 'That does seem to fit the facts, miss.'

'Is there any reason,' I asked Jeeves, with perhaps an iota of chagrin, 'why you chose to keep all this from me? Only this morning you claimed to have no inspiration whatsoever. There was talk, I recall, of "considerable disquiet".'

'I must beg your pardon for the subterfuge, sir. Since we could not be certain that the plan would come off, I was anxious not to give Mr Travers false hope or risk disrupting the proceedings at Shipley's. As I may have mentioned, in ventures such as this I am of the opinion that—'

'Verisimilitude cannot be overestimated?'

'Precisely, sir.'

'Even so, Jeeves, I think you might have tipped me the wink – especially now that I'm in the Ganymede cabal. But how did the auction – the *fake* auction, I mean – come to take place here?'

'That's where I come in,' said Iona. 'As you'd expect, the Junior Ganymede is pretty well connected inside London's telephone network. Before I met you this morning I popped into the Mayfair exchange and had a word with the "hello girls". They promised that any calls to Shipley's originating from Trollope's switchboard would be redirected here.'

'But how did you know he'd be calling from the bank? He could have telephoned from anywhere.'

Despite there being only three of us in the room, Jeeves lowered his voice. 'The Cabinet Office scheduled a telephone call between Sir Gilbert and the Chancellor of the Exchequer just as the auction began. This mitigated against Sir Gilbert attending Shipley's in person, and made it likely that he would bid via the bank's switchboard.'

'The Chancellor, eh? Friends in high places.' I turned to Iona. 'And you, I take it, were the voice of Shipley's?'

She dropped her enchanting Edinburgh brogue and slipped into the idiosyncratic intonation of a London telephonist: '*Good* morning, caller, *Shipley's* telephone bidding, *may* I be of assistance?'

'Impersonations as well! Is there no end?'

'*You should hear my Aunt Dahlia!*' she boomed in a voice that had my much-loved relative down to a tee. '*You fiend in human form!*'

'And the parliament of ravens?' I asked Jeeves, pointing to where the flash-mob of Ganymede members had been roosting. 'What were they in aid of?'

'That is what radio engineers call "presence", sir. I thought the occasional cough, murmur, or shuffling of paper from a group of people would add atmospheric authenticity. Also, I judged that Sir Gilbert would be reassured by a round of applause on finally securing the tantalus.'

I had to hand it to Jeeves, even by his egg-headed standards this was a pretty neat scramble. Although, did I detect a flaw?

'So, Jeeves, what happens when Sir Gilbert turns up at Shipley's to collect his booty? What then?'

'I imagine confusion will abound, sir. However, Sir Gilbert has no proof he purchased the tantalus, which was, after all, auctioned off in full view of . . . ?'

'About a hundred.'

'. . . about a hundred unimpeachable witnesses.'

'So, this is a culprit-less crime?'

'Is it a crime, sir?' Jeeves mused. 'Sir Gilbert has not been deprived of his money, nor has Shipley's been deprived of its commission.'

I cocked a sceptical eyebrow.

'I concede, sir, that a strict reading of the 1868 Telegraph Act might indicate certain irregularities, but nothing, I venture, that could be substantiated.'

Iona raised a finger. 'And, Bertie, if your uncle has a telegram from Sir Gilbert promising not to bid in the auction—'

'—he can hardly claim he's been duped! Well this is elegant indeed. Perhaps it's true, you can't deceive an honest man.'

'I suppose they'll have to rewrite the Greek myth now,' said Iona.

'Eh?'

'Banner headline in the *Hades Times*: "GANYMEDE SAVES TANTALUS!"'

'Oh, *very* good, miss,' said Jeeves, approvingly.

'Yes,' I bluffed, utterly mystified. 'Splendid.'

A clock chimed, and Iona looked at her wristwatch. 'Gracious, I should be leaving. I have to pack.'

'Actually off to Edinburgh this time?'

'On tonight's sleeper, so I will bid you both farewell. Jeeves, it's been an apprenticeship to watch you work.' She handed me her card with a heart-stopping smile. 'I hope our paths cross again soon, Bertie – and don't forget what I asked you earlier.'

Iona tripped off down the stairs, leaving master and manservant alone.

'Are those the club books?' I pointed towards a set of twelve leather-bound volumes neatly stacked in a glass case.

'Yes, sir.'

'Terrifying,' I shuddered. 'Like unexploded ordnance – they could go off at any time.'

'Only in the wrong hands, sir. Might I offer you a drink? The bar is downstairs.'

'That's decent of you, and don't think I'm not gasping, but I have been summoned by Monty to the Gaiety Theatre to spectate the dress rehearsal of *Flotsam*.'

'Very good, sir. Would you have any objections if I remained here for a while?'

'None whatsoever. You have more than earned it. In fact, please order champagne for all and sundry and send me the account.'

'Thank you, sir.'

As we descended to the front door, I was assailed by a qualm, assuming such things are sold to the public in the singular.

'Jeeves?'

'Sir.'

'I don't wish to appear ungrateful – and, really, that was a pippin – but ought we to have unleashed the heavy brigade of the Junior Ganymede and the Chancellor of the Excheq. merely to settle a score for Uncle Tom?'

'In the normal course of events, sir, no. The Junior Ganymede takes a dim view of using club assets in a private capacity. However, Sir Gilbert has for some time been of interest to the government.'

'MacAuslan did mention that.'

'And, on occasion, sir, inconspicuous vexation is a most effective strategy.'

'Is it?'

'Assuredly, sir. The Junior Ganymede's founding charter from 1878 expressly commands the organisation to "frustrate their knavish tricks".'

'I say! *Knavish tricks.* That's awfully good. Where have I heard that phrase before?'

'The National Anthem, sir?'

*   *   *

The Gaiety Theatre was locked and bolted when I arrived to meet Monty, but there was a handwritten note stuck to a window directing all callers to the Stage Door. There I found a cheerful old codger ensconced in a cupboard and dragging on a Woodbine.

He looked up from his paper. 'Evening, squire. Can I help?'

'I'm here to see Montague Montgomery. Is he about?'

'Might be. What's 'e look like?'

'Erm, a bit like a tall tweed lamp-post.'

'Oh, 'e's here, all right. Go straight through and take two lefts and a right. Keep shtum, mind, they've just started the dress.'

I followed these instructions to the letter and, after a few dead ends, found myself standing in the wings next to a remarkably pretty redhead.

'What-ho, mermaid.'

'I'm not a mermaid.'

'Really? You do realise you're dressed as a mermaid?'

'I'm an undine. It's a mystical water nymph who has to marry in order to acquire a human soul.'

'I see.'

'But they only had mermaid costumes. Also, I have a song about waterfalls in the third act.'

'I shall look forward to that. Have you seen a tall chap in a tweed suit? He's probably been hanging around backstage for a week or two, annoying people.'

'D'you mean Monty? He's in the prompter's box.'

She pointed towards the footlights where, underneath an arched canopy, decorated for some reason like a seashell, Monty's head emerged from a hole in the stage.

'How does one get to him?'

She began to explain before realising it would be simpler to show me. We backtracked through the maze of turns and climbed down a rickety staircase into the dark. It was evident from the thudding of footsteps and creaking of boards above that we were directly under the action.

'He's over there,' she whispered, gesturing to a wooden platform on which stood a pair of legs illuminated by a dazzling shaft of light from the stage above.

I picked my way carefully through the darkness, weaving around a tangle of ropes, pulleys, and levers. When I finally arrived at the cuffs of Monty's trousers it wasn't immediately clear how my presence might be announced, so I tapped him lightly on the toe of his left shoe.

He peered down. 'Bertie, you came! Climb up and join me.'

Monty shuffled over to one side and hoisted me onto the platform, where we stood shoulder to shoulder, like two shy coconuts, gazing out across the boards.

A crew of nautical-looking extras was milling about hammily upstage, while downstage left a swarthy seaman was coiling rope and describing to the empty theatre, in a thick Cockney accent, the privations of life on the ocean wave.

'What's going on, Monty?' I whispered.

'It's Act I, Scene One. That's Able Seaman Benskin Muchmore with his opening speech. Any minute now Lady Cynthia Mandrake will arrive and beg him to help her stow away for the fateful voyage to Peru.'

'I mean, what are you doing in the prompter's box?'

'You get much the best view from here.'

'I can see that.'

'And I get to avoid Lord Sidcup. He's always hanging around Florence, reminding her of his sizeable investment in a leering sort of way.'

'I can see that, too.'

'Also, I've appointed myself prompter.'

'Where's your script?'

'Don't need one. I know the play by heart. Better than half the cast, I should say.'

By this time, Benskin Muchmore had wandered downstage right, and was describing '*waves as high as cathedrals, waves as the likes no man has survived*'.

'How long does this hogwash last, Monty?'

'Not including interval, three hours.'

I whistled in astonishment. 'That's two plays where I come from.'

Monty gasped, spun round in an awkward circle, and spat three times between his legs. 'Please, Bertie! No whistling – it's deadly bad luck to whistle in a theatre.'

And, as if to prove his point, who should enter upstage left but Florence Craye – dressed as a Victorian flower-seller and carrying, for some reason, a lobster pot.

'Heavens! What's she doing?'

'She plays Lady Mandrake. Didn't you know?'

I most certainly did not. I knew she'd written this three-hour leviathan, but not that she'd cast herself as leading lady. That said, Florence did have a certain *je ne sais something* onstage, not to mention a voice almost as nerve-jangling as Aunt Dahlia's.

There'd be no complaints from the back row about her projection, although those in the stalls might endure a month or two of tinnitus.

The same could not be said for the actor playing Benskin Muchmore, who suddenly dried and, after an agonising pause, was forced to call out, 'Prompt!'

Without a second's hesitation Monty furnished the line – '*Lummy, miss, there ain't many who can take the spume*' – and the action continued.

I glanced at my wristwatch and decided that any more of this nautical bilge would create expectations for supper too great for any restaurant to fulfil.

'Right, Monty, time for me to shemozzle.'

'But it's only just begun!'

'That's what worries me. I think once round the park will be more than enough for *Flotsam*. I will see you in the bar tomorrow evening for a pre-fight sharpener.'

I was clambering back down into the dark, folding and unfolding my limbs like a trapped spider, when a foot stomped on the stage directly above my head. Startled by this percussive explosion just inches from my ear, I lost my balance and stumbled into a wooden contraption that broke my fall with a creak.

'Hush!' shushed Monty, waggling an annoyed foot in my direction.

Regaining my equilibrium, I inched cautiously to the staircase and ascended to the well-lit safety of the wings. Here, once again, I discovered my amiable mermaid.

'Three hours, eh?'

She grimaced. 'Plus an interval. I'll be lucky to get out of here by midnight.'

'But at least you'll end the day with a human soul.'

'No such luck. Lady Mandrake steals my man in the final scene, so I remain an undine forever.'

'But a very charming undine.'

She hit me playfully with a flipper. 'Get away with you!'

I was on my way to the Stage Door when I heard an almighty collision followed by a cry of agony far too convincing to be anything performed by Mandrake or Muchmore. I dashed back to the wings to find Florence Craye peering down a hole in the middle of the stage.

'Are you all right?' she asked the void.

'No, I am not all right,' the void replied, furiously. 'I've broken my damn leg. Some idiot left a trap open, and when I find out who it was I will break both his dammed legs and much else besides.'

The voice was that of Benskin Muchmore, and it didn't take long for me to link the scene unfolding onstage with the wooden contraption into which I had stumbled below stage.

'Can you walk?' Florence enquired.

'With a broken leg? Are you completely deranged?'

'That's that, then,' she said hopelessly. 'We have no Benskin. We have no play. Closed before the opening night! *Flotsam* will have an even shorter run than *Spindrift*.'

There was a flurry of movement from the footlights and, with all the zeal of a ferret seeking freedom from a Yorkshireman's trousers, Monty scrambled out of his box and up onto the stage.

'I'll play the part!' he shouted, grinning and breathless.

'Oh, will you, Monty?' Florence laughed. 'You, who have never before acted, step in at the dress and take over from the leading man?'

'He's not really the leading man—'

'Yes I am!' shouted the void.

'I admit Benskin Muchmore has by far the most lines,' conceded Monty, 'but if you consider the play's subtext—'

'Subtext? We haven't got time for subtext!'

'Look here, Florence, I know the play, I know the part, and the curtain goes up tomorrow. What other choice do you have? The show must go on.'

She shook her head. 'An illiterate deckhand from the Isle of Dogs played by *you* – a public schoolboy with an accent that could scratch diamond? I don't think so, Monty. This isn't Noël Coward.'

There is a tide in the affairs of men, which taken at the flood, struts and frets its hour upon the stage. Or something like that, I forget the specifics. Suffice to say, cometh the hour, cometh the Cockney.

Monty tossed his jacket to the stage and rolled up his shirtsleeves. Stepping forward into the full glare of the footlights, he adopted a heroic pose and declaimed from memory, in a perfect East End accent, Benskin Muchmore's opening monologue.

You could have heard a programme drop. Florence was the image of incredulity, and I was pretty gasted by the flabber myself.

It occurred to me that while Monty had never actually trodden any boards, he was a naturally versatile chameleon. Each of his three jobs required him to adopt a persona and, when I had seen him in action, his portrayals were spot on the button.

As the closing line echoed around the empty auditorium, all that could be heard was a furious actor banging his head in resentful frustration on the floor under the stage.

Monty turned to Florence. 'Have I won the part?'

'Oh, Monty, you have.'

And it would have been obvious, even to those up in the cheap seats, that he had won much, much more.

'Attention everyone,' Florence called out to her cast and crew. 'We go again in fifteen minutes with Mr Montgomery taking the part of Benskin. Beginners in fifteen, please.'

As the stage was reset, I beckoned Monty to the wings.

'I say, that was quite the audition. You must have greasepaint in the blood.'

'It was thrilling, Bertie. Electric. I always knew I was destined for the spotlight.'

'And now you have a fourth job.'

'About that, Bertie – might you be able to ...?'

'It would be a privilege, Monty. I will walk your sandwich in the mornings, wash your bottles all afternoon, and assume your hosting duties at the Hot Spot in the evenings.'

'Really? I say, that's dashed sporting of you.'

'Of course not, you muttonhead! I have done my lifetime's allocation of good deeds for the Widcombe Montgomeries. From here on in, old bean, you are firmly on your own.'

He eyed me coolly. 'Oh, it's to be like that, is it? I see. Well, what if I were to tell Florence it was you who opened the trapdoor? What then?'

'Then I would be obliged to tell Florence *and* Spode about your flirting with Madeline Bassett this morning.'

His mouth flapped open like a landed carp.

'I think the word you're hunting for, Monty, is "checkmate". And now I am off to Simpson's, where I shall stow away a steak and kidney pud while drowning a bottle of claret. Tinkety-tonk.'

'But, Bertie—'

'You may stick your three jobs, Montague, where the monkey hides the nuts. Tinkety-*tonk*.'

I was strolling briskly towards the exit with a that's-that sort of feeling, when a plaintive voice rang out from the void:

'I say ... did anyone call for an ambulance?'

* * *

I was not late back to Berkeley Mansions, and Jeeves welcomed me home sporting the apron and white gloves he dons to polish silver. I divested myself of various items of outerwear as I made my way to the sitting-room and collapsed appreciatively onto a long-suffering divan.

'Have you dined, sir? Or would you care, perhaps, for an omelette?'

'I have been deliciously stranded at Simpson's, thank you, but might I trouble you for a nightcap? It has been a long and wearisome day.'

As he decanted the necessary fluids, I put to him the question I'd been cogitating since we parted. 'Jeeves, do you have any idea how much the tantalus sold for? In the real world, I mean.'

'Yes, sir. The winning bid was seventeen thousand pounds.'

'Hell's bells, what riches! Uncle Tom must be jigging a hornpipe.'

'So I should imagine, sir.'

'And the bidder? Some foreign potentate with pockets crammed with doubloons?'

'I believe, sir, that the lot was secured by Sir Watkyn Bassett.'

I set down my drink, and swung from the recumbent to the sedentary.

'Jeeves, tell me you're joking.'

'No, sir.'

'But I didn't see Bassett at the auction. How did he do it? Did *he* bid by telephone?'

'Actually, sir, there was no telephone bidding at today's sale.' He paused to let the irony of this statement ripple out. 'I am informed that Sir Watkyn participated in the auction disguised as a vicar.'

'A vicar! I call that low, Jeeves, very low indeed. And quite possibly heretical.'

'Sacrilegious, sir?'

Either way, this was most definitely an earwig in the eyewash.

Sir Watkyn Bassett CBE is, as the surname hints, Madeline Bassett's father. But this is merely a hobby, since 'Pop' Bassett's true vocation is as personal nemesis to the clan Wooster. Me, he has persecuted for years in his roles as Justice of the Peace and legal-minded stickybeak. Devoted readers may recall that Sir Watkyn once fined me five quid for pinching a policeman's helmet on Boat Race night, despite my spirited defence that bluebottles, as a rule, treat such copper-sloshing as good-natured sport and all in a day's plod.

Uncle Tom, on the other hand, has been hounded by the Bassett for decades. Time after time, his innocent attempts to trade some precious silver trinket have been foiled by Sir Watkyn, who once plotted to steal away the services of Anatole. *Anatole!* Belief is truly beggared.

It was, therefore, a gold-plated certainty that however much Uncle Tom did not want Sir Gilbert to grab the tantalus, he wanted Sir Watkyn Bassett CBE to grab it less.

'So, Jeeves, after all your ingenious artifice, we leapt out of the whatsit-called into the thing?'

'Yes, sir.'

'Rats! Do you think Uncle Tom knows?'

'I could not say, sir. It would depend on the effectiveness of Sir Watkyn's ecclesiastical dissimulation.'

'Well, I didn't spot him. Let's hope Tom never finds out.'

'Yes, sir.'

'And, lest we forget: seventeen thousand smackers. Which is more than double what Sir Gilbert originally offered. As silver linings go, I'd call that pretty muscular.'

'Quite so. Incidentally, sir, did you see the package that arrived in this afternoon's post?'

'Package? I saw no package.'

'I positioned it in a prominent spot next to the aspidistra. If you would wait one moment, sir.'

He vanished for a second before rematerialising with a rigid square envelope, inside of which was a 78 r.p.m. recording of 'You're the Sweetest Girl This Side Of Heaven' by Guy Lombardo and His Royal Canadians. Carefully written on the disc's glossy black shellac, in yellow wax pencil, was the telephone number *Gulliver 1432*, and the words OLD MANIAC.

'OLD MANIAC?' I ruminated. 'It might refer to any of a hundred people we know.'

'Indeed, sir.'

'It must mean *something*, Jeeves. I mean, people don't go sending cryptic dance tunes for no good reason.'

Jeeves cleared his throat. 'Might it be an anagram, sir?'

'You mean like ... MANILA COD? ... CAN DO MALI? ... AN IDOL MAC? ... AM ICON LAD? ... DIAL MA CON?'

'Actually, sir, I was thinking of NOMADICAL.'

'Zing!' I cried. 'Exacto perfecto! So *this* is my special song, and Gulliver 1432 is the secret telephone number. Bless the cotton socks of Baron Chuffnell. It looks like I've acquired another club.'

7

TUESDAY

'Have you ever wondered,' I enquired over the toasted soldiers, 'why chickens and pigs, who rarely see eye to eye in the farmyard, are so utterly congenial on the plate?'

'No, sir.'

'It's a mysterious thing.'

'Is it, sir?'

I gestured to my plate. 'Eggs and bacon. Chicken and pigs.'

'Will there be anything else, sir?'

'Actually, yes. I promised Iona MacAuslan I would seek your guidance.'

'Sir?'

'She's looking to engage a gentleman's personal gentleman, and I wondered if you could think of any suitable candidates?'

'I would be pleased to give the matter some consideration, sir, although one name does immediately present itself.'

'Is it a secret?'

'Mr Crawshaw, sir.'

'Great minds! That's who popped into my head. Where is Crawshaw now?'

'With a gentleman in Coombe Bissett, sir. Wiltshire.'

'Could he be lured up to Edinburgh, do you think? And, first things first, would he object to working for a dame? Some chaps are fairly dusty on that subject.'

'I cannot speak for his geographical inclinations, sir, though I foresee no difficulties in the latter regard. Mr Crawshaw once resigned a position when he learned his employer had opposed the cause of women's suffrage in the House of Lords.'

This sounded like just the sort of modern man Iona was after, and so I asked Jeeves to dip an elbow into the bathwater.

'I will make enquiries, sir.'

'Thank you. Although, I did also wonder whether Archie Rathbone might suit Miss MacAuslan? Even with his inebriate tendencies.'

'I'm afraid Mr Rathbone has gone away, sir.'

'Oh, yes, that does strike a chord. Somewhere like Paris, wasn't it? Or Provence? Penrith?'

'Pentonville, sir.'

'Ah. For good?'

'For six months, sir. Without the option.'

'Double carpet! Well then, let's hope Crawshaw manages to keep himself unlocked up. And now, as they say in Victorian novels, I have important business at the club. Might you be so kind as to determine the whereabouts of *mon chapeau*?'

It cheered the spirits no end to ambulate down Dover Street and spy the Drones Club emerged from its summer hibernation: windows unshuttered, door agape, and gas *flambeaux* ablaze in celebration.

I bounced gazelle-like into the lobby and, with a triumphant '*Olé*', tossed my titfer with deadly precision onto the hat-stand.

'Good morning, Mr Wooster,' said Bashford, collecting my trilby from the floor.

'Ahoy there, Bashers. I trust you had a splendid holiday?'

'We visited the wife's family, sir.'

'Oh, I am sorry. I bet you're glad to be back.'

'I'm looking forward to the relative silence, sir.'

'Jolly good. Did a Gorringe arrive? Tall chappie, side-whiskers? The furtive snuffle of a professional ink-slinger?'

'Yes, sir. He's waiting in the billiard-room, as you requested.'

And so he was, all six foot two of him, strolling around the table, puffing on a small cigar, and casting an admiring eye over the club's impressive collection of sporting memorabilia, only some of which had been stolen.

'What-ho, Percy!'

'Does that still apply?' asked Gorringe peremptorily, waving his cheroot at a hand-painted sign:

Only Billiards May be Played
During the National Hunt Season

'Oh no, that's not us. That item was liberated from the Victoria Club a few years ago by my ne'er-do-well cousins, Claude and Eustace. They have a remarkably light-fingered touch those two – especially once you observe the thing's attached to the wall with thirty-six screws.'

'So we can play snooker-pool?'

'Snooker-pool, Percy? Just how ancient are you? No one calls it snooker-pool any more. We shall simply be playing snooker.'

Gorringe spotted the colours as I racked the reds.

I offered him the cue-ball. 'Care to break?'

He placed the white between green and brown, and chalked his cue thoughtfully.

'Is there something odd about this table, Bertie?'

'Odd? How so, odd?'

'I'm not exactly sure. But it seems distinctly odd.'

'Nothing odd about it as far as I know,' I said blithely, lying through my teeth.

What Gorringe had sensed, but not understood, was that the Drones Club snooker table is quite a bit larger than your standard full-size model. It is, to be strictly accurate, one-fifth larger. The table was bequeathed to the club by Milo Hamilton, a giant of a man who had commissioned it at eye-watering expense in order to obtain a decidedly unsporting advantage from his seven-foot height and corresponding wing-span.

Many visitors suspect there is something fishy about the set-up, but surprisingly few ever guess what – a state of affairs that gives the Drones Club snooker and billiards teams a significant, if dishonourable, home advantage.

Gorringe broke off, glancing the pack with the finest of edges and returning to baulk, leaving nothing that even resembled a viable red. The cue-ball slid to a halt touching the top cushion, directly in line with the green.

This gave me pause.

I enjoy a frame of snooker as much as the next man, assuming the next man isn't Gussie Fink-Nottle – whose horn-rimmed spectacles make cueing the simplest of shots a ceremony of pantomimic proportions. (Any occasion where the white ball is further than three inches from its target is known in the Drones as a 'Fink-Nottle Snooker'.) Although I've never made it onto any club team, I've assembled the occasional four-ball break and have, once or twice, assisted by a following wind, inched into the high teens at a single visit.

My original plan, therefore, had been to sweeten Gorringe by gracefully shepherding him to well-contested, yet slyly certain victory. But now he had shown himself to be quite the cue-man, it was clear I'd have to be at the top of my game to salvage even the sorriest crumbs of honour.

I played off the side cushion and settled safely into the pack.

Gorringe strolled round the table, crouching low to examine the angles. He lined up a shot that made no sense to me whatsoever, before neatly planting a red to the corner.

'Play often, Percy?'

'I dabble,' he replied, smoothing the cloth with an expert hand before feathering an impossibly thin black and landing bang on a red he had previously nudged loose.

That's the problem with writers, I thought to myself. Forever searching out excuses not to write, they end up expert in pursuits like snooker and darts, which ought, by rights, to be the exclusive province of clubmen and *boulevardiers*.

Before I had begun to pay proper attention, Gorringe was well into double figures and I was in the jaws of the pocket nearest the yellow.

'What am I meant to do with this, Percy?'

'You're corner-hooked, old chap. Not much you can do, except make an attempt and concede the points.'

I did as suggested and my opponent showed no mercy, sinking a red so long that it was almost imperceptible down the deep end of the table.

After the usual authorial chit-chat about his latest novel, the parlous state of publishing, the perfidy of critics, and the scandalous dearth of royalties, I decided to commence manoeuvres.

'Ever thought of joining this place, Percy?'

Gorringe gazed at me in awe, as if, by simply chalking his cue, he had summoned a wish-granting genie.

'I won't lie, Bertie, I'd love to join the Drones. My club is the absolute pits. They insist on laying out fish-knives, they've banned smoking in the smoking-room, and they've just blackballed two members of the England cricket team.'

'Hell's teeth!'

'It's becoming more and more like a railway hotel each week. They threatened to halt the playing of billiards on Sundays, but instead have decreed that play will be permitted so long as no score is kept.'

To indicate just what he thought of this puritanical humbug he hammered the white into the pack, sinking two reds simultaneously.

It seemed like the ideal moment to thicken the plot. 'You know I'm on the membership committee here?'

'I didn't. Interesting.'

'And a Craye-shaped bird told me you might be keen to join.'

'Florence?' He looked up from the table. 'It's been an aeon since we intersected. How the dickens is she?'

'Punching well above her weight, I should say, and even brainier than usual. Although she does have some anxieties at the moment.'

'About *Flotsam*, I expect.' He edged the pink into the centre. 'And, by the way, what kind of name for a play is *Flotsam*?'

I was hoping he'd be the first to introduce this topic. 'Funny you should mention *Flotsam*.'

'Funny, how? Other than its idiot title.'

'I gather you are to write tomorrow's first-night review for the *Evening News*?'

'Not I,' he said innocently, tapping a red into the green-corner pocket.

I sighed. 'Very well, Percy, the review is being written by Mr Rex West. With whom, I believe, you are on unusually friendly terms, in that you inhabit the same body.'

By way of a silent riposte, Gorringe struck a delicate three-cushion safety that deposited the cue-ball tight in behind the brown. I played off the top cushion, and was astonished when the white cannoned off the blue and fluked a red into the middle.

'What are the ethics of all this?' asked Percy, patently irked by my stroke of luck. 'Writing a good review in order to obtain club membership?'

I felt pretty confident that this was the first time the subject of ethics had ever been raised in the Drones Club billiard-room. That said, had Florence Craye been a fly on the wall she would have buzzed with gratification. This was precisely the sort of gum-flap the old girl relished, so much so that she has tried (and failed) on numerous occasions to get me to read a brick of a book seductively titled *Types of Ethical Theory*.

I met my foe on his own terrain.

'You pose an excellent philosophical question, Percy. Let me ask you one in return.' I sank the blue and came off the angle for a cushy red. 'What are the ethics of pseudonymously reviewing *Flotsam* when you used to be engaged to the author, and when you dramatised its forerunner, *Spindrift*?'

I flubbed the cushy red.

'When you put it like that ...' said Percy, pocketing my red with a stun shot that left him his choice of colours.

'I'm sure I could get Bingo Little to second your nomination,' I enticed. 'And a legion of chaps to sign your page in the book.'

Percy toyed pensively with his cube of chalk. 'The thing is, Bertie, I couldn't possibly be seen to compromise the independence of the press.'

'Heavens no! Wouldn't dream of asking such a thing.' I paused for a beat, like detectives do before finally unmasking the murderer. 'But what of ... Rex West?'

Percy sank a ludicrously long blue and came off two cushions to rest inches from a red. 'Rex is a horse of a different colour.'

'Would Florence be safe in betting on Rex?'

Gorringe didn't answer. Instead he got down to the serious business of racking up points. As colours followed reds like dominoes, any hope I had of salvaging a decent score evaporated like so much cigar smoke.

I applied another ratchet of pressure. 'Tough crowd, Percy, the membership committee. Unpredictable. Capricious. Devilish with the blackballing. Positively cruel. And, of course, Rule Fifteen states that if you've been blackballed once, well, that's that. Forever.'

By the time Gorringe again acknowledged my presence he had all but cleared up. Only the black remained.

'Let me put it like this, Bertie ...'

He paced round the table towards the white.

'Imagine the black ball is a glowing Rex West review of *Flotsam* ...'

He lined up the shot.

'And that corner pocket is the theatre page of the *Evening News* ...'

He drew back his elbow, squinted one eye, and slammed down the cue with formidable might.

I know what he intended to happen. What actually happened was very different. The white, outraged at its grievous assault, kicked hard against the black, which flew straight off the table and made a bee-line towards a cabinet of silver trophies.

Countless halcyon schooldays spent fielding in the slips had trained me for this moment, and I caught the errant missile left-hand, backhand without thinking or blinking.

'Well held!' exclaimed Percy, astounded at my feat of instinctive sinisterity – for this was no cakewalk catch.

I took a bow and gave the black a quick polish. 'So, where does this leave us?'

'Put it back on the spot and I'll have another go.'

Percy potted the black on his third attempt and, with our *quid pro quo* thusly sealed, I escorted him up to the front door and reassured him that the next time he entered the Drones it would be as a fully-fledged member.

Back in the lobby, I decided it would only be charitable to help assuage Florence's first-night nerves.

'Bashers, have you such a thing as a telegram pad?'

'Here you go, sir. And a pencil.'

I scribbled off a quick salvo. 'Can you get this to Lady Florence Craye, care of the Gaiety Theatre, as soon as poss?'

'"Gorringe says no lemon,"' read Bashford. 'Very good, sir. I'll send Robinson out with it straight away.'

'I'm obliged. Now, is the rest of the committee here?'

'Yes, sir. They're upstairs.'

'Jolly good. See you shortly.'

I pushed open the creaking door of the Silence Library to find Bingo Little, Tuppy Glossop, Freddie Bullivant, Barmy Fotheringay-Phipps, and Catsmeat Potter-Pirbright standing in a circle. Each had a teaspoon balanced on his nose.

'What-ho, Crumpets!'

'Shaddup,' growled Bingo through gritted teeth.

'Who's losing?'

'Shadd-up!'

Time passed, then all of a sudden Tuppy's spoon thudded to the carpet and the rest of the gang exhaled sighs of relief.

'Right,' said Bingo, 'Glossop's in the chair. Over to you, Tuppy.'

'Spooning for chairman?' I asked. 'This is new.'

'Freddie couldn't find the straws, so we improvised.'

Chairmanship of the Drones Club membership committee cuts both ways. On the one hand, you get to steer which names from the nomination book go forward to the quarterly elections. On the other, it is your disagreeable responsibility to inform unsuccessful candidates that they have been blackballed. To ensure the heavy yoke of office is shared, the committee selects a new chairman at the start of each season by drawing straws. I was excluded from today's spoons only because my chairmanship had just ended.

Tuppy summoned the meeting to order by tapping his signet ring against an ashtray. 'I say, chaps, a little decorum, if you please.' He consulted the agenda. 'First order of business: Apologies for absence from the fifth Baron Chuffnell. A gross act of impertinence for which the committee will fine Chuffy a case of ...?'

'Claret?' suggested Barmy.

'Claret it is. So ordered. Second, I can't help noticing that one of us is incorrectly attired for this meeting, noose-wise.'

'Sorry about that,' said Bingo, nervously adjusting his tie, which was the only specimen not in the club's approved shade of plum. 'Won't happen again.'

'Drinks are on Bingo,' adjudicated Tuppy. 'And now, to the candidates. Because of the summer vac, we've only three names before us. Each is nominated under a technicality, so we should be back in the bar *toot sweet*.'

The first candidate was a shoe-in, being as he was Freddie Bullivant's youngest brother, just down from Cambridge.

Under Rule Two (g), brothers of members in good standing are elected to the club by acclamation alone, assuming their nomination is supported by the brother in question. And so it came to pass, with a hearty drumming on the table, that Phineas 'Piebald' Bullivant became the latest in a long and dubious line of Bullivants to darken the door of the Drones.

'The second candidate,' read Tuppy, 'is one Fitzgerald Quent, who is before the committee under Two (f).'

Rule Two (f) states that a Dronesman who resigns his membership for whatever reason may stand for re-election without first seeking formal nomination.

'Mr Quent is a complete mystery to me,' confessed Tuppy. 'It says here that he resigned eleven years ago after objecting to the introduction of electric lighting. But that's all I have. Does anyone else know anything about him?'

'Damfino,' said Barmy.

'I've asked around,' I said, 'and it seems that Quent wants to rejoin the Drones because he's just been kicked out of the Paternoster.'

'How in hell does one get kicked out of that mausoleum? I thought they were all stretchered out.'

I cleared my throat. 'The story, as I was told it, goes like this. Leaving the Paternoster after a goodish lunch, and seeing the sky was ominous, Quent spun back to the cloakroom to fetch his umbrella. Discovering his usual peg was empty, he concluded that he had been the victim of theft. The red mist descended and he commenced an orgy of retributive destruction. Working methodically down the row of pegs, he seized each umbrella in turn, opened it up to its fullest extent and then, with size eleven hobnails, kicked it inside out. With every vandalous thrust of his heel, he is said to have shouted, "Brolly bad show!"'

'I like the sound of this Quent,' exclaimed Catsmeat. 'Looks like we have a new opening batsman.'

'By the time the Paternoster's secretary arrived to diffuse the scenario, Quent had annihilated more than a dozen of Mayfair's most expensive *parapluies*. It didn't help his case when the head porter produced the brolly that Quent had left in the front-hall stand earlier that day.'

'He sounds gruesome, if you ask me,' said Barmy. 'A man's club peg is hallowed ground.'

Bingo concurred. 'Do we need yet more hooligans in the Drones?'

'Let us ballot Fitzgerald Quent,' said Tuppy, placing on the table in front of him the Drones Club voting machine.

If you've never seen such a device, picture in your mind's eye a wooden box about the size of a largish tomcat, or smallish bulldog. The box has two hinge-lidded compartments, front and rear. These are divided internally by a partition into which is cut a hand-size hole. One by one, voters lift the lid of the front compartment and secretly select one of the white or black balls contained therein ('white elects, black rejects'). Then, placing their hand through the hole, they drop their chosen ball into the rear compartment, where a 'clunk' registers delivery. Once every vote has been cast, the rear compartment's lid is lifted and the totals are tallied.

Different clubs have different rules, but at the Drones a single black ball is fatal. Quent had six.

(To be strictly accurate, Quent had six brown sugar cubes. This is because, every December, Dronesmen pinch the black balls to drop into the toes of Christmas stockings in place of lumps of coal.)

'Quite the pilling for Quent,' said Tuppy, less than gruntled at the prospect of breaking such bad news to one so quick to violence.

'Shame!' jeered Catsmeat. 'Shame!'

'Catsmeat, old cock,' I pointed to the unanimous vote, 'you pilled him too.'

'Oh, yes. So I did. *Shame!*'

'Last but not least,' said Tuppy, 'we come to Graydon Hogg, Member of Parliament for East Looe.'

'Whiner the Poo?' asked Freddie, bemused. 'He's already a member! In fact, I passed him earlier on the stairs.'

'Rule Two (b),' said Tuppy. 'A few weeks ago.'

The Drones is not, strictly speaking, a bachelors' club. There are many married members, and many more members who aspire one day to marry. However, under Rule Two (b), any Dronesman who stumbles into wedlock *ipso facto* forfeits his membership and is obliged to stand for re-election.

(It's also true that Dronesmen occasionally resign from the club at the insistence of their fiancées. This explains, for instance, why Horace Pendlebury-Davenport hasn't been seen alive since he imprudently heaved a diamond at Valerie Twistleton.)

Some have suggested that Rule Two (b) was no more than a drunken caprice by the founders of the Drones and should, therefore, simply be ignored. Yet, over time, the loophole has proved a useful way to fill the club's coffers, since with the prize of re-election comes the penalty of a new admission fee.

'Does anyone know who Hogg married?' asked Bingo.

'Tibby Spode,' I reported.

'Lord Sidcup's niece?' gasped Bingo. 'Heavens. How did they get mixed up together?'

'Hogg has become quite the Spodean,' I said. 'Have you not heard him orate on the topic of Britain's blue passports?'

'Thankfully no, and long may I pass freely from that tedious subject without let or hindrance.'

'I'm rather upset about Tibby,' grumbled Freddie. 'She was on my list.'

'You have a list?'

'My aunts keep one for me. But names get struck off it almost weekly.'

'I propose,' announced Tuppy, in a chairman-like sort of voice, 'that since Hogg is nominated under Two (b), he is entitled to be re-elected by acclamation. Any objections?'

I raised my hand.

'For what reason, Bertie?'

'I've just spent the weekend with Hogg and, quite frankly, the man is an unutterable blister. This whole Spode business he's mixed up in is enough to put any decent Dronesman right off his cheese and biscuits.'

'The thing is, Bertie,' said Tuppy, with a thirsty glance at his watch, 'the spirit of Rule Two (b) is that married members are re-elected automatically. On the nod.'

'That is as maybe. But since when has Graydon Hogg cared for anything but the strictest letter of the law?'

'Bertie has a point,' agreed Barmy. 'Hogg once called on the Home Secretary to hang an innocent man because the pardon document contained a typo.'

'I used to fag for him,' said Freddie, 'and he was a slave-driver. He absolutely insisted I do his washing-up in alphabetical order.' Freddie impersonated Hogg's pinched vowels: '"*Cups, forks, glasses ... knives, plates, spoons.*" If I made the smallest mistake, I had to start all over again.'

'Didn't he once sue his barber for cutting his hair too short?' Bingo added.

'Very well,' said Tuppy. 'Let us ballot Graydon Hogg.'

The voting box did the rounds, disgorging two white sugar cubes and four brown.

'Guilty!' I cried in triumph, for the jury had clearly been swung to a majority verdict by the persuasive oratory of the prosecuting counsel.

'This is going to be fun,' grumbled Tuppy, who had good reason to lament the smoothness of his nose.

Our solemn duty discharged, the committee dissolved down to the bar where McGarry was ablur with the cocktail shaker.

Some twenty minutes later, as we were settling into a second round of especially arid martinis, a vast, saturnine man stomped into the bar with the combative air of one who had just clocked off from a long and tiring day punching horses.

He looked around the room before stalking up to our table. 'Are you the membership committee?' he demanded.

'We are,' replied Tuppy, with calm condescension. 'I am its chairman.'

'And *I* am Fitzgerald Quent.'

You could hear the martinis sweat.

'Well?' he scowled. 'May I take it that I have been re-elected?'

Tuppy swallowed hard. 'As it happens ... no. You were blackballed.'

'*Black*balled?' said Quent, rolling the word around his mouth. 'How very *interesting*. How very *remarkable*. I wonder ... were there *many* black balls?'

This called for quick thinking. If Tuppy let on that Quent had been pilled unanimously, then this increasingly sinister confrontation was unlikely to end happily for any of us. However, if just a single black ball had been cast, the needle of guilt would be lost, so to speak, in a haystack of suspects.

'Actually,' I said, attempting a what's-done-is-done, the-die-is-cast sort of tone, 'there was just one black ball.'

'Just one, eh?' Quent mused, before turning on Tuppy and barking, 'Was it you?'

'Er, no.'

He pointed to Bingo. 'Or you?'

'Absolutely not.'

Quent was about to interrogate Catsmeat when his face registered a devious thought. 'Did *any* of you blackball me?' he asked, with wheedling menace. 'Because I strongly suspect that *none* of you blackballed me. I strongly suspect it must have been a *trick of the light*. A white ball that only *appeared* to be black. Do you follow me?'

I had not anticipated this depth of low cunning.

'In which case, gentlemen,' he concluded, 'I must have been re-elected after all. Is that not so?'

There was only one way out of this trap.

'As a matter of fact, Quent, old man,' I said, leaning back in my chair with as much aloofness as I could muster, 'I blackballed you.'

My fellow committee members stared at me in bewilderment – stunned by my reckless course of self-destruction, yet relieved I seemed willing to hurl myself in front of the horses.

Quent stepped closer and loomed over me, his ungainly bulk plunging the table into shadow. 'Oh, *did* you now?'

'I did. And d'you want to know something else? I'd do it again. With knobs on.'

He smiled a twisted little smile. 'And who, might I enquire, are you?'

I drew a gasper from my cigarette case, tapped it casually on the lid, and enflamed it with a nimble match. 'The name's Hogg. Graydon Hogg. With two "G"s . . . three, actually.'

'Very well then, Mr Graydon Hogg,' said Quent icily, removing from his pocket a coin. 'Heads or tails?'

'What?'

'I said, heads or— It doesn't matter. I call tails.'

Quent spun the shilling into the air, caught it with his right hand, and inverted it onto the back of his left. 'Damn,' he said, pocketing the coin. 'Heads! Well then, Mr Hogg, you can expect to hear from my solicitors first thing tomorrow morning.'

His business apparently complete, Quent spun on his axis and strode away.

'What was tails?' I called out to his rapidly departing form.

'The horsewhip!'

I turned to the barman, who had been spectating this exchange with wry amusement.

'McGarry, might you inform Bashers that Fitzgerald Quent has absolutely *not* been re-elected to the club, and if he ever again attempts to trespass, the constabulary should be summoned forthwith.'

'Certainly, Mr Wooster. It will be my pleasure.'

'That was magnificent!' cried Bingo. 'For a moment I feared Quent was about to umbrella you.'

'I propose,' said Tuppy, who evidently saw a path to safety, 'that Bertie be elected chairman of the membership committee in perpetuity.'

'Oh, no.' I shook my head. 'Not for all the coconuts in Kerala. I will chance my spoon with the rest of you, but I will do no more.'

'Right,' declared Freddie, sinking his martini and rising to his feet, 'that sharpened the appetite.'

Lunch was a bibulous affair, and I knew from previous lunches that were I to push on through to the port and walnuts I would arrive in no fit state to tackle Spode at the Gaiety, or to collect Madeline's newly engraved snuff-box. The hurdle I faced, how-ever, was that cutting out of a membership-committee bean-feast prior to the arrival of the undertakers is unanimously condemned as shocking bad form.

Accordingly, so as not to rouse the ire of my colleagues, I bided my time for a suitably distracting incident – Tuppy attempting 'Auld Lang Syne' on the wine-glass orchestra – before taking the subtlest of French leaves and legging it up Dover Street before anyone could send up a flare.

As I made my way along Bond Street towards Lambert Lyall, I was alive to the very real risk of bumping, once again, into Monty. It was probable, of course, that the Cockney charmer would be deep in rehearsals for his debut performance, but one can never rest easy with entrepreneurial types. And so, with no appetite for another encounter, I used the reflections in shop windows to keep a wary eye for anything resembling a sandwich-board.

One of the windows into which I glanced was that of the lingerie purveyor Eulalie Sœurs, where I was startled to see, fold-ing lacy unmentionables behind the counter, Tabitha Hogg.

I stepped inside, and lifted my lid in salaam.

'Bertie! What are you doing here?' Tibby smirked. 'On the hunt for something slinky? You rogue, you!'

'Er, no,' I blushed, 'I was on my way to see your neighbour, Lambert Lyall, when I thought I glimpsed you through the glass. You don't work here, do you?'

'In a sense: I own the place.'

Not knowing if Tibby knew that I knew all about Eulalie Sœurs, I played it dumb. 'How splendid. Did you set up the shop or ...?'

'Oh no. I took it over from Madame Eulalie herself – a darling old Parisienne who established the label with her sister in the 1880s.'

It required all of my self-control not to snort loudly into this tissue of lies, for not only were there no Sœurs, there was, in fact, no Madame Eulalie. The shop in which I was standing had been opened just a few years prior by Roderick Spode, and he'd only disposed of the business when it became impossible to reconcile his dreams of popular tyranny with designing ladies' underwear.

Blackmail is, of course, a dirty word, but I am happy to make an exception in the case of Lord Sidcup. Before he got out of lingerie, if you will forgive the image, there was a brief but golden age when a rampaging, spittle-flecked Spode could be stunned into the meekest submission merely by whispering the name 'Eulalie'. As incantations go, it was right up there with abracadabra.

How did I know all this? Jeeves, of course – who divulged the incriminating intelligence that had been added to the Junior Ganymede club book under the wicked stipulation of Rule Eleven. What I didn't know, however, was that Spode had kept

Eulalie Sœurs in the family by chucking the business at his niece.

'I must congratulate you, Tibby! It's an exceedingly elegant shop, if a tad *risqué*.'

'Oh, come now, Bertie. We must move with the times.'

'Must we? It seems to me that "the times" should occasionally be given the sharpest of elbows.'

'You wouldn't say that if you saw my charmingly modern shop girls.'

'And where are these damsels? Stitching lace by candlelight in the attic?'

'Célestine and Marie-Thérèse have the afternoon off. Which is why I am stuck bandying words with strange men in offensive purple ties.'

'Célestine?' I raised an eyebrow. 'And Marie-Thérèse?'

'Well, Irene and Betty. But what is lingerie if not poetic licence?'

The telephone tootled and, with an apologetic smile, Tibby answered it. Judging by her grim reaction, whoever had called had been the embodiment of discontent, and she replaced the receiver crossly.

'Problems?' I asked.

'Customers, so, yes. Look here, can you do me a favour?'

'Certainly.'

'Would you mind the shop?'

'Why would I mind? It may not be my partic—'

'No, Bertie, would you *look after* the shop? I have to deliver an urgent gift for a troublesome regular and there's no one else to stand guard. Fifteen minutes? Twenty at the most. You can time me.'

I do what I can to oblige, and never let it be said that a Wooster passes by on the other side while a fair maiden is jostled by dragons. But hang it all, this was pushing chivalry to the *louchest* of limits.

'Tibby, what do I know of flogging lingerie?'

'I'm sure you will rise to the challenge. Anyway, you owe me a favour after that disgusting meal on Saturday night.'

'Hang on,' I protested, 'that meal was Aunt Dahlia's doing. I was as innocent a bystander as you.'

'I doubt that, Bertie. Anyway, I'm holding you jointly and severally liable.' She grabbed her hat, scarf, handbag, and gift-box and headed for the door. 'I'll be back before you know it. Just don't scare away too much trade. Also, and I'm deadly serious about this, no discounts!'

And with that, she scarpered – leaving, as Jeeves is apt to say, not a wrack behind.

I was in the process of taking a quick inventory of the goods on display when in strode a silver-haired chap in the approved regalia of a City gent: bowler hat, leather briefcase, tightly furled brolly, and salmon-pink *Financial Times*. His confident footsteps faltered when he espied, behind the counter, me.

'Are you,' he quavered, '*here?*'

'I am, sir. Good afternoon. May I be of service?'

He swallowed uneasily and tugged at his cuffs. 'I'm, er, looking for something ...'

'A good start, sir.'

'... for my wife.'

'Excellent.'

'It's our silver anniversary next week, and I thought, well ...'

'Of course, sir. Congratulations.'

'Thank you.'

He paused. Time passed. I decided I should probably say something. 'Might I enquire, sir, what kind of things your wife ... enjoys?'

'Gosh, hard to say ... What do you suggest?'

'Well, sir, is she the sort of woman who ...?'

'Not really.'

'Ah.'

'She's very ... you know ...'

'Is she, sir? Perhaps in that case ...' I gestured to one of the racks.

His face fell.

'Or perhaps not.'

He pointed the ferrule of his umbrella at a glass case. 'Do you think, possibly, something like that?'

'They are quite ... well ... you can see for yourself.'

'Oh yes ... they *are*, aren't they? ... Hmm.'

'Would she ever ...?' I indicated a range of items clipped to a revolving display.

'Good God, no! She's never done anything quite like ... *that*.'

'Ah.'

He had a thought. 'Do you have anything in the way of ...' and he outlined an unfathomable contour with his hands.

'I don't *think* we do, sir.'

'No ... you wouldn't. Can't be much call for that sort of thing nowadays.'

There was a long, protracted silence during which we both peered around the shop, studiously avoiding eye contact.

Finally, he spoke. 'I think, on reflection, it might be better to give her a book.'

'A book? Oh, yes, sir – a good book is always a treat.'

'Hatchards?'

'I'd say so, sir. You can't ever go wrong there.'

'Excellent. I'll be saying goodbye, then.'

'Goodbye, sir.'

'And thank you for your assistance. You've been most ... understanding.'

'Of course, sir. My pleasure.'

This might not have been the most lucrative transaction in the annals of trade, I mused, but at least I hadn't given him a discount. Just then the door swung open and two elderly matrons stepped inside, clutching their handbags like shields.

'Good afternoon, ladies. May I—'

'That's *quite* enough from you, young man,' the older of the ladies snapped. 'We will *just* be browsing, thank you, and wish to do so *un*molested.'

As they shuffled round the shop, closely inspecting flimsy garments through pebble-thick specs, a soberly dressed man stepped furtively through the door. He was so preoccupied in scanning the street behind him to ensure he hadn't been followed that he tripped over his feet and fell straight into my arms.

Our eyes locked, and he froze in terror. He, too, had not been expecting to encounter a man in such a feminine establishment, especially not a man he recognised but couldn't for the life of him place.

I, on the other hand, knew exactly who he was. If the goatee hadn't given him away, the Turkish cologne was a clincher.

'Sir Gilbert, we meet again! Is it a half-day in the world of banking? I do hope Trollope's will survive your absence.'

'I'm afraid you have the advantage of me, Mr ...?'

'Wooster.'

'Of course! Forgive me, I think I must be in the wrong shop.'

'Really? You seemed quite certain when you came in.'

'Is this the, er ...' his eyes darted about in search of inspiration before settling on a pile of correspondence '... post office?'

'The post office, Sir Gilbert?'

'Yes. I need to buy some ... stamps.'

'Really?'

'I have a small package, you see.'

'*Do you?*'

'But this is not, you say, the post office?'

'No. This is Eulalie Sœurs.'

'Oh.'

'We sell undergarments.'

'Ah.'

'For ladies.'

'I see.' He clenched and unclenched his hands anxiously. 'How careless of me. What could I be thinking?'

'It's hard to say.' I let him perspire for a while. 'I'm pretty sure the nearest post office is on Queen Street.'

'Of course. Yes. Good. Thank you. I'll be on my way then, Mr Wooster. So sorry to have troubled you.'

'No trouble at all, Sir G. And be sure to keep an eye out for counterfeit postal orders!'

His attempt at a swift and inconspicuous exit was greatly encumbered by Tibby's simultaneous return, and the two of them tangoed inelegantly in the doorway before Sir Gilbert Skinner finally broke free and bolted down the street at a sprint.

'What a strange and clumsy man,' she said, reclaiming her station behind the counter.

'I'm surprised you didn't recognise Sir Gilbert from Saturday night. He's my new bank manager.'

'That figures, they're never any good with withdrawals. Now, how did you fare? I see you have at least been occupied.'

'No sales to report, I'm sad to say. But on the plus side, no smash-and-grab attacks. So I think, on balance, a win.'

'It was kind of you to stand in for me, Bertie, but now you should be popping off. I must attend to those ladies, and they won't buy a thing with a scoundrel like you lurking about.'

She pecked me on the cheek and headed off to the back of the shop where my two elderly matrons sat shoeless on a chaise longue, massaging their fallen arches. I departed Eulalie Sœurs, ambled twenty yards up the street, and jingled once again into Lambert Lyall.

'Shop!'

'Good afternoon, Mr Wooster.'

'And a fine pip emma to you. Is she ready?'

'Of course, Mr Wooster, I have it here.' He took out from under the counter a small, tastefully wrapped gift-box. 'The inscription came out very nicely, we think, all things considered.'

'Ha! I'd forgotten about that. How many "O"s did you manage to squeeze in?'

'It's interesting you should ask, sir. The engraver told me that he could have fitted thirteen, but in the end we settled on twelve. It seemed to me that Miss Bassett was likely to count the "O"s and if she was a superstitious sort of person ... well, we wouldn't want that, would we?'

'You are a shrewd connoisseur of character, Lambert.'

'Thank you, sir. Jeweller's intuition, we call it. Will you be at the wedding?'

'If invited, I shall attend. If not invited, I shall sneak in – primarily to ensure that no idiot puts anything asunder before bride and groom are taken down to the cells. But, you know, I still harbour significant doubts that a wedding will take place. As you saw for yourself, Madeline approaches romantic commitment with all the steadfast resolve of a cuckoo clock.'

He chuckled. 'By the way, I asked around about the seventh Earl of Sidcup and, if you will pardon the liberty, I reckon they deserve each other.'

'Did I ever mention, Lambert, that you are a shrewd connoisseur of character?'

*　　*　　*

I had agreed to meet Lord MacAuslan for a drink at the Beefsteak, to finalise the plans for our theatrical attack and generally 'synchronise watches' – something I've always wanted to do. And so, after a quick nap and brush-up back at 3A Berkeley Mns., I scrambled eagerly into the monkey suit and flagged down a taxi to Irving Street.

The Beefsteak is, first and foremost, a dining club. Apart from a couple of bedrooms and a galley kitchen, the place comprises a single, soaring timber-beamed hall with a communal table that seats about two dozen. The white wood-panelled walls are decorated with fine silver and club memorabilia, and if it looks like nothing has changed since 1896, it's because very little has.

I was admitted by the steward, Charles, and directed to the far end of the room where Colonel Stroud-Pringle sat alone, staring out of the mullioned windows. His mood had not improved.

'You're late!' he barked.

'I don't think I am, Colonel.'

'Yes, you are. We said five o'clock. Sharp.'

I consulted my wristwatch. 'And it's just before five.'

'Don't talk rot, man. You're swinging the lead. Dodging the column. That's the problem with civilians – no sense of discipline, NBG whatsoever.'

I could have kissed the mantelpiece clock when its hour hand clicked loudly into place and five delicate chimes rang out.

'Damned thing's slow,' fumed the Colonel. 'Has been ever since some ninnyhammer muffled it when Queen Victoria died.'

'Is Lord MacAuslan not with us?'

'He's on the telephone, not that it's any of your business.'

I stood awkwardly for a while as he glowered at the timepiece.

'Lovely weather we're having?' I suggested.

'No it's not. Too damn humid by half. Not like the dry heat of India. Now there's a heat. You've never been to India, have you, Wooster? Never left W1, I'll be bound.'

Having failed miserably with the conventionally benign topics of temperature and time, I chanced a final throw of the conversational dice. 'By the way, Colonel, thank you for arranging the Worcestershire Regiment on Sunday. It was, as you may have heard, a riot!'

The impact of this innocent remark was astonishing. Colonel Stroud-Pringle's stony facade cracked into a sunbeam, and the man actually giggled with delight. 'That was glorious, wasn't it? Jeeves is quite something. I wish I'd been there to witness it.'

'You should have seen Spode's face when the band marched into view.'

'Confused, was he?'

'Bewildered! And then he had the nerve to pretend the military salute was there for him.'

'Well, in a way, Mr Wooster, it was! Now, why are you standing there without a drink? We can't have that.' He called out down the room. 'Charles, might you bring a tankard of champagne for my young friend?'

He rubbed his hands together conspiratorially. 'Take a seat and tell me all about it, Mr Wooster, from the beginning. Spare nothing. I especially want to hear about the piggies!'

I related the events of Sunday afternoon in as much detail as I could recall, and by the time I got to Spode waving a miniature Union Jack, the Colonel had become entirely incapable with laughter – scarlet in the face, shaking like a blancmange, and clutching one hand to his stomach with the other raised in agonised submission.

This was the scene that greeted Lord MacAuslan as he strode down the room to join us. 'Is everything all right, Mr Wooster?'

'I hope so. I was just telling the Colonel about Sunday afternoon.'

'I see.'

Colonel Stroud-Pringle was gasping helplessly for breath. 'A ... tiny ... little ... flag ... on ... a ... tiny ... little ... stick!'

'That's right, Colonel,' said Lord MacAuslan. 'And he was waving it in time to "The British Grenadiers".'

This supplementary detail tipped Colonel Stroud-Pringle over the precipice and the poor man toppled crying out of his chair and staggered from the room, gasping for air.

'Do I detect a thaw, Mr Wooster?' Lord MacAuslan smiled.

'Stumps me. Perhaps there was something in his drink?'

'Oh no, I think you've unlocked dear old Cuthbert, which is not something many live to achieve.'

After a few minutes of small talk, a partially restored Stroud-Pringle returned, begging us to say nothing further about Sunday's events. 'I'm far from a young man,' he warned, screwing back his monocle. 'And death by laughter is no epitaph for a soldier.'

'To work then,' said Lord MacAuslan. 'Are you primed and ready for tonight, Mr Wooster?'

'I think so. Perhaps we could run through the mechanism a final time? Last Friday seems a lifetime ago.'

'But of course. The eight private boxes at the Gaiety Theatre are identified by letters. Boxes A to D are situated house right, or stage left. Boxes E to H mirror them, house left, or stage right. Lord Sidcup has taken Box B; we have taken Box G opposite. Madeline Bassett will be shown to Box G, which we have re-labelled Box B. Lord Sidcup will arrive late and be shown to Box B, which will, of course, also be labelled Box B.'

I began to wish I hadn't drunk most of my tankard of fizz.

'I will be in Box C,' said Colonel Stroud-Pringle, 'and you will join Miss Bassett in the bogus Box B – in reality, Box G.'

I closed my eyes in concentration, and drew with my finger an imaginary cat's cradle. 'The Colonel is in Box C. Spode is in Box B. I am in Box G with Madeline, who thinks she is in Box B.'

'Perfect.'

'C-B-G-B.'

'A catchy mnemonic,' said Colonel Stroud-Pringle.

'And where will you be, Lord MacAuslan?'

'Here and there,' he offered, enigmatically. 'Hither and yon.'

I raised a finger. 'There may be something we've overlooked.'

'What is that, Mr Wooster?'

'Everything hinges on Spode being late and not meeting Madeline before the show. But what if he fails to be late? What if he's on time, or even early? How then can Madeline be shown to the wrong box?'

'Lord Sidcup will be late. We have arranged for him to witness a minor motor accident, in approximately an hour. Nothing serious, no one hurt. But the police will be called, and statements will be taken, and as a result Lord Sidcup will sadly miss the opening moments of Act I.'

'Lucky chap. Though that still leaves him two hours and fifty-something minutes of *Flotsam*.'

'The rest of the plan is considerably less algebraic. You will, in your own inimitable style, inspire Lord Sidcup to leave the theatre before the interval, and Jeeves will do the rest.'

'I have a style?'

'Oh, you do, Mr Wooster. And it's inimitable.'

*　　*　　*

I had planned to pass the time before *Flotsam* began Dutching my courage in the obscurity of the upper circle bar, but Colonel Stroud-Pringle advised that even there, up among the gods, I would not be safe. So, instead, I spent a wretched hour dozing in a pitch-black broom cupboard tucked away behind the dress circle.

I was released from this cell by an usher who, with a wink and a shush, led me through a series of turns until we were standing outside Box B – the box formerly known as G. Unable to see the auditorium, I was reliant on the hubbub of the audience to time my entry.

As a hush fell, I opened the door.

'Bertie!' Madeline whispered. 'What are you doing here?'

Before I could answer, the curtain rose to reveal Montague Montgomery – alone onstage, dressed in rags, casually applying whale grease to a jumble of lobster pots. After a minute or two's intense, silent labour, he chucked his brush to the floor, strode to the footlights, and addressed himself to the audience.

'There's them that says spindrift starts with a gale. And there's them that says flotsam starts with an huricano. But Able Seaman Benskin Muchmore – that's me, m'lords and m'ladies – Benskin Muchmore says they both starts here . . . in a man's heavy heart.'

'You're in the wrong box,' whispered Madeline.

'No. You're in the wrong box. This is my box. Box G.'

'This is Box B! Box-B-for-Bertie, Bertie. Still, it's nice to see you.'

'It's nice to see you too. Do you have any binoculars?'

Muchmore, meanwhile, was giving it the beans.

'For there be no true sailor who don't believe in mermaids! There be no true sailor who don't believe in undines! The sea be a wicked mistress, and she has secrets to share with thems who risk their very humanity at her cruel mercy.'

I raised Madeline's opera glasses to my eyes, and trained them across the darkness towards the real Box B. As I adjusted the focus wheel, what had been a blur gradually resolved into the pin-sharp image of Lord Sidcup, who was scanning the front rows through his own opera glasses, doubtless on the prowl for first-night wreckers.

Evidently sensing he was being watched, Spode shifted his scrutiny upwards until two rheumily bloodshot eyes were glaring directly into mine. We both instantly swung our specs away, and then gradually inched back our gazes.

I've never attended a Swiss finishing school, but I would bet £ to fr. that few of our gilded youth are trained to master this sort of social predicament: locked in a long-distance staring contest with an ape-like loony while you share a private box with his affianced. It's one up from walking in circles balancing slim volumes of poetry, or knowing how properly to address a maharajah.

Out of the corner of my eye I saw a flash. Redirecting my glasses to starboard, I spotted Colonel Stroud-Pringle in Box C waggling his monocle to reflect the light. Seeing he had secured my attention, the Colonel pointed to his wristwatch and jerked his head as if to say, 'Get on with it, man!'

So I did.

I edged my chair closer to Madeline, close enough that an onlooker, Spode for instance, might surmise that the two of us enjoyed an 'understanding'.

'Oh, Bertie,' she whispered, 'you are an angel.'

'One does try.'

'And I know how sad you must be.'

'Oh, of course. Cut to ribbons.'

'What about Iona?' she enquired archly.

'Who?'

'Oh, *Bertie*!'

, 'The thing is, Madeline, I wanted to say how pleased I am that, though not with me, you have found true happiness with Spo— Lord Sidcu— Roderick.'

'Bertie, I can't be yours. It was not meant to be. The flower bed foretells all – and I am, as you know, a lily of the valley.'

'Which reminds me, I collected your gift this afternoon.'

I took from my pocket the Lambert Lyall box and presented it to her with such formality that an onlooker, Spode for instance, might surmise that it contained a plover's egg.

'Oh, Bertie! I'm so happy with my dear, darling foxglove,' she sighed, 'but the Michaelmas daisy will always have a special place here …' She took my hand in hers and placed it delicately over her heart.

The effect was instantaneous. From across the auditorium came a clatter of chairs and the resounding 'thud' of a tall man overestimating a low door. Since this coincided with an especially quiet moment onstage, there was no missing the echoing roar of 'WOOSTERRRRRRRR!'

That was my cue.

I bade Madeleine good night, and zipped out of the box. Reasoning that Spode must attack my left flank, I made off to the right – through a heavy velvet curtain that led to a narrow, winding staircase decorated with framed posters from the heyday of music hall. I took the stairs two at a time, no mean feat in patent leather pumps, but was soon aware of thundering beetle-crushers behind me.

Like many oversized men, Spode is inexplicably light on his feet, and I found myself back in the upper foyer only a length or two ahead. I slid down the short brass banister, as any Dronesman would, and plunged headlong into the revolving door, which ejected me, reeling, onto the pavement.

Jeeves, somehow, was standing calmly at the kerb alongside a chugging taxi. He guided me into the back with a nonchalant 'Good evening, sir,' and tapped the roof imperiously.

I sped away.

It quickly became apparent that Spode was not content to be left standing on the street, claret-faced and open-mouthed, lest he be mistaken for the pillar box he so plainly resembled. My clue was a second taxi, closing in on our exhaust, out of which a Peer of the Realm was hoisted slantingdicular, bellowing at the top of his prodigious voice, 'WOOSTER, YOU ABSOLUTE WORM!'

Passers-by, every compound plural of them, stopped and stared as his insults rang out over the traffic's roar.

'Friend of yours, is 'e?' smirked my driver.

'Ish,' I replied, anxiously assessing the rapidly narrowing gap between our two vehicles.

''E seems in a right two-and-eight.'

'A misunderstanding over a fiancée.'

'Ah, *cherchez la femme*.'

'I say, driver, does this cab go any faster?'

'For you, guv, and for the course of true love, she most certainly does.'

He accelerated urgently and we cornered King Street at such an m.p.h. that, for a brief, unsettling moment, the taxi tipped up onto two wheels.

'I was engaged once, y'know,' he reminisced, oblivious to our helter-skelter slalom down Bedford Street.

'Really? I'm pleased for you. Look, I don't mean to be insensitive, but you do know we're being pursued by a madman?'

'I sees 'im ... I hears 'im, too.'

'You seem awfully relaxed about it.'

'Well, we get this kinda thing a lot.'

'You do?'

'Oh yeah, all the time. Chases, races, every kind of pursuit. You'd be amazed at the number of people who jump in the back and shout "Follow that cab!"'

'Really?'

'See, people love a caper. That's what I've found, in my line of work. People love a caper!'

It dawned on me that I had no clue as to our destination. 'By the way, do you know where we're headed?'

'Ha! See what I mean? Caper-bleedin'-mad! Yeah, I knows all right: the Athenaeum Club, on Waterloo Place. Designed by Decimus Burton, it was.'

'Who?'

'Decimus Burton. 'E designed the Athenaeum in the neo-classical style. Above the portico there's a statue of Athena. She's who the club's named after – the goddess of wisdom.'

'How do you know all this?'

'Well, cabbies are expected to have a bit of *spiel*, ain't they? It's all part of London's rich pageant, so they say.'

'But is this even the right way to the Athenaeum?'

'Not specially. But your pal in the bowler told me to take the long way round, in case we was followed.'

'I see.'

'Except 'e said, *"in the hun-likely event of a ve-hic-ular pursuit"*.'

'That does sound like him.'

'Funny sort of cove, your pal.'

'Hilarious.'

As we turned into the Strand, I noticed that Spode had abandoned his vocal assault and was back in his seat, no doubt sharpening his knuckles for the rib-roasting to come.

'His driver's not half nippy, guv. Mind if I get clever?'

'Not in the slightest.'

We swung left past Nelson's Column and down into Whitehall. 'Hang on, chief,' he yelled as we swerved across the flow of traffic into the narrow yard of Horse Guards. Here our progress was brought to an abrupt stop by two fiercely armed members of the King's Life Guard.

'HALT!' they screamed, to the delight of the gawping tourists. 'Who goes there?'

'Easy, lads,' soothed my driver, waving out of the window an oval ivory pass. The soldiers stamped to attention and saluted as we sped through the archway and emerged onto the wide expanse of Horse Guards Parade.

'How?' I exclaimed, incredulously.

'Wheels within wheels, you might say. Should stymie the co-respondent party, I reckon.'

I turned to confirm his reassurance, and was disheartened to see Spode's taxi hurtling through the arch in our wake. 'I wouldn't be quite so sure.'

'Coo! How'd 'e get a pass?'

We turned left onto the Mall and accelerated up towards Buckingham Palace.

'I don't suppose you've got anything that gets us in there?'

'Not today, guv, the boss is home.' He pointed to the Royal Standard which fluttered gently in the breeze.

We drove up Constitution Hill, round Wellington Arch, and down along Piccadilly – past Iona's Lyceum Club and the Ritz. At every turn Spode was on us like flypaper.

'This may be the best we get,' my driver said, as we approached Fortnum & Mason. 'Mind if I head for the club?'

'Not at all!'

My stomach lurched as he stamped on the brakes and we swung right into Duke Street, sped past Jermyn Street and Rider Street, and turned left into King Street. Spode was within spitting distance as we entered St James's Square, but then something unexpected occurred: whereas my driver turned left (as directed by custom and practice, common sense, and the Highway Code), our pursuers turned right – slap-bang into the path of onrushing cars.

As we raced round the square in opposite directions, regaled by a cacophony of protesting horns, it felt as if we were being drawn inescapably towards one another. Every yard brought us closer to an autocidal collision, and soon I could make out the contour of Spode's gruesome head through the glass of our two windscreens.

We were headlamp to headlamp when, at the last possible moment, my driver averted disaster with a molecular flick of his wheel.

As our vehicles cannonballed past each other, separated by no more than a gimme, I heard Spode's thunderous roar and caught a fleeting glimpse of his driver, who, even with his collar up and flat cap down, reminded me of someone I was pretty sure I knew.

'Blimey,' exhaled my driver, 'that was a shaver! Ain't love grand?'

We dog-legged across Pall Mall into Carlton Gardens, and swung into Carlton House Terrace. Blurring past a long stretch of greenery, we turned left onto Waterloo Place and pulled up abruptly in front of the Athenaeum.

'Good luck, chief! I hope she's worth it.'

'She's not,' I said, thrusting a fiver into his hand, and hotfooting it up the steps.

I heard Spode's taxi squeal to a halt, and sensed him at my heel.

I wasn't exactly jubilant to spy my old adversary on doorman duty, and I braced myself for another frosty Athenaeum reception. Instead, to my abundant relief, he ushered me inside with a knowing wink, just in time to slam the door in my pursuer's beetroot face.

'Let me in,' Spode bellowed through the glass.

'Are you a member, sir?' asked the doorman impassively.

'No, I am not.'

'Are you, perhaps, the guest of a member?'

'No, but—'

'I am afraid, sir, that this is a private club.'

Spode cocked his head and eyed me malevolently, his hot breath steaming against the windowpane. It's fascinating the power that institutions hold over men like Lord Sidcup. A lesser vandal would have elbowed the door, swept the porter aside, and gone straight for the Wooster jugular. But Spode, brutish as he undoubtedly was, could not conquer the instincts of nursery, school, church, and state. This doorman, though less than an ant to a climber like Spode, represented the Club, which in turn represented Society, Order, and all that was Holy. Confronted by a figure of authority, Spode was quashed – which isn't to say he wasn't jolly angry.

And then he was struck by a demonic flash.

'Actually,' he declared, 'I *am* the guest of a member.'

'Might I enquire which member, sir?'

Spode grinned maliciously. 'Lord Forbes of Pitsligo.'

'I regret to inform you, sir, that his lordship died some years ago.'

'I'm sorry, I meant to say Professor Mainwaring.'

'He died before Lord Forbes, sir.'

Spode was dismayed. 'Good God! What about the Bishop of Lindisfarne?'

'Regrettably, sir, no.'

This exchange had become something of a *memento mori* for Lord Sidcup, who began to wobble slightly and persp. freely about the upper lip.

'Er ... How about Sir Watkyn Bassett? He must still be alive, surely?'

'Happily, Sir Watkyn is with us – although not in the sense of being in the club at present. You would, of course, be welcome to wait for him in the library.'

Spode stared at the door, which remained conspicuously unopened. 'Well?'

'I'm sorry, sir, but the Athenaeum does require members and their guests to be properly attired.'

'What?' he spat. 'I am properly attired!'

'The club rules state that a necktie must be worn, sir.'

'Are you blind?' Spode jabbed at his collar, his face an apoplectic balloon. 'This is a necktie!'

'Actually, sir,' the porter replied with cool regret, 'you appear to be wearing an ascot.'

Spode snapped and, enunciating each word with savage intent, bellowed: 'IT'S. THE. SAME. THING!'

There are some outrages a man can let pass without comment. Not every game, you understand, is worth the candle. But as the author of 'What the Well-Dressed Man is Wearing' – a well-received article for *Milady's Boudoir*, Aunt Dahlia's erstwhile sixpenny journal – I could not permit such sartorial poppycockery to stand.

I stepped up to the glass.

'Really, my dear Spode, it's not the same thing at all. Look at it! It's not even tied into a proper knot. Now, if you had been wearing a stock, or a cravat, or even a solitaire – that we could discuss sensibly, like gentlemen. But an ascot? I ask you! Who wears an ascot to a club?'

It took a moment or two for the full effect of this dressing-down to percolate through Spode's nervous system. Very

gradually his face faded from crimson to purest white, and I
began to fear spontaneous human combustion.

'I intend,' he seethed through clenched jaw, pointing a fleshy
digit in my direction, 'to tear that man's head clean off his body!'

'Very good, sir,' said the doorman.

'He is a treacherous, parasitic never-sweat who cannot be
trusted with other men's fiancées.'

'If you say so, sir.'

'And I will stand right here until he leaves.'

'As you wish, sir. But might I ask you to stand on the pavement? The portico is club property.'

Spode shook with rage as he descended the steps backwards,
like a courtier withdrawing from a king. He didn't take his eyes
off me for a second.

'I can wait all night, Wooster,' he shouted up. 'I can wait all
night.'

I could feel my pulse, well, pulsing. 'Are there any other ways
into the club?' I asked the doorman.

'No, sir. Not at this hour.'

'Good. Although that also means there's no other way out,
except past . . .' I gestured to the pavement tornado.

'If monsieur would allow me,' said an absurdly French accent.
I spun round to see the maître d', who beckoned me to follow
him with a profoundly Continental wink.

I'd like to report that the atmosphere of the Athenaeum's dining-room had warmed up a degree, but the same solitary men
were reading the same yellowed pages in the same funereal
silence. Despite Spode's pyrotechnic pleasantries at the front

door, not a single head turned as we hoofed it across the carpet to the open French windows and, through them, onto the balcony, which overlooked a large, well-tended garden.

For those readers who are not *au courant* with the anatomy of London's clubland, here is the basic posish. Most of the top spots huddle for warmth in and around St James's. Here we find blue-blood haunts like Brooks's, Boodle's, and White's – which is a year older than the Bank of England, and almost as heaving with gold. Orbiting these are a swathe of more humane clubs, such as the Pelican, the Senior Conservative and, of course, the good old Drones. In addition to a crop of new ladies' clubs – Iona's Lyceum being the grandest – there are a number of far-flung establishments of note, including the theatrical Garrick, located in Covent Garden, and the raffish Chelsea Arts, out towards the wilds of Fulham.

Along the south side of Pall Mall lies 'club row'. Travelling west to east, from St James's Palace towards Leicester Square, one finds: the Oxford and Cambridge, the Royal Automobile Club, and the Carlton. And then, in one impressive enfilade of stone, the Reform, The Travellers, and the Athenaeum. These last three clubs share the communal garden past which my taxi had just sped, and into which I was about to step.

'If you will follow Repton, monsieur.' The maître d' gestured down the stone steps towards a gardener who was looking up at us, cap literally in hand.

I descended the stairs, and followed my man a few yards across the lawn to where a white-jacketed steward was waiting.

''Ere you go, m'lord,' winked the gardener, handing me over like the baton in an unusually well-dressed relay race.

'Welcome to The Travellers, sir,' the steward bowed, leading me down a few steps, through some French windows, and into a bar that was so full of boozy congeniality and pink gin it might have been a Gillray cartoon sprung to life.

'I say! Is it always this buzzing down here?'

'Reciprocals, sir. They say you can tell when the Garrick is closed, because there's laughter in the bar of The Travellers.'

I ignored this inter-club badinage, and followed my chaperone up a staircase.

I suspected we were headed to the library, but we continued up another flight to the third floor.

'This way, if you please, sir.'

'To the bedrooms?'

'No, sir.'

He guided me along a cramped passage to a plain oak door that, when unlocked, faced an identical oak door just a few feet away. He unlocked this, and we stepped out into what I soon saw, from its soaring glass-roofed atrium, was the next-door Reform.

'I say, adjoining clubs? How bally convenient. Like a hotel room!'

'Precisely, sir. Although ironically, The Travellers and the Reform no longer enjoy any form of reciprocal understanding.'

'No?'

'Not since "The Drones Club Event" of '02.'

'Ah,' I said, self-consciously. 'Was that a particularly uppish scrag?'

'I'd say so, sir. Both clubs' secretaries stood down and questions were asked in Parliament.'

'No casualties, though?' I jested.

'Seventy-eight, sir.'

Throughout this repartee, we had been pacing along the carpeted upper balcony, which looked down onto the mosaic floor far below. A few members glanced up from their newspapers and sniffed officiously, but we were mainly disregarded. At the end of the balcony stood a studded-leather door, which swung open to reveal an aproned steward decanting a magnum of burgundy over a stub of candle.

I was directed to the room's far corner and shown a hole in the wall.

'What's this?'

'A cellar lift, sir, for conveying wine bottles up – and you down.'

It looked fearfully small. 'Will I fit?'

He appraised me dispassionately, as a leopard might size up a warthog. 'Oh, I'd say so, sir. We've had much stouter gentlemen in here before, and the apparatus only rarely gets stuck.'

Far from reassured, I accepted a leg-up onto the rusty metal platform and concertinaed myself into the claustrophobic hollow.

'I'll bid you good night then, sir,' said the steward with a wink, sliding shut the safety gate and deploying the release.

'Good night,' I replied, as the darkness began to engulf me. 'Er ... what happens next?'

'I'd keep your knees and elbows well chested, if I were you, sir. Last week the Duke of Mudeford lost a toe.'

My descent down the Reform Club rabbit hole was comically slow and alarmingly accompanied by the twanging of distant wires. After what felt like days, the gimcrack apparatus spasmed to a halt and I fell base over apex into a cavernous vault.

Many tales are told of club wine cellars extending hectares underground, but I had never seen anything quite like this. Tempted though I was to explore the dimly lit and no doubt highly drinkable racks, I concluded it would be expedient, *vis-à-vis* Spode, to decamp up the staircase to my right, towards a door marked simply 'S. R.'

Not knowing where 'S. R.' might lead, I turned the handle gingerly and was delighted to find myself in the smoking-room.

I've enjoyed many a pre-luncheon cigar in this elegant, double-height chamber over the years, but had never before noticed the door from which I was exiting – flush as it was with the walnut shelving. Despite the urgency of my mission, I paused briefly to peruse the titles, and was pleased to see such classics of the concealed-library-door genre as *A Damsel in His Dress*, *The Blot Thickens*, and *Goodbye to All Cats*.

It was the work of seconds to cross the smoking-room, cut along the edge of the atrium, and exit the Reform Club past the porter's cubbyhole.

Once again, Jeeves was waiting at the kerb with a taxi, although this time it contained the tartan presence of Lord MacAuslan. As we climbed aboard I recognised at the wheel my driver from earlier. He let fly the handbrake, double-declutched, and waggled his eyebrows.

'Capers, eh? What a palaver!'

It took me a beat or two to regain the composure for which we Woosters are renowned. Much had transpired in the half-hour past, and I couldn't help thinking it had been quite some time since I'd last had a snifter.

Jeeves was of his usual clairvoyance. From beneath his fold-down dicky seat he extracted the cocktail case Aunt Dahlia had grudgingly given me last Christmas, and set about decanting something palliative into silver cups.

'I think you might have one yourself, Jeeves, all in all.'

'Thank you, sir.'

The three of us did our best to raise a toast as the taxi shuddered along Pall Mall.

'This is a remarkable drink, Jeeves,' said Lord MacAuslan, swirling the cocktail around his mouth like a vintner.

'I am gratified to hear that, m'lord.'

'Do I detect a dash of ginger wine, maybe?'

'I could not say, sir,' he demurred, ever vigilant of Guild secrets.

'Well, it's a fitting tribute to a job well done. Mr Wooster, you played your part magnificently.'

'I'm glad you think so,' I replied after a longish gulp. 'I don't know how I'll ever face Spode again. I wonder if he's still standing in wait.'

'He is. But he'll give up soon enough – he needs to get back to the theatre.'

'Oh, yes, to collect the Bible code from under his interval drinks.'

'Which Jeeves has already copied for us. It's not a full message, just a single reference.' Lord MacAuslan handed me a slip of paper on which was written: *Heb. xii. 1.*

'Aha! Well, I did not win the Malvern House prize for Scripture Knowledge for nothing. This refers to Hebrews, Chapter 12, Verse 1.'

'Well, yes. That much was reasonably clear. But do you know how that verse runs?'

'Not a clue. Jeeves?'

Jeeves took out a pocket Bible, and opened it to a page he'd marked with a silk ribbon. 'The verse begins: "*Wherefore seeing we also are compassed about with so great a cloud of witnesses—*"'

'Hang on,' I said. '"Cloud of witnesses"?'

'Yes, sir. Which I suggest may be a reference to *À la recherche du temps perdu.*'

'*À la* who *du* what?'

'It is a seven-volume novel series, sir, by Marcel Proust. It addresses the "cloud"-like themes of memory through a heterogeneous cast of characters or, perhaps, "witnesses"?'

When Jeeves is on form, he's peerless – a *raisonneuring raisonneur*, you might say – but there are times, and this was a peach, when the man's brainpower is simply overmatched to life's more trivial challenges. If you require a visual parallel of this hammer-to-nut disparity, imagine approaching an erupting volcano hoping to coddle an egg.

'It *might* be Proust,' I said, with the tone he adopts when I've confused, say, heresy and sacrilege. 'But I can't really see Spode dipping into that particular jar of French mustard, can you?'

'Perhaps not, sir.'

'No. I'll bet a pound to a peanut that "so great a cloud of witnesses" refers to a Lord Peter Wimsey whodunnit entitled *Clouds of Witness*.'

'Dorothy L. Sayers?' Lord MacAuslan asked, understandably alarmed to be taking my counsel over Jeeves's in matters of cryptography or literature. 'Are you sure?'

'Yup. I read it when it came out a few years ago, and it turns out – well, I won't spoil it for you – but it turns out pretty neatly. That Dorothy L. S. is fiendish clever.'

Neither of my companions appeared in the slightest persuaded.

'By all means have your boys double-check, MacAuslan, but I stand by my theory. And think about it, which would be less suspicious: Spode lugging about a seven-volume French albatross, or Spode back-pocketing detective fiction starring the son of a duke?'

We dropped Jeeves off in Berkeley Square, and drove on for supper at Lord MacAuslan's club, which, I shouldn't have been surprised to learn, was the High Highland.

'I've never been here before,' I said, as we entered the tartan-tiled lobby. 'It's like a little Scottish embassy.'

'Och aye? You'll be very welcome, will he not, McTavish?' Lord MacAuslan addressed a kilted doorman, who replied in the affirmative with an astonishingly thick Welsh accent.

'All the doormen at the High Highland are called McTavish,' Lord MacAuslan explained. 'Even Llewelyn here.'

Lord MacAuslan excused himself to make a telephone call, and I wandered about the bustling lobby. I don't think I've ever seen so much tartan in one place. Like a shortbread tin magicked into existence, the entire club was enveloped in plaid and overrun with red-headed men in kilts, trews, and tam-o'-shanters.

Yet even within this kaleidoscope of multicoloured checks, stripes, houndstooth, and herringbone, Lord MacAuslan's suit stood out as quite remarkably vivacious – just as there's bound to be one zebra in every herd who gives his pals a crashing migraine.

'Is that MacAuslan tartan you're wearing?' I asked on his return.

'We MacAuslans traditionally wear Buchanan, being a sept of that clan,' he said, delighted that someone had plucked up the courage to enquire. 'However, this particular cloth is my own creation. It combines the yellow and white stripes of Drummond of Strathallan, the red ground of Ogilvie, and the pale blue patches of MacLaine of Lochbuie. With just a touch of Balmoral grey to give monarchy its due.'

'They can't say they didn't see you coming.'

'They never do, Mr Wooster, they never do.'

After a wee dram at the bar, Lord MacAuslan led me into the dining-room, where the tartan-clad walls were adorned with a necropolis of stags' heads somewhat callously interspersed with the armoury of weapons that had been used to slay them.

A glance at the menu indicated that High Highland's chef was similarly taking no prisoners. Various cuts of Scottish salmon, Scottish lamb, and Scottish beef were listed in abundance, alongside cock-a-leekie, Cullen skink, Arbroath smokies, finnan haddie, stovies, skirlie, black pudding, white pudding, something called red pudding, and, of course, haggis.

'I might need some translation,' I said. 'Rumbledethumps?'

'Bubble and squeak.'

'Cranachan?'

'Eton mess-ish.'

'Crappit heid?'

'It's an acquired taste.'

'Is the wine list similarly ... partisan?'

'Jings, no, we're not monsters! Except when it comes to whisky, mind, where you'll find us truly brutal. You'll not see a *whiskey* for searching.' Although his accent and vocabulary were becoming more Scottish by the minute, he gave the distasteful 'e' in 'whiskey' a distinctly Dublinesque twang.

We ordered (me timorously, he bestially) and settled into a fine bottle of Montrachet.

'So, Mr Wooster, have you enjoyed working with the Junior Ganymede?'

'I think I have, yes.'

'Do I sense misgivings?'

'Perhaps. It was all very thrilling and white-knuckled and such, and I'm happy to do my bit to assist His Majesty in impeding the carbuncular Spode. But I can't help wondering—'

'If it was all strictly necessary?'

'Exactly. I mean, surely Jeeves could have copied the code during the first half of *Flotsam*, while Spode was correctly Box B'd with the Bassett.'

'He could have, yes.'

'So why involve me? Why the theatrical boxing, the near-death chase, and the clubland escape?'

Lord MacAuslan smiled. He had clearly been expecting this question and was looking forward to providing the answer. 'Two reasons. The first, I suppose, one might call a test.'

'To see how I ran when the going was heavy?'

'To ascertain whether you had a thirst for the Junior Ganymede's game.'

'And the second reason?'

'The second reason very nearly ran you off the road not half an hour ago.'

'You mean Spode's taxi driver?'

'Except that he's not a taxi driver.'

'He was assuredly driving that taxi!' I protested.

'True enough. But he is actually the Member of Parliament for East Looe.'

'Graydon Hogg?' This was one of those newsflashes best digested with a large dose of anaesthetic, and so I reached for the Montrachet. 'I don't credit it! How is such a thing even possible?'

'I suspect he was banking on just such a reaction. Mr Hogg has been leading a double life for many years. Hiding in plain sight, you might say.'

'Hiding in the limelight, more like. Can you be certain it was him?'

'We can. Shortly after he dropped Lord Sidcup at the Athenaeum, Mr Hogg was stopped for reckless driving.'

'I don't call that much of a charge sheet after he nearly killed me.'

'Perhaps not, but it was sufficient to arrest and search him, whereupon we discovered three items of interest. First, a substantial quantity of gold coins. Second, an octagonal cloakroom token of unknown origin. And third, a Glisenti Model 1910.'

'Which is?'

'A nine-millimetre semi-automatic pistol, issued to Italian servicemen.'

'Not a very patriotic gat.'

'Also, notoriously underpowered and unwieldy. Nevertheless, an ominous possession for an MP who has sworn the Oath of Allegiance.'

'Hang on, what was the second thing you mentioned?'

'An octagonal cloakroom token. Engraved with the number 458. Sadly, we don't yet know to what it pertains, and Mr Hogg is declining to enlighten us.'

This was deuced coincidental. I fished out my wallet, and extracted the octagonal token that I had been meaning to return for days. 'Does it look anything like this?'

'It certainly matches the description. Wherever did you find it?'

I recounted, briefly, how Monty's sandwich-board had been transformed into an umbrella by the cloakroom attendants at the Ritz, and Lord MacAuslan excused himself to make another call.

'Well,' he said on his return, 'we shall soon see if your octagonal token matches Mr Hogg's octagonal token. Also, I owe you an apology.'

'I can't think why.'

'Our cipher department agrees with you about Hebrews, Chapter 12, Verse 1.'

'Dorothy L. Sayers?'

'A fine piece of deduction, Lord Peter Wooster.'

'Elementary. Though I'm still trying to deduce Hogg as a traitor.'

'We have been concerned about Mr Hogg for some time. We suspect he was recruited while studying Modern Languages at Cambridge.'

'Cambridge!'

'Well, quite.'

Lord MacAuslan explained how Hogg's director of studies had been an Italian academic with some deeply unsavoury political connections in Naples and Rome. After graduation, Hogg had spent a year in, surprise surprise, Naples and Rome before returning to London and establishing himself in finance and politics.

'Isn't Hogg famous for hardly ever attending the Commons?' I asked, poking at my tatties and neeps.

'It's true that Mr Hogg was, until recently, a very backwoods kind of backbencher. He spends most of his time in the City, where, we have reason to believe, he is circumventing various foreign-exchange controls through the unlawful transfer of gold.'

This was all very perplexing. 'If Hogg's a money man, then why was he driving Spode about in a taxi?'

'We don't know.'

'Was Spode aware that his driver was Hogg?'

'We don't know.'

'Are they in league?'

'We don't know.'

'We don't seem to know very much,' I laughed.

'Not knowing, Mr Wooster, is not the same as not *knowing*.'

'Eh?'

'Knowing what you don't know is a form of knowledge, and very different to the ignorance of not knowing what you don't know. The Junior Ganymede is as concerned with unearthing questions as supplying answers.'

This presumably meant something to someone, but it confounded me and it failed to explain Tibby's appearance in the triangle. 'But Hogg just married Spode's niece, so presumably there's more to this than sinister design.'

Lord MacAuslan took a sip of wine. 'A little puzzling, that marriage, wouldn't you say?'

'I admit that Hogg is an unlikely choice for a charmer like Tibby – but who among us can pick the lock of love? Maybe it's a marriage made in heaven.'

'Or somewhere else.'

It seemed to me highly unlikely that any such arrangement would be tolerated outside of royal dynasties and stud farms, but Lord MacAuslan begged to differ.

'Our surveillance of Mr Hogg shows that he was not exactly faithful to Miss Spode during their engagement, nor has he been faithful to her in the few weeks since their wedding.'

'I saw evidence of that whilst strolling with Iona last Sunday.'

'And I've seen the photographs. So, we have to ask ourselves, why did he marry her at all?'

'Love?'

Lord MacAuslan smiled. 'But love of *whom*? Love of *what*? One thing we do know is that since Mr Hogg began courting Lord Sidcup's niece about a year ago he has been much more active in Parliament, and vocal in his support of the Black Shorts.'

'So, Hogg has become Spode's megaphone in the Commons?'

'That seems to be the case. Unless, of course, Lord Sidcup manages to discard his title to stand for Parliament.'

'Oh no, Spode's not going to become an MP. Madeline Bassett has kiboshed that pipe dream completely.'

'How interesting. Thank you.'

A clan of kilted waiters descended on our table to clear away one course and deposit the next. I topped up our glasses, and raised a question that had been bothering me all night.

'What's with all the winking?'

Lord MacAuslan groaned. 'Oh dear. Was there a good deal of winking?'

'A contagion. Nearly all the people I came across squink-eyed like myopic badgers. I assumed it was some form of Junior Ganymede signal.'

'We tell them not to wink. Really, we absolutely insist, but it seems to escape out of them. The thrill of the chase, I suppose.'

'All these people can't be *in* the Junior Ganymede, can they?'

'Assuredly not! They're what we call "bob-a-nobs" – part-timers we engage when required, and tip generously for their discretion.'

'Aren't they ever ... *suspicious*?'

'Occasionally. But we tell them we're divorce agents investigating marital infidelity. It's best not to stray from the clichés in these matters.'

I considered this to be an eminently sensible approach, since divorce is at a feverish pitch among the married classes. Strolling around London one forms the distinct impression that every shifty-looking chap enjoying a solitary cuppa, or perusing the newspaper in a shop doorway, is a private eye amassing evidence or scheming to serve writs of citation.

'What about my cabby? Is he a bob-a-nob?'

'George Jones? Oh, no, he's been with the Ganymede longer than I have; he's almost part of the furniture. George is what we call a "streetologist" – an expert in back-doubles, shoptalk, con games, and have-ons. And, as you saw, he can drive like the wind.

He's uncommonly versatile, George, if you don't mind – how would he put it? – the *rabbit*.'

'I bunged him a fiver as I left the cab. I trust that was sufficient?'

'It was very generous, but you really didn't need to – George is paid well enough. Although I'm always amazed by the hinges you can grease with the timely deployment of a five-pound note.'

'You seem to have half of London's domestics on your books. It must cost a fortune.'

'And not just London. The Ganymede does, however, have a unique and rather unlikely source of income …' He trailed off, as if encouraging me to guess.

'Blackmail?'

He laughed. 'Not a bad idea, but no. The Junior Ganymede is funded by hypothecating the income derived from the taxation of canine ownership.'

I felt that shot of gratification you get on discovering the mislaid portion of a half-eaten cucumber sandwich. 'You don't mean dog licences?'

He nodded.

'I knew it! I've always thought there's something fishy about dog licences. I mean, that you have to pay to keep a pug, but not a parrot. Or, come to think of it, a dachshund, but not a donkey. And now it makes sense.'

'About three million licences are issued each year, and at seven shillings and sixpence a dog, well …' He spread his hands like a magician.

'Every time I see a schnauzer, MacAuslan, I will think of you.'

'Mr Wooster! If you please: a Highland terrier.'

I looked up, and saw the man I now knew to be George Jones approaching our table. He was carrying a small parcel and grinning with the delight of a chap who has found a long-lost gold watch in the grass beside a lake.

'Mr Wooster, I believe you've met George Jones.'

'Evening, guv,' he winked. 'Quite the merry fandangle, eh?'

Lord MacAuslan flinched as he observed the 'secret' signal. 'Is this from the Ritz, George?'

'Certainly is, chief. I shoved that token across the counter, adding a quid of palm oil just in case, and got this bundle in return. No names, no pack drill. Easy meat. Will there be anything else?'

'I think that's all, George, thank you.'

'I'll be tipping off then. Enjoy your grub.'

'Care to do the honours, Mr Wooster?'

I took the package and delicately unsealed one of its flaps with a tine of my fork. Inside, wrapped in the front page of the *Deutsche Allgemeine Zeitung*, were seven unnumbered, blue British passports.

'Well, I mean to say! It's all gone a bit *Kartenhaus, Kartenhaus, Kartenhaus*, what?'

Lord MacAuslan agreed.

'Are they printed with Mr Smee's patent Bank Black ink?'

He took a passport and held it open to the light. 'It certainly looks like it. The technical boys will know for sure.'

'So, what does it all mean?'

'We don't yet know what it all means. It might explain the coincidence of Mr Hogg and Sir Gilbert being at Brinkley Court at the same time.'

'Honeymooning in Market Snodsbury is definitely iffy.'

'And it will certainly help my colleagues who are at this very moment encouraging Mr Hogg to cross the floor.'

'You mean, swap parties?'

'Swap countries.'

'And spy on the Italians while he's meant to be spying for the Italians on us?'

'Or,' said Lord MacAuslan, prodding his knife at the passports, 'Germany.'

'Or both?'

'Whichever it is, Hogg finds himself in an invidious position. He can either betray what I assume are his principles to work with us, or be ruined here, in Italy, and in Germany.'

'*Zugzwang*!' I exclaimed, like a bingo player calling 'house'.

Lord MacAuslan looked perturbed.

'Long story. Ask Jeeves.'

'I will. And I will thank him at the same time. For it was his idea to bring you into the Junior Ganymede. And without you, we would not have drawn Lord Sidcup out of the theatre, drawn Mr Hogg out of the shadows, or thought of drawing a line to Sir Gilbert.'

'Oh no, really,' I protested.

'It's true. Without Jeeves and Wooster, we would have nothing but rumour and suspicion.'

'It's a jolly good thing we kicked Hogg out of the Drones this morning.'

'*Did* you?' flashed Lord MacAuslan. 'Might I enquire why?'

I explained the idiosyncrasies of Rule Two (b), but he remained concerned.

'Do you know if Mr Hogg has yet been informed of his blackballing?'

'It depends whether Tuppy Glossop has written to him. Given Tuppy's hasteless approach to bureaucracy, my guess would be no. He's pretty slack, Tuppy.'

A look of disquiet passed across Lord MacAuslan's usually placid features – the look of a bridegroom when the priest asks the congregation whether any person present knows of cause or just impediment.

'Mr Wooster, I hesitate before presuming to encroach on the affairs of another man's club.'

'But?'

'But, it would be highly advantageous if Mr Hogg remained a member of the Drones.'

'Any particular reason? Or do you just want to stop him joining this place?'

'Men like Mr Hogg feel uniquely at ease at their club. They uncoil, unwind. They drop their guard. And, once in a while, they allow their carefully constructed public masks to slip entirely. As you now know, the real work of the Junior Ganymede happens behind closed doors – behind doors as closed as the Drones'.'

I saw his point. Like a well-worn pair of shoes, or a nib that has curved to your scribble, few things are more conducive to repose than a club where you are chummy with members and staff alike. The first few years in a new establishment can be a touch chilly, but once you know the neighbourhood dogs it's all cream.

'Might you be able to pull some strings?' Lord MacAuslan asked.

This was by no means a simple request, given my passionate (and, I might add, persuasive) opposition to Graydon Hogg just hours earlier. But I was determined not to let down the side at this eleventh hour. 'It may not be easy, but I shall try.'

'Excellent. And now you understand, perhaps, the unorthodox channels through which the Junior Ganymede sails.' He consulted his fob-watch. 'Sadly, though, Edinburgh beckons, and I must depart for the sleeper. But we shall be in touch, Mr Wooster, have no fear of that.'

'I look forward to it.'

'Oh, one last thing,' he said, taking out his wallet. 'I thought you might like to have this.' And he handed me a ticket stub for the debut performance of *Flotsam* – Box B.

8.

WEDNESDAY

I woke unusually early and unexpectedly refreshed, the way people pretend you do after a long cross-country run.

The events of the previous night crowded my mind, though, and it remained almost impossible to credit that Graydon Hogg had traitorous entanglements with not one but two foreign powers – or that he could operate a taxi at such speeds.

I made a mental note to speak to Tuppy about the membership dilemma at a more enlightened time of day. A telephone call at the ungodly hour of eight would hardly warm his ear to my special pleading – not that I had the faintest idea of how my request could be couched without blowing the Junior Ganymede's gaff.

I decided to canvass the Oracle of Mayfair over the marmalade.

'Jeeves, I find myself impaled by a dilemma.'

'I'm troubled to hear that, sir.'

'It involves the Drones Club membership committee, of which Tuppy is this season's chairman.'

'I see, sir.'

'Yesterday, I successfully rallied the troops into blackballing Graydon Hogg *en masse*, but last night Lord MacAuslan enjoined me to ensure Hogg remains as a member. Do you grasp the predic?'

'I do, sir. Would I be correct in assuming that Mr Hogg's membership was put to a ballot under the constitutional stipulation of Rule Two (b)?'

You see what I mean about Jeeves? He really is The Master.

'Two (b) is indeed the hidden sand-trap.'

'Has Mr Hogg been informed of his ejection, sir?'

'Almost certainly not, which definitely helps, since it's tactless in the extreme to chuck a man overboard and then reel him back in. But, to put an additional monkey in the wrench, I promised Percy Gorringe that I would crowbar him into the Drones without delay.'

Jeeves pursed his lips. 'Is the committee likely to look unfavourably on Mr Gorringe's nomination, sir?'

'Quite the reverse, I expect he'll breeze in – they all love a good detective yarn. However, the waiting list is nearly two years long, and I may have given Percy the impression it would all be over by Christmas.'

'There is one solution, sir, though I fear it may not appeal.'

'Does it require eating anything cooked by Aunt Dahlia?'

'No, sir.'

'Then fire away.'

'You have previously mentioned, sir, that becoming chair of the membership committee is something of a Pyrrhic victory.'

'If by that you mean no sane man would touch it with a ten-foot punt pole, then yes.'

'In which case, sir, if you offered to assume the mantle of chairman for, say, a year, this would presumably gratify Mr Glossop, assuage your fellow committee members, and provide you with sufficient latitude to accelerate Mr Gorringe's election.'

Jeeves was right, it didn't appeal – but it was unquestionably shrewd. I could see Tuppy jumping at an honourable discharge, and everyone else thrilled to be out of the front line for a spell.

'Does it have to be for a whole year?' I asked.

'I anticipate any shorter duration would be considered insufficiently self-sacrificial, sir.'

'You're probably right. And, come to think of it, Tuppy suggested only yesterday that I wear the crown of permanent chairman, so I can give him the credit for your idea.'

'An astute embellishment, sir.'

'But will it be enough? I mean, asking the committee to renege on a blackballing is pretty unheard of.'

'In which case, sir, I wonder if it might also be fruitful to make a frank and somewhat calculating appeal to the committee's amorous self-interest.'

'In English?'

'In English, sir: what if one of them ever got married?'

This was crafty. A number of the chaps were impatiently eager to bother the clergy and they might be persuaded that ejecting Hogg under Rule Two (b) would set a dangerous precedent that might come back to bite them.

'By Jeeves, I think you've got it. Thank you. I will telephone Tuppy as soon as the clock chimes a more civilised hour.'

'Very good, sir.'

'Hang on a sec, I almost forgot! Did you get the papers?'

'Yes, sir.'

'And? How were the *Flotsam* reviews?'

'There were no reviews, sir.'

'No reviews?' I was taken aback, and fleetingly wondered if I had simply hallucinated last night's brouhaha. 'None at all?'

'I expect that because of the show's uncommonly *ambitious* duration, sir, the reviewers were unable to meet even their off-stone deadlines.'

'Ah, so the sword dangles over Florence until tonight's *Evening News*.'

'Yes, sir.'

'At what time does that rag hit the streets?'

'The first edition is at midday, sir. However, I do not antici-pate Mr West's review will appear before the six-thirty printing, or possibly even the "late extra", sometime after seven o'clock.'

'She must be on tenderhooks.'

'Tenterhooks, sir? I expect so. Excuse me, sir, the front door.'

After some murmuring and the jingle of coins, Jeeves shim-mied back in with the silver salver.

'Telegram?'

'Telegrams plural, sir. Three, in fact.'

'Read away, Jeeves.'

'The first, sir, is from Lord Sidcup: WOOSTER OLD MAN. MADELINE INSISTS SHE BLAMEWORTHY BOXWISE. INSTRUCTED TO APOLOGISE FOR WORM SLANDER. ALSO NECK WRINGING. ALSO PARASITE. TRUST BYGONES. WEDDING INVITATION TO FOLLOW. RODERICK.'

'"Old man," eh?'

'Yes, sir.'

'And "Roderick"?'

'Indeed, sir.'

'I expect he wrote that with Madeline's hat-pin to his head. Anyway, I shall slumber more soundly knowing that Spode has been pacified by imminent matrimony.'

'It must also be a comfort, sir, to know that Miss Bassett is, if you will forgive the idiom, out of circulation.'

'I should coco. Who was it who said marriage exists not only to punish the guilty but also to protect the innocent?'

'I believe the maxim is more usually applied to prison, sir, although one can appreciate the parallels. The second telegram is from Mr Montgomery: BERTIE PLAY SMASH SUCCESS THREE CUR-TAIN CALLS STANDING OVATION MOBBED AT STAGE DOOR IF REVIEWS GOOD WILL REPAY CASH SOONEST ALSO AM ENGAGED INSIST BEST MAN MONTY.'

'He gets confused by punctuation.'

'That would explain his breathless style, sir.'

'And, if he's engaged also, that takes care of Madeline and Florence. I might suggest a double wedding – kill two birds with one sermon.'

'The third telegram is from Mrs Hogg.'

'Who?'

Jeeves blenched slightly, if blenched is the word I want. 'Tibby, sir.'

'Mrs Hogg, of course. It's still not easy to square that romantic ellipse. What does Tibby have to say?'

'The telegram reads: IN NEED OF A SHOULDER. MIGHT WE MEET?'

'Poor old thing. I wonder if she's got wind of her husband's villainy, or simply acquired cold feet. I fear this will be an uncomfortable rendezvous.'

The doorbell rang again, and Jeeves trickled out.

I forked another sausage. 'Further communications?'

'A delivery, sir. From Mr Travers. He has sent a case of the 1911 d'Yquem. A most remarkable vintage, if I may say so, coinciding as it did with the Great Comet.'

'Did this comet appear with a note?'

'Yes, sir. It reads: *A little something to celebrate the sale. I don't know what Jeeves did, but I sense he must have done something. Cheers to you both.*'

'Good old Tom. You should take the lion's share of that case down to the Junior Ganymede.'

'That is especially generous of you, sir. D'Yquem is a particular club favourite.'

The doorbell rang once again.

'Is it me or are things getting unduly campanological around here?'

Jeeves returned momentarily. 'Two further telegrams, sir.'

'Do you think the delivery boy is rationing them out to amplify his tips?'

'The thought did occur to me, sir, and so on this occasion I declined to remunerate him.'

'I bet he was miffed.'

'I venture "miffed" does not do justice to the vocabulary of his reply, sir.'

'Did you fetch him a clip round the ear?'

'Sadly, sir, he proved too nimble. The first telegram is from Mrs Travers: SAUCY BOY. NEW RECIPES DEVISED. EXPECT YOU BRINKLEY FRIDAY FOR TASTING. UNDER NO CIRCUMSTANCES TELL ANATOLE. NOR TOM. DO YOU HEAR ME BERTIE YOU CLOT? TELL NO ONE. LOVE TRAVERS.'

'Heavens! More recipes?'

'So it would seem, sir.'

'Did you ever get to taste any of them?'

'I did, sir. As you will recall, the events of last Saturday were somewhat turbulent, and there was insufficient time to prepare a separate servants' hall supper. As a result, we dined on the same dishes as the party upstairs.'

'Good Lord, I had no idea. Was it as hellish for you as it was for us?'

'I have had more enjoyable meals, sir.'

'I've had more enjoyable medicine. You know, I'm genuinely surprised that no one needed the professional services of Prebendary Miller.'

'It is hardly my place, sir, but it did occur to me that Mrs Travers might like to know one of the ingredients I felt was missing from her experimentations.'

'A bucket of sand?'

'Soy, sir.'

'Sorry?'

'No, sir, soy. Soy sauce. An ancient Chinese condiment derived from fermented soybeans. I sensed this particular flavour was lacking in many of her dishes, and I gather it is a key – one might even say "secret" – ingredient in Lea and Perrins.'

'Let's keep that one up our sleeve, eh? I really don't think Aunt Dahlia requires any further ammunition for her culinary howitzer.'

'Very good, sir.'

'Was there a second telegram?'

'There was, sir. It is from the Cabinet Office: PRIVATE FOR WOOSTER K-C. POSSIBLE DEVELOPMENT IN EDINBURGH. HOPEFUL WE MIGHT COUNT ON REPEAT ASSISTANCE. SLEEPER TONIGHT? MACAUSLAN.'

'Scotland, eh? It's quite a distance.'

'Indeed, sir.'

'And it's been quite a week.'

'Undeniably, sir.'

'What do you say, Jeeves?'

'Edinburgh can be very agreeable at this time of year, sir.' He brushed a mote of dust from his sleeve. 'And Loch Leven offers some notably scenic trout fishing.'

'Trout, Jeeves?'

'Brown trout, sir. *Salmo trutta*.'

I enjoy fish as much as the next man, assuming the next man is not Gussie Fink-Nottle, whose passion for all things aquatic is positively delirious. Even so, Edinburgh seemed a high road to hike for a dish that the Drones serves grilled to perfection with a dab of Montpellier butter.

Jeeves pressed his case; the man was loopy for the rod. 'And if I may make the observation, sir, if you accepted his lordship's invitation to Scotland, it would be impossible for you to accept the invitation from Mrs Travers to sample her new sauces.'

'Even though, technically, Aunt Dahlia's summons was served first?'

'Was it, sir?' he murmured. 'I don't recall.'

'That rather simplifies things, does it not?'

'I would say so, sir.'

'Telegram MacAuslan, secure first-class berths, and commence packing.'

'Certainly, sir.'

'You hover, Jeeves. Was there something else?'

'Yes, sir. I wonder if you will be requiring your new slippers?'

His voice was steady, but something in his countenance communicated genuine distress. After all he had done for me – dash it, after all he had done for Uncle Tom – well, who would break such a stately wheel on a mere sartorial butterfly.

'I think not, Jeeves. Tartan to Scotland has the ring of coals to Newcastle, wouldn't you say?'

'Assuredly, sir.'

'Do you think you'll be able to find them a loving home?'

He coughed very gently. 'I donated them yesterday, sir, to the Knightsbridge Society for Thrift.'

*   *   *

I was lounging in the first-class bar of the Edinburgh sleeper, sipping a perfect Rob Roy and watching the lights of London blur past, when in flowed Jeeves with a newspaper.

'You tracked down an *Evening News*?'

'Yes, sir. It took some time, but I finally located a copy in one of the luggage cars. Mr West's review appears on page three.'

'Page three? Ack. That's either very good or very bad. Look, since there's no one here, *squattez-vous* and read me the worst.'

Jeeves glanced about uneasily before sitting on the edge of the seat opposite. 'The headline, sir, is "FLOTSAM FLOATS TRIUM-PHANT", and the article begins as follows: *There was a moment during the opening scene when I feared that* Flotsam *– the must-see new play by Lady Florence Craye – had fallen victim to the 'first-night wreckers'. However, the piercing cry of torment that erupted from the auditorium only minutes into the show was just the first of many imaginative staging innovations that this superb production pulled off with aplomb.*'

'Ha! They'll have to do it every night now. I do hope Spode is available.'

'Shall I continue, sir?'

'I'll skim the rest later. I predict "floats triumphant" and "must-see new play" will keep Florence solvent, and they more than cover Gorringe's side of the table. Oh, wait a jiffy, did he say anything about Monty?'

'He was most complimentary, sir. This is from the body of the review: *Making his debut was Mr Montague Montgomery, of the Widcombe Montgomeries, whose virtuoso performance in the leading role of Able Seaman Benskin Muchmore displayed an empathic sensitivity to the emotional depths of an East End Jack Tar with the wind in his hair and salt in his soul.*'

'Praise indeed. There'll be no talking to Monty now. Did Rex West make any mention of "unmoored epistemological musings"?'

Jeeves looked puzzled. 'No, sir. Were you expecting such a criticism?'

'Florence was.'

I hailed a passing steward. 'Care for a gargle, Jeeves?'

'That would be very welcome, sir.'

'Same again for me,' I instructed, 'and one for m'colleague.'

As I took out my wallet to extract some largesse for the waiter's return, a fold of paper spiralled from my jacket to the floor. I picked it up, read it, and spotted something unusual.

'Jeeves, I've just had a look at MacAuslan's telegram, and there's a dashed peculiar annotation.'

'Sir?'

'See, here, where it says "PRIVATE FOR WOOSTER K-C".'

'Sir.'

'K-C? Is that a transmission error?'

'I don't think so, sir.'

'Some sort of telegraphese?'

'I would venture to suggest, sir, that K-C is a Junior Ganymede Club code name.'

'You have code names?'

'Senior officers do, sir.'

'Just odd pairs of letters?'

'No, sir. Ganymede code names are premised on playing cards from the traditional French deck designed in Rouen.'

'That seems uncharacteristically playful for Stroud-Pringle.'

'They were devised by the Earl of Winchester, sir, who was a close friend and Oxford contemporary of Lewis Carroll. He adopted the codes after being inspired by *Alice's Adventures in Wonderland*.'

'"The Queen of Hearts, she made some tarts, all on a summer day"?'

'Quite so, sir. The Earl took as his *nom de guerre* the Knave of Hearts.'

'Aha! "Frustrate their knavish tricks"?'

'Precisely, sir.'

'So if my code is K-C, then I must be ... the King of Clubs?'

'That is what I infer from Lord MacAuslan's telegram, sir.'

'And MacAuslan himself, which card was he dealt?

Jeeves leaned forward and lowered his voice. '9-D, sir.'

'The nine of diamonds? Hoots, mon! "The Curse of Scotland" – how very fitting. Do you have a Ganymede code name, Jeeves? Being a senior officer, and all.'

'I do, sir.'

I stared at him expectantly. 'And?'

Jeeves never has cause actually to be embarrassed, but I detected the very slightest pinking of his earlobes. 'A-H, sir.'

'A-H, eh? A-H ... I say, A-H!'

There was an interlude.

'Any particular ...?'

'*No*, sir,' he said, emphatically.

'Of course. Quite understand.' I took a sip. 'But, even so, A-H. At-a-boy!'

'The codes *are* confidential, sir,' he urged.

'Understood, A-H. Strictly sub-fedora.'

This was all very crispish and new. I've been called one or two things in my time, not least at school where nicknaming was a ruthlessly pursued blood sport, but never before had I been given an honest-to-goodness code name.

It was also pretty chuffing to be a face card rather than a mere pip. Although, on reflection, Lord MacAuslan was a humble nine, and Jeeves an elevated ace. Unless aces were low through this particular looking-glass? In which case, what? Were there wild cards? Did suits signify anything in particular? And, if they did, what were trumps in the Junior Ganymede deck?

I was mentally shuffling these questions when somewhere in the back of my mind a synapse pinged.

'I say, Jeeves, whatever happened to that horse I backed on Monday?'

'Privateer, sir?'

'That's the nag. Was she placed?'

'She did not finish, sir.'

'Shot in the paddock, I expect. Hey-ho, that's twenty I'll never see again.'

Jeeves churched his fingers. 'I feel I owe you an explanation, sir.'

'Do you?'

'Yes, sir. While effectuating the necessary transactions with the turf accountant, I inadvertently added your stake to mine and placed them both on Treadgold.'

'Was *she* placed?'

'She won, sir. By two lengths.'

'At what odds?'

'Thirty-three to one, sir.'

'Double carpet!'

This was a suspiciously fortuitous act of 'inadvertence', and one that many employers, I have no doubt, would view as outright insubordination. Or is it *downright* insubordination? Jeeves would know. And, you see, that's the key to Jeeves: one must take the rough with the smooth. And, in this instance, the rough was actually some six hundred and sixty quid.

'How on earth did Treadgold merit such vertiginous odds yet finish so strong?'

'As you may know, sir, Treadgold is a distinctive chestnut roan with white blaze, four white stockings, and a high tail carriage.'

I affected equestrian acumen.

'Her owners took great pains to locate a filly with virtually indistinguishable markings, which they trained on the gallops in full view of the touts. Naturally, this ringer was significantly slower than Treadgold, a fact which doubtless influenced the setting of the odds.'

'Well that explains how Bingo's man Fred went so completely astray. And you knew about this duplicity, how?'

'My Uncle Charles, sir, who works for the horse's owner, Mr Esmond Haddock at Deverill Hall.'

'Charlie Silversmith, of course! Please remember me to him, and thank him for his tip.'

'I will, sir.'

'You know, I really did fancy Privateer.'

'In fairness, sir, Treadgold was assisted by the especially hard going at Kempton Park.'

'It's true, some fillies do fly on a tough deck.'

And then a lightning bolt struck. Which, if it meant what I thought it meant ... well, I didn't know quite what I thought it meant. But it surely meant something, and that was enough to get the old ticker beating a tarantella.

'Brace yourself, Jeeves.'

'Sir?'

I put down my drink and set out my hypothesis.

'The Ganymede's "deck" of code names?'

'Sir?'

'If you are the Ace of Hearts ...'

'Sir.'

'MacAuslan is the Nine of Diamonds ...'

'Sir.'

'And I am the King of Clubs ...'

'Sir?'

'Then doesn't Iona's family nickname, the one MacAuslan used at Brinkley Court, take on a rather different complexion?'

Jeeves said nothing, he merely raised an eyebrow.

'Kewcee? ... Q-C ... So, Iona is ...'

It was my turn for the pink-earlobe treatment.

'Yes, sir,' said Jeeves. 'The Queen of Clubs.'

IT IS AN incomparable honour to follow – *strive* to follow,
I think, old bean – in the patent-leather footsteps of the
greatest humourist in the English language.

I've been captivated by P. G. Wodehouse ever since an
Aged Relative placed a well-thumbed copy of *Carry On, Jeeves*
into my tender, unsuspecting hands. That book, and the
characters therein, unveiled an empire of comic writing on
which the sun has never set.

Jeeves & the King of Clubs is, therefore, an homage to
The Master – an attempt to deploy the pulleys, levers, gears,
and knotted rope of Plum's creative brilliance, and construct
a novel that might both entertain his legions of devoted fans
and introduce new generations to the caper-strewn uplands
of Brinkley Court and Berkeley Mansions.

I am indebted to the Wodehouse Estate for their gracious
permission to borrow the Crown Jewels – and especially to
Sir Edward Cazalet, Plum's step-grandson, for his thoughtful
and generous support.

I hope this book might inspire readers to return to the
fountain of Wodehouse's peerless oeuvre – not just Jeeves
and Wooster, but Psmith, Ukridge, Emsworth, Mulliner,
Uncle Fred, and the Oldest Member.

Nothing can cap perfection; my aim has been to establish
base camp in the foothills of Plum's genius, and direct climbers
up towards the peak.

Tinkety-tonk!

BEN SCHOTT · xi 2018

NOTES ON THE TEXT

GENERAL

The *Oxford English Dictionary* currently employs 1,525 P. G. Wodehouse quotations to help define entries ranging from 'Aberdonian' to 'Zowie' – including 'first base', 'lallapaloosa', 'palsy-walsy', and 'screwball'.

Within this collection are twenty-six words where Plum is credited with the 'first quotation':

Billiken (*n.*; 1914) · **Crispish** (*adj.*; 1930) · **Cuckoo** (*adj.*; 1923) · **Cuppa** (*n.*; 1925) · **Fifty-fifty** (*adv.*; 1913) · **Gruntled** (*adj.*; 1938) · **Ilag** (*n.*; 1941)· **Lame-brain** (*adj.*; 1929) · **Not-at-all** (*v.*; 1936) · **O' goblin** (*n.*; 1909)· **Oojah-cum-spiff** (*adj.*; 1930)· **Persp.** (*n.*, 1923) · **Plonk** (*n.*; 1903)· **Pottiness** (*n.*; 1933) · **Raisonneur** (*v.*; 1963) · **Right-ho** (*v.*; 1936)· **Ritzy** (*adj.*; 1920) · **Scenario** (*v.*; 1923) · **Scrag** (*n.*; 1903) · **Shimmy** (*v.*; 1923)· **Snooter** (*v.*; 1923) · **Unscramble** (*v.*; 1923) · **Upswing** (*n.*; 1922)· **What-the-hell** (*v.*; 1924)· **Whiffled** (*adj.*; 1927) · **Zing** (*int.*; 1919).

All of these words are included in the book, in one form or another.

1. WEDNESDAY

The In & Out · This is the long-established nickname of the Naval and Military Club, founded in 1862. It derives from the vehicular directions ('IN, 'OUT') painted in large black capitals on the stone pillars guarding the entrances to the courtyard of Cambridge House, the club's former home on Piccadilly. When the club moved to 4 St James's Square in 1999, these directions were waggishly inscribed on the columns either side of the new front door.

Shall we go straight through to dinner? · The 'wise king' alluded to here is the novelist, critic, and enthusiastic boozer Kingsley Amis. [See, for example, Keith Waterhouse, *The Theory and Practice of Lunch* (Michael Joseph, 1986), p. 32.]

Temperance Corner · In reality, this was an ironic epithet that referred to the area of the Athenaeum's dining-room wherein the hoaxer and clubman Theodore Hook would sit and drink heavily. To save the blushes of the Athenaeum's extensive ecclesiastical membership, Hook would ask the waiters for refills of 'tea', 'lemonade', and 'toast-and-water'. [See, for example, Frank Richard Cowell, *The Athenaeum: Club and Social Life in London, 1824–1974* (Heinemann, 1975), p. 44.]

Eggs, Beans, and Crumpets · A triad of Wodehousian nicknames for chums and clubmen, and the title of a collection of Plum's short stories, first published in 1940.

Spindrift · The title of Florence Craye's successful novel and unsuccessful play, 'spindrift' is the fine spray that blows off wave crests in gale conditions – specifically, Force 7–8 winds by the Beaufort Scale.

Flotsam · The floating wreckage of a ship, or its cargo, more commonly associated with the devastation of a Force 12 hurricane, as Benskin Muchmore later informs the audience.

Sharp-Shine Joe was Cockney from loaf to Bromleys · The rhyming slang translates as: '*loaf (of bread)* = head'; '*Bromley(-by-Bow)* = toe'. Bromley-by-Bow is a district in East London. The back-slang '*pu to the kalat*' means 'up to the talk'.

2. THURSDAY

Ack emma · A (military) communications term for 'a.m.' (*ante meridiem*) to ensure precision during transmission. **Pip emma** was similarly used for 'p.m.' (*post meridiem*).

Boil-washed coins · Several gentlemen's clubs – including, apparently, Boodle's, Brooks's, and Arthur's – did indeed boil silver coins before handing them back to members in change. [See, for example, Sir George Arthur, *A Septuagenarian's Scrap Book* (Thomas Butterworth, 1933), p. 291.]

Turkish cologne · An 1880 etiquette manual gives the following formula for Turkish cologne: 'Tincture Canada snake root, eight ounces; tincture orris root, twenty-four ounces; oil of bergamot, oil of lavender, oil of lemon, each twelve drachms; essence musk, oil of neroli, oil of cinnamon, oil of clove, each two drachms; orange spirits, six quarts. After mixing, the cologne should be allowed to stand several days before pouring off into bottles.' [Anon., *The Manners That Win* (Buckeye Publishing Co., 1880), p. 411.]

Sir Gilbert Skinner · Sir Gilbert is loosely inspired by Montagu Collet Norman, the longest-serving Governor of the Bank of England (1920–44).

A dandyish, self-regarding, and supercilious old Etonian, Norman was as famed for his foppish Vandyke beard as his neurotic ill-temper. He cultivated an air of cloaked mystery by actually wearing a cloak, and regularly travelled under the pseudonym 'Professor Clarence Skinner' in an attempt to outfox the press, in whose attentions he also basked. (He was, for example, on the cover of *Time* magazine in August 1929.)

Described as a 'banker's banker' and the 'first modern central banker', Norman has also been accused of being a 'Nazi sympathiser'.[1] He was certainly a close friend of Hjalmar Schacht – Hitler's Reichsbank President and Minister of Economics – and, in 1939, he travelled to Berlin to become godfather to one of Schacht's grandsons.

In the early years of the Second World War, Norman told a friend that 'Hitler and Schacht are the bulwarks of civilisation in Germany',[2] and in 1942 President Roosevelt sent a telegram to Winston Churchill alerting him to suspicious contacts between Norman and Schacht.[3]

As the historian David Blaazer explores in detail, Norman was centrally involved in the highly controversial transfer of Czechoslovakia's London gold holdings to the Nazi Reichsbank following Germany's invasion in 1939. Whether Norman was a Nazi sympathiser, an appeaser, or just a cynical capitalist is the subject of debate. Blaazer writes: 'The Czech gold affair … provide[s] an insight into crucial moments in appeasement's unravelling. Appeasement had been a cohesive, multi-stranded effort by Britain's gentlemanly order to keep Germany within the international fold so as to maintain a peaceful order in which Britain could prosper and progressively restore the global financial hegemony which had been the basis of gentlemanly capitalism's power.'[4]

[1. Isabel Vincent, *Hitler's Silent Partners: Swiss Banks, Nazi Gold, and the Pursuit of Justice* (Knopf Canada, 2011), ebook; 2. Liaquat Ahamed, *Lords of Finance: The Bankers Who Broke the World* (Windmill Books, 2010), p. 488; 3. Scott Newton, *Profits of Peace: The Political Economy of Anglo-German Appeasement* (Clarendon Press, 2003), p. 194; 4. David Blaazer, 'Finance and the End of Appeasement: The Bank of England, the National Government and the Czech Gold', *Journal of Contemporary History*, vol. 40, no. 1 (January 2005), pp. 25–39.]

Ye Olde Cheshire Cheese · One of London's most famous pubs, the Cheshire Cheese was established sometime in the sixteenth century and rebuilt after the Great Fire of 1666. Its inclusion is a nod to a letter Plum wrote to a friend on 12 February 1927: 'Isn't it curious how few people there are in the world whom one wants to see. Yesterday, I looked in at the Garrick at lunch time, took one glance of loathing at the mob, and went off to lunch by myself at the Cheshire Cheese.' [*P. G. Wodehouse: A Life in Letters*, ed. Sophie Ratcliffe (2011) (Arrow Books, 2013), p. 183.]

Eclipse Stakes · 1 mile, 1 furlong, 209 yards – run at Sandown Park since 1886. No horse called Jiggery-Pokery has ever won.

Smyth's for Snuff · This fictional establishment pays homage to the legendary tobacconist G. Smith & Sons, a London landmark at 74 Charing Cross Road between 1869 and c.2012. (It's said that the building's lease stipulated the shop must sell tobacco.) All of the snuffs named in the book – Golden Lavender, Irish High Toast, Cock of the North, etc. – come from a 'Smith's for Snuff' catalogue of unknown (but pre-decimal currency) date.

Toad-in-the-hole · This was indeed the term for a sandwich man 'when his person is confined by a four-sided box'. [John C. Hotton, *The Slang Dictionary* New Edition (Chatto & Windus, 1874), p. 277.]

Pass the mustard · 'Few men who earn their living in the streets are better abused and more persistently jeered at than the unfortunate individuals who let themselves out for hire as walking advertisements. The work is so hopelessly simple that any-one who can put one foot before the other can undertake it, and the carrying of boards has therefore become a means of subsistence open to the most stupid and forlorn of individuals ... The boardmen have therefore become a general butt, and it is considered fair play to tease them in every conceivable manner. The old joke, the query as to the whereabouts of the mustard, has now died out, and it is considered better sport to bespatter the "sandwich men" with mud, or to tickle their faces with a straw when the paraphernalia on their backs prevents all attempts at self-defence.' [J. Thomson and Adolphe Smith, *Street Life in London* Part 1 (Sampson Low, Marston, Searle, & Rivington, 1877), p. 69.]

Less Passion From Less Protein · This is a profoundly anachronistic nod to the much-missed eccentric Stanley Owen Green, who, from 1968 until his death in 1993, tramped London's Oxford Street with a placard decrying the moral perils of protein, specifically fish, meat, bird, egg, cheese, peas, beans, nuts, and (curiously) sitting.

Had Napoleon been an aunt · For more on Plum's numerous references to Napoleon Bonaparte see Tony Ring and Geoffrey Jaggard, *Wodehouse in Woostershire* (Porpoise Books, 1999), p. 37.

Knut · The *Oxford English Dictionary* defines 'knut' as 'a fashionable or showy young man'. Although the term was in use *c.*1911, it was popularised in 1914 by the actor Basil Hallam, who performed as 'Gilbert the Filbert' and sang the lyric: 'I'm Gilbert the Filbert, the Knut with a K / The pride of Piccadilly, the blasé roué.'

In 1973, Plum wrote: 'I was never myself by knut standards, dressy as a young man (circa 1905), for a certain anaemia of the exchequer compelled me to go about my social duties in my brother's cast-off frock coat and top hat bequeathed to me by an uncle with a head some sizes smaller than mine, but my umbrella was always rolled as tight as a drum and though spats cost money, I had mine all right.' [*A Life in Letters*, p. 533.]

Renounce your peerage · There is an anachronism in Plum's oeuvre, which I have fudged somewhat. The question of Lord Sidcup renouncing his title in order to stand for Parliament was first mentioned in *Much Obliged, Jeeves*, published in 1971:

'... You remember me telling you he couldn't be a Member of Parliament because he was a peer. Well, he wants to give up his title so that he will be eligible.'

'Can a fellow with a title give it up? I thought he was stuck with it.'

'He couldn't at one time, at least only by being guilty of treason, but they've changed the rules and apparently it's quite the posh thing to do nowadays.'

[P. G. Wodehouse, *Much Obliged, Jeeves* (1971) (Arrow Books, 2008), p. 150.]

The 'change of rules' to which Plum refers is the Peerage Act 1963, which passed into law rather late in the day for Lord Sidcup. The Act was championed by the 2nd Viscount Stansgate, better known as Tony Benn, who renounced his title on the day the law changed.

First-night wreckers · Towards the end of the nineteenth century, 'first-night wreckers' were a genuine menace to certain theatrical productions.

As the *Saturday Review* noted in 1886: 'The Destroyer – or, as he is technically called the Wrecker – is no angel, but a common cad. He has no special education, and no peculiar gift of understanding. His vocation is to sell cheese, or measure tapes, or distribute greengrocery; at the best he is only an unsuccessful dramatist, and it is out of mere lightness of heart that he takes to the business of making first nights hideous … His work being over, he puts off his apron, joins his comrades at the playhouse door, fights his way to a place, and does his loudest to confound success with failure. He hoots, he howls, he bellows; he makes the ancient privilege of hissing, a thing abominable to man. It matters nothing to him that the question is artistic and literary, and that in his wake the air is clouded with the spectres of murdered and of misbegotten aspirates. He has come to amuse himself, and amused at better men's expense he assuredly is.'

[Anon., 'First Night Wreckers', *Saturday Review of Politics, Literature, Science and Art*, vol. 62, no. 1,625, 18 December 1886 (Spottiswoode & Co.), pp. 805–6.]

3. FRIDAY

Grrgghh · There are, Plum informs us with a specificity that implies keen experience, 'six varieties of hangover – the Broken Compass, the Sewing Machine, the Comet, the Atomic, the Cement Mixer and the Gremlin Boogie.' [P. G. Wodehouse, *The Mating Season* (1949) (Arrow Books, 2008), p. 34.]

Third circle of Hell · In Dante's *Inferno*, this realm is inhabited by gluttons and wine-bibbers.

Screech of his peacocks · This is a nod to the composer Sir Edward Elgar, who would telephone home from Brooks's Club specifically to hear his dogs barking back in Worcestershire. [See, for example, Stephen Klimczuk and Gerald Warner, *Secret Places, Hidden Sanctuaries* (Sterling, 2009), p. 240.]

Found a pearl in a restaurant oyster · Established in 1929 by Giovanni Quaglino, the restaurant known as 'Quag's' and 'Quaggies' was an immediate society success – and was the first private restaurant ever visited by Queen Elizabeth II.

According to legend, a woman named Barbara did indeed discover a pearl in a Quaglino's oyster sometime in the early 1930s. That woman was Barbara Cartland. [See, for example, Alex Witchel, 'At Lunch With: Sir Terence Conran; The Titled Champion of Democracy', *New York Times*, 28 July 1993, C1.]

Your pal Nietzsche · In *Carry On, Jeeves*, we learn that Florence Craye intended to educate Bertie by burdening him with the work of Friedrich Nietzsche. Jeeves – who had just been fired and could, therefore, 'speak freely without appearing to take a liberty' – warns: 'You would not enjoy Nietzsche, sir. He is fundamentally unsound.' [P. G. Wodehouse, *Carry On, Jeeves* (1925) (Arrow Books, 2018), p. 36.]

The 'new' dinner jacket · The longevity of a bespoke suit is both a selling point on Savile Row and a point of pride – as John Hitchcock, former head cutter of Anderson & Sheppard, said: 'A ten-year-old suit is considered a *new* suit.'[1] That said, as his colleague Dennis Hallbery also observed: 'If a customer walked out of our shop and he met a friend who said, "What a splendid new suit," we would not be pleased. A suit should not look new.'[2]

[1. David Kamp, 'A Style is Born', vanityfair.com, 21 October 2011; 2. Henry Porter, 'The Unkindest Cut', *Illustrated London News*, 1 August 1987, p. 39.]

And will we be dancing or just dining? · A dinner jacket cut for dancing will be slightly looser round the scye (i.e., armhole).

The Nomadical · Although this is a fictional establishment, the idea of an illegal, peripatetic, and parasitic gambling club is based on fact. As the historian Ralph Nevill wrote: 'Some of the most decorous-looking [Mayfair] mansions could tell queer tales. The high play which took place within their walls has been known to go on without the consent or even the knowledge of the owners. This was especially the case just before the Great War, when it became the practice of certain sporting individuals, appreciative of the financial benefits of the *cagnotte* [owner's share], to pay a big rent for six months in order to be able to entertain a select clientele fond of baccarat.'

Nevill tells of an Englishman who, walking along the Rue de la Paix in Paris, ran into a friend who crowed that he had recently won £500 playing baccarat in his own London drawing-room.[1]

According to *The Times*, similar illegal enterprises flourished also after the Great War, albeit on a less extravagant scale: 'During the 1920s professional gamesters rented flats for discreet sessions of roulette, *chemin-de-fer* and poker, charging table-money according to the stake and risking loss from their clients' failure to pay card-losses. The premises were frequently changed and there was little danger of a police raid.'[2]

[1. Ralph Nevill, *Mayfair and Montmartre* (Methuen & Co., 1921), pp. 141–2; 2. Edward Mayer, 'Crockford's: the rise and fall of a card club', *The Times*, 29 August 1977, p. 6.]

'Tulip Time in Sing Sing' · A song written by Jerome Kern and P. G. Wodehouse for their 1924 musical comedy, *Sitting Pretty*.

Even-Odd · So great was the press and public uproar surrounding this rudimentary (and ruinous) form of roulette that, in 1782, the 'EO Table Bill' ('The Act to Prevent the Pernicious Practice of Gaming') was brought before Parliament. Although, for various technical reasons, the Bill failed to become law, the authorities cracked down hard on gaming houses that offered Even-Odd tables. [See, for example, Donna T. Andrew, *Aristocratic Vice: The Attack on Duelling, Suicide, Adultery, and Gambling in Eighteenth-Century England* (Yale University Press, 2013), p. 206.]

Engaged twice over · 'The first Simplon-Orient Express left Paris for Istanbul on 15 April 1919, taking ninety-six hours over its journey.' [*Geographical Journal*, vol. 97 (Royal Geographical Society, 1941), p. 288.]

Alpine Joe · The criminal moniker Jeeves bestows on Bertie in *Stiff Upper Lip, Jeeves*. It refers to a controversial Alpine hat ('blue … with a pink feather') that Bertie recklessly purchased. [P. G. Wodehouse, *Stiff Upper Lip, Jeeves* (1963) (Arrow Books, 2018), p. 17.]

Chief Inspector Witherspoon · The police moniker Jeeves adopts in *Stiff Upper Lip, Jeeves*. As Bertie notes: '"Why Witherspoon? On the other hand," I added, for I like to look on both sides of a thing, "why not Witherspoon?"' [Ibid., p. 100.]

Red threes · In the game of canasta, such cards are worth 100 points (or 200, if all four are collected).

Eyes within that hedgerow · The first half of the 'walls have ears' proverb seems to have come adrift over the decades: 'They say, Hedges have Eyes, and Walls have Ears.' [Jonathan Swift, *A Complete Collection of Genteel and Ingenious Conversation* (Motte & Bathurst, 1738), p. 199.]

4. SATURDAY

Maiden speech · The first speech an MP gives on being elected to the Commons. Maiden speeches tend to be uncontroversial and witty, and pay tribute to the outgoing incumbent as well as to the glories of the constituency.

East Looe · When this Cornish constituency was abolished by the 1832 Reform Act it represented just 167 houses and 38 voters. [J. Holladay Philbin, *Parliamentary Representation, 1832* (Yale University Press, 1965), p. 28.]

Coratch Sauce · All these sauces did, at one time, exist – so too did Rowland's Macassar Hair Oil, from which we derive the word 'antimacassar'. [See, for example, William Shurtleff and Akiko Aoyagi, *History of Worcestershire Sauce 1837–2012* (Soyinfo Center, 2012).]

Because Mr Giovanni hails from northern Italy · Jeeves is, naturally, correct: the dialects of northern Italy tend to elide double consonants into single sounds. [See, for example, Gianrenzo P. Clivio and Marcel Danesi, *The Sounds, Forms, and Uses of Italian* (University of Toronto Press, 2000), p. 179.]

5. SUNDAY

What was his name? · Prometheus.

Bruichladdich · According to the distillers, the anglicised pronunciation of this celebrated single malt is *brook-laddie*, although West Coast Gaelic speakers say *brew-ah-kladdie*.

Bank Black · Alfred Smee FRS was one of those remarkable, almost fictional, nineteenth-century polymaths: surgeon, chemist, metallurgist, educationalist, astronomer, philosopher, physiologist, oculist, electrical engineer, statistician, satirist, and experimental horticulturalist.

It's not clear when Smee became interested in the chemistry of printing substrates – although it seems likely that the need for an ink that remained black over time might first have been suggested by his father, William, who in 1829 was appointed chief accountant to the Bank of England. (Smee himself was elected surgeon to the Bank in 1841, a position created especially for him.)

Smee perfected 'Bank Black' in 1842 – and the knowledge he accrued on the subject of ink allowed him to provide an expert opinion in a number of criminal cases. Perhaps the most notorious was the 1848 Stanfield Hall Murders, in which Isaac Jermy and his son Isaac Jermy Jermy were shot to death in the hallway of their Norfolk home by their tenant farmer James Bloomfield Rush. (Rush foolishly undertook his own legal defence; it took the jury less than ten minutes to find him guilty, and he was hanged a week later.)

The recipe for 'Bank Black' is given in Appendix IX of a memoir of Smee written by his daughter.

RECEIPT OF A WRITING INK made by ALFRED SMEE
56 nut-galls to 50 gallons of water; specific gravity 22
15 lbs copperas to 5 gallons of water
15 lbs of gum to 5 gallons of water
1 gallon of pyroligneous acid
¼ lb corrosive sublimate

Hot water to be poured on the gall-nuts, and this is to be allowed to stand about twenty-four hours.

The infusion of galls is then to be poured off, and the gum (previously mixed with the five gallons of water) to be first added; then the copperas, which also has been previously mixed with five gallons of water, the pyroligneous acid

and the corrosive sublimate are all to be mixed together. The whole to stand till the ink is dark enough for writing, when bottle off.

The specific gravity of ink when made to be 35–37.

The ink should be run through sieves four or five, or even six times, to make it clear.

[Elizabeth Mary Odling, *Memoir of the Late Alfred Smee, FRS* (George Bell & Sons, 1878)]

Associated Civil Service · Both this club and the Northcote-Trevelyan are fictional, but the idea of a club dissolving and re-forming itself just to expel one offensive individual is, splendidly, not.

In 1824, London's Stratford Club – the home of whist and, later, bridge – was plagued by a disreputable member, identified by *Cassell's Weekly* as 'a certain General Charitie'. This Charitie – 'a gallant solider', 'noted duellist', and 'inveterate gambler' – was so adept at extracting money from 'various young sprigs of the nobility' that the Stratford Club became increasingly fearful of society scandal. 'Eventually, one afternoon, a meeting of the members was held upstairs in the card-room, and the Stratford Club was dissolved. The meeting was then adjourned to the downstairs room, where a new Club was formed under the title of the Portland Club, and all the members of the old club were re-elected, with the single exception of General Charitie.'[1]

That almost no biographical information exists about 'General Charitie' may be due to a typo. The soldier who caused the dissolution of the Stratford Club seems to be Major General

Thomas Charretie – a remarkable man of 'wild orgies and escapades' who fought under Wellington in the Peninsular War, was present at Vitoria, Pamplona, and Toulouse, and led a troop of Life Guardsmen at Waterloo.[2]

As well as being a noted equestrian and poacher, Charretie was 'a very capital hand at billiards, cards, and pigeon-shooting' who would take on the most outlandish wagers. In 1842, he bet that he could win a shooting match, come first in the Imperial Steeplechase, and play the Duke of Gloucester in *Richard III* at the Cheltenham Assembly Rooms, all on the same day. According to his obituary in *The Field*, Charretie once memorised – and repeated word for word – an entire issue of the London *Morning Post*, including adverts.[3]

[1. Anon., 'Clubs and Clubbing', *Cassell's Weekly*, 28 March 1923, p. 52; 2. Edith Mary Humphris and E. C. Willoughby, *At Cheltenham Spa* (Alfred A. Knopf, 1928), pp. 190–2; 3. William C. A. Blew, *A History of Steeple-Chasing* (John C. Nimmo, 1901), pp. 46–9.]

Northcote-Trevelyan · The 1854 Northcote–Trevelyan Report, by Stafford H. Northcote and C. E. Trevelyan, led to the creation of the British Civil Service.

Taxi for Sir Charles · Variations on this joke have been attributed to a number of clubs over the decades, most often Boodle's.

Pushed the ankle-biter Oswald off the bridge · In *The Inimitable Jeeves* (1923), Bertie hatches a plan to help Bingo Little woo Honoria Glossop (and thereby thwart Aunt Agatha's attempts to fix him up with said girl). The scheme involves pushing Honoria's pestilential brother Oswald off a stone bridge into the lake below, at which point Bingo – hiding in a clump of bushes – will dive in, rescue the child, and win Honoria's heart. Things, needless to say, go awry.

6. MONDAY

Privateer · This was the horse favoured by Bertie in the opening pages of *The Inimitable Jeeves* (1923) and even then Jeeves did not consider the stable to be 'sanguine'.

Treadgold · The name of this horse was suggested by one of Plum's housemasters at Dulwich College. According to Robert McCrum's magisterial biography, T. G. Treadgold was a 'walrus-moustached disciplinarian' under whose tutelage the young Wodehouse 'rapidly became one of those all-rounders, thriving in sports as much as school work, who stride across the pages of his school stories'. [Robert McCrum, *Wodehouse: A Life* (W. W. Norton, 2004), p. 33.]

Lionel Dennis Freeman · This name was suggested by Plum's letters, in which, as the editor Sophie Ratcliffe notes: 'The unidentified figure of "Dennis Freeman" stands ... as a cipher for the sort of man Wodehouse detested, the sort who ... would spend his time "twittering all over the place, screaming: 'Oh, Lionel!'"'' [*A Life in Letters*, p. 225.]

The fifteenth of October · Plum's birthday.

Floromancy · The bar for what constitutes 'divination by flowers' does not seem to be all that high. According to *The Fortune-Telling Book*, 'plucking the petals from a flower while saying the words "She (or he) loves me; she loves me not," until the last petal, is a form of floromancy.' [Raymond Buckland, *The Fortune-Telling Book* (Visible Ink Press, 2003), p. 206.]

Anatomical snuffbox · 'The anatomical snuffbox [is] formed by the tendons of the extensor pollicis brevis and abductor pollicis longus laterally and the tendon of the extensor pollicis longus medially.' [Elizabeth Burns, et al., *Oxford American Handbook of Clinical Examination and Practical Skills* (Oxford University Press, 2011), ebook.]

The Lyceum · Founded in 1903 by Constance Smedley, the Lyceum Club on Piccadilly was 'for women of any nationality who either have published any original work in literature, journalism, science, art, music, or have university qualifications, or are wives or daughters of distinguished men'. The Lyceum did indeed have a system of *à la carte* and *table d'hôte* menus designed to cater for 'many a woman who hides a slender purse under a brave aspect'. [Dora D'Espaigne, 'The Lyceum Club for Ladies', *Lady's Realm*, vol. 16 (May–June 1904), pp. 602–9.]

Aunt Minnie · This has long been a spy term for (amateur) photographs that inadvertently contain useful intelligence.

As the historian Paul Winter explores, in 1942 Director of Naval Intelligence Admiral John Godfrey asked the BBC to broadcast an appeal for holiday snaps taken along the coast of Europe at sites of 'potential military interest'. The overwhelming response, some 80,000 replies, was 'of immense value to Allied planners for "pictures taken at eye level can be more informative than obliques taken from aircraft" mainly because they can "show the gradient [of a beach], whether the surface is sand or shingle", as well as indicate the "height and construction of sea walls, groins, and breakwaters".'[1]

The etymology of the term 'Aunt Minnie' is unclear. It may originally have been a vague American 'stock' characterisation – similar to 'Uncle Jack' or 'Cousin Billy' – and its first associations with espionage seem to derive from a 1941 article for *Collier's* in which the intrepid journalist Alice-Leone Moats warned against taking photographs in Japan: 'Even staying on the ground and training a lens on Aunt Minnie may incur difficulties with the police. They might admit that Minnie is no fortified zone, but they are sure to insist that the background – whether bank, department store or wind-swept beach – is one.'[2]

In 1982, William Colby, Director of the CIA between 1973 and 1976, spoke of the importance of such amateur intelligence: 'Even such a trivial thing as a photo of somebody's Aunt Minnie on a beach in a bathing suit [is put to use]. If experts noted she was standing by a truck, for example, they would know that the beach was firm enough for military or espionage vehicles.'[3]

[1. Paul Winter, *D-Day Documents* (Bloomsbury, 2014), pp. 76–7; 2. Alice-Leone Moats, 'Beware, Honorable Spy! Super-snooping, the new Japanese national pastime', *Collier's*, 16 August 1941, p. 18; 3. Barbara Bernstein, 'Former CIA Chief Defends Agency Role', *Deseret News* (Salt Lake City), 5 February 1982.]

Alpine hats · See: **Alpine Joe**, above.

Out-Ginger the deftest of Rogers · In *Joy in the Morning*, Bertie boasts that 'as a dancer I out-Fred the nimblest Astaire'. [P. G. Wodehouse, *Joy in the Morning* (1946) (Arrow Books, 2013), p. 46.]

Two thousand two hundred · In common with many non-fictional auction houses, the bidding increments at Shipley's increase as the total rises. This also explains why Jeeves jumps from £5,500 to £6,000 in one go.

Hello girls · A long-standing nickname for female telephone-exchange operators. As Mark Twain wrote: 'The humblest hello-girl along ten thousand miles of wire could teach gentleness, patience, modesty, manners, to the highest duchess.' [Mark Twain, *A Connecticut Yankee in King Arthur's Court* (Harper & Bros., 1889), p. 111.]

Flash-mob · The *Oxford English Dictionary* notes that 'flash-mob' was first used in 1832 to describe 'a group of thieves, confidence tricksters, or other petty criminals, esp. ones who assume respectable or fashionable dress or behaviour'.

Knavish tricks · The full verse is: 'O Lord our God arise, Scatter his enemies, And make them fall, Confound their politics, Frustrate their knavish tricks, On Thee our hopes we fix: God save us all.' [See, for example, *A Collection of National English Airs*, ed. William Chappell (Chappell and Simpkin, Marshall, & Co., 1840), p. 88.]

Some idiot left a trap open · There are numerous accounts of actors (and animals) falling through stage traps – occasionally to their deaths. This scene is loosely based on the accident that befell Catherine Hogarth, wife of Charles Dickens. In November 1850, husband and wife were due to perform together in Ben Jonson's play *Every Man in His Humour* when, during a rehearsal, Catherine (described by many as 'clumsy', and by Charles as 'a donkey') fell through a trapdoor, sprained an ankle, and was unable to continue. [See, for example, Frederic G. Kitton, *The Life of Charles Dickens* (T. C. & E. C. Jack, 1902), p. 194.]

7. TUESDAY

Double carpet · In traditional British prison slang, a sentence of three months is a 'carpet' and six months is 'double carpet'. The folk etymology seems to be that it took three months of prison labour to make a carpet. [See, for example, Stuart Wood (pseud.), *Shades of the Prison House: A Personal Memoir* (Williams & Norgate, 1932), p. 42.]

Only Billiards May be Played · This sign, and its thirty-six screws, are an invention – although the Victoria Club, founded in 1860, did indeed prohibit the playing of snooker during the National Hunt Season. The club's billiard table, made for Queen Victoria, was 'unique' in that it had four instead of six slates, and unusually narrow 3¼-inch pockets. [Charles Graves, *Leather Armchairs: The Chivas Regal Book of London Clubs* (Coward-McCann, 1963), p. 86.]

Types of Ethical Theory · We learn in *Joy in the Morning* (1946) that Florence Craye gave Bertie this two-volume study by James Martineau in an attempt to improve his mind. Martineau – Professor of Mental and Moral Philosophy and Political Economy – could have no idea that, almost half a century after his death in 1900, *Types of Ethical Theory* would be selected by P. G. Wodehouse as the most turgid book imaginable.

The club's approved shade of plum · The Drones Club tie is 'a rich purple' – 'there was talk at one time of having it crimson with white spots, but the supporters of that view were outvoted.' [P. G. Wodehouse, *Aunts Aren't Gentlemen* (1974) (Arrow Books, 2008), p. 170.]

Brolly bad show · This tale of umbrella destruction was suggested by the antics of the poet (and old Etonian) Algernon Charles Swinburne (1837–1909), who was expelled from the Arts Club in Hanover Square for vandalising hats. Various versions of the story are told, though all of them have Swinburne drunk.

According to Swinburne's friend Coulson Kernahan, the poet removed all of the members' hats ('silk, opera, bowlers') from their pegs before placing them on the floor in two parallel lines. 'Then, Swinburne and his friend each standing on his right foot at the end of one row of hats, his left ankle clasped in his left hand, the word: "One – Two – Three. Go!" was given, and away in a wild, single-footed Frog's Dance the two racers went, each hop meaning the pancaking of a hat.'[1]

A slightly less energetic account was given by F. N. Broome in 1875: '[Swinburne] was expelled for crushing the hats in the hall because he could not find his own hat, the fact being that he had lost his hat putting his head out of a cab window on his way down to the club.'[2]

[1. Coulson Kernahan, *Swinburne as I Knew Him* (John Lane, 1919), pp. 40–3; 2. The Hon. F. N. Broome, Colonial Secretary, Natal, 'Literature and Art in London at the Present Day', *Evening Hours* New Series, vol. 2 (1875), p. 769.]

Drones Club voting machine · There are various types of 'voting machine' or 'ballot box' – some, as here, use white and black balls, others use balls of a single colour which are covertly dropped into a 'Yes' or 'No' compartment.

The Shakespeare Society at Gonville & Caius College, Cambridge, has long used **sugar cubes** when voting on new members at the annual May Week elections. Two sugar cubes serve to reject a candidate and, as the current president recalls, 'one not madly popular senior member of the college once got ten sugar cubes and several grapes'. The society was presented with a new box of cubes after the end of sugar rationing.

Rule Two (b) · The idea for this rule was suggested by the now defunct Bachelors' Club in Piccadilly – which is often cited as one of Plum's sources for the Drones, along with Buck's and the Bath Club. Members of the Bachelors' who married were obliged to stand for re-election and, if successful, faced a 'fine' of £25 – later, apparently, £50. Only single men could sit on the club's committee, and the chairman had to be unmarried. Ironically, by all accounts, the Bachelors' was uncommonly welcoming to female guests. [See, for example, Anon., 'Club Chatter' *To-Day*, vol. 22, 13 April 1899, p. 347.]

Without let or hindrance · British passports have long included this legalistic doublet. The current wording is: 'Her Britannic Majesty's Secretary of State requests and requires in the Name of Her Majesty all those whom it may concern to allow the bearer to pass freely without let or hindrance and to afford the bearer such assistance and protection as may be necessary.'

And I am Fitzgerald Quent · Fitzgerald Quent is loosely based on George Robert FitzGerald – a notorious duellist (and old Etonian) known as 'Fighting FitzGerald'.

According to the *Compendium of Irish Biography*, 'an account of his wild freaks and lawless excesses would fill a small volume. Most of his life was spent on his paternal estate in the County of Mayo. There he hunted by torchlight, terrified his friends by keeping bears and other ferocious animals as pets, erected a fort and set the law at defiance, and even held his father to ransom for a sum of £3,000.'[1]

As Charles Marsh recounts in *The Clubs of London*, having been rejected by numerous London establishments, FitzGerald persuaded (i.e. threatened) Admiral Keith Stewart to propose him for Brooks's. After three ballots in which he was comprehensively blackballed (including by his proposer), FitzGerald stormed into the club and aggressively interrogated each elector in turn. When self-preservation ensured that no one admitted to voting against this violent maniac, FitzGerald declared: 'You see, gentlemen, that as none of ye have blackballed me, I must be chose.' He then ordered and drank three bottles of champagne before storming out of the club – apparently never to return. FitzGerald was eventually hanged for murder in 1786, aged about 38.[2]

The surname Quent refers to a gambling club of that name that opened in 1962 at 22 Hill Street, Berkeley Square, London – the former home of the Earl of Sandwich. It has been suggested that 'Quent' was 'a password used by friends of the gambling Earl' – though it might just be a corruption of 'quaint'.[3]

[1. Alfred Webb, *Compendium of Irish Biography* (M. H. Gill & Son, 1878), p. 195; 2. Charles Marsh, *The Clubs of London*, vol. 1 (Henry Colburn, 1828), pp. 25–40; 3. Graves, *Leather Armchairs*, p. 178.]

Pip emma · See **Ack emma.**

I was admitted by the steward, Charles · All of the stewards and waiters at the Beefsteak are called Charles. (At Pratt's the waiters are called George.) The doormen at the **High Highland** might all be called **McTavish,** were the club not fictional.

The eight private boxes at the Gaiety · I have taken many liberties with the number, arrangement, and labelling of the boxes of the Gaiety Theatre, which stood on Aldwych from 1864 to 1956.

Waving out of the window an oval ivory pass · Vehicular passage (carriages, cars, horses) through the arch between Whitehall and Horse Guards Parade is reserved for members of the Royal Family and a limited number of VIPs (politicians, diplomats, clergymen, aristocrats, etc.) who possess and can show an ivory (now plastic) pass – granted by the sovereign and issued, nowadays, by the Home Secretary.

Prime Minister James Callaghan recounted the following story in the House of Commons in 1976: 'I am reminded of the Conservative Prime Minister, Mr. Disraeli – Lord Beaconsfield – who, I am told, when asked whether he could give someone an ivory pass to go through Horse Guards, said "No. You may have a dukedom but not an ivory pass."' [HC Deb, 2 December 1976, vol. 921, cc.1153–5.]

Boozy congeniality and pink gin · This is a nod to le Carré: 'Percy showed it to him last night – over a pink gin, was it, Percy, at the Travellers'?' [John le Carré, *Tinker Tailor Solider Spy* (1974) (Penguin, 2011), ebook.]

Laughter in the bar of The Travellers · This oft-repeated slight delights members of the Garrick as much as it irks members of The Travellers. [See, for example, Anthony Sampson, 'The Mystique of British Clubs', *Harper's Magazine*, November 1962, p. 42.]

I say, adjoining clubs? · Sadly no such passage exists – though The Travellers and the Reform do now share a garden, with the Athenaeum.

Concealed-library-door genre · There is a long tradition of using fake book spines (with humorous titles) to camouflage library doors. The titles here were inspired by Plum's own oeuvre: *A Damsel in His Dress* is based on his novel *A Damsel in Distress* (1919); *The Blot Thickens* is based on *The Plot That Thickened* (1973) – the American title of *Pearls, Girls and Monty Bodkin* (1972); and *Goodbye to All Cats* is the actual title of a short story published in *Cosmopolitan* in 1934.

About three million licences · In the year ending 31 March 1929, exactly 2,953,018 dog licenses were issued in Great Britain. [HC Deb, 30 January 1930, vol. 234, cc.1206–7W.]

Found a long-lost gold watch · In the latter part of 1941, when Plum was staying with the Maxtone-Mailer family, he went for his usual afternoon walk, which took him past a local lake. Seeing something glinting on the ground, he bent down and discovered a gold fob watch. On returning to the house, he showed the find to his hostess – who was thrilled, since the watch belonged to her late husband, who had lost it on a similar perambulation.

8. WEDNESDAY

Soy sauce · 'Soy sauce remained the main secret ingredient [in Lea & Perrins] until World War II, when supply problems caused it to be replaced by hydrolyzed vegetable protein.' [*History of Worcestershire Sauce*, p. 5.]

Ganymede code names · The Junior Ganymede's playing-card code names were inspired not only by Lewis Carroll, but also by the infamous double- (tri-ple-?, quadruple-?) agent Sidney Reilly – the 'Ace of Spies'.

Reilly's improbable and flamboyant life has been the subject of numerous biographies (and a television mini-series), although, fittingly, sources are often at odds even on fundamental details, from the year (1873? 1874?) and place (Poland? Russia?) of his birth, to the precise number (Three? Four? More?) of his bigamous marriages, and the circumstances of his death (1925? Moscow? Execution?). What is (relatively) certain is that Shlomo ben Hersh Rozenblium (his birth name?) was a courageous and avaricious adventurer: a crook, con-man, profi-teer, womaniser, murderer (?), fanta-sist, lie-peddler, and *agent provocateur* who eagerly offered his services as a spy to a range of foreign powers, including Russia, Japan, and Great Britain – from whom (in 1899?) he obtained a passport in the name of (Irish-born?) Sidney George Reilly, without (some say) ever becoming a naturalised subject.

Reilly seems to have been based in Port Arthur, China (1890–1905?), St Petersburg, Russia (1906–14?), and New York (1914–17?), before joining the British Air Force in c.1918. He was recruited by the British Secret Intelligence Service in the same year, and in 1919 was awarded the Military Cross – according to some accounts for repeatedly parachuting into Germany during the First World War. Among *many* other (actual, exaggerated, and imagined) escapades, Reilly has been implicated in: 'forging' the Voynich manuscript; the 1904 'D'Arcy Affair' to secure Britain's petroleum supply; the 'Lockhart Plot' to assassinate Lenin in 1918; and the publication of the 'Zinoviev letter' in 1924.

The 'Ace of Spies' is often cited as a source for Ian Fleming's 'James Bond', although he seems to have far more in common with John le Carré's creations 'Toby Esterhase' and 'Otto Leipzig'.

[See, for example: Jeffery T. Richelson, *A Century of Spies: Intelligence in the Twentieth Century* (Oxford University Press, 1997), pp. 12–13; Rodney Carlisle, *Encyclopedia of Intelligence and Counterintelligence* (Routledge, 2015), p. 528; *The Palgrave Dictionary of Anglo-Jewish History*, eds. W. Rubinstein and M. A. Jolles (Springer, 2011), pp. 795; Richard B. Spence, 'Reilly, Sidney George [formerly Shlomo ben Hersh Rozenblium] (1874–1925), spy', *Oxford Dictionary of National Biography*, https://doi.org/10.1093/ref:odnb/40834.]

The Curse of Scotland · Brewer's *Dictionary of Phrase and Fable* explores six theories for why the nine of diamonds has this nickname: (1) In the card game 'Pope Joan', the nine of diamonds is nicknamed 'the Pope' – 'the Antichrist of the Scotch reformers'. (2) The winning card in the game 'comete' (also 'commette', 'comet', etc.) was the nine of diamonds, and the game (popularised by Queen Mary) ruined many Scottish families. (3) 'Curse' is a corruption of 'cross', which refers to the St Andrew's Cross. (4) The nine of diamonds was the card on which the Duke of Cumberland (the 'Butcher Duke') wrote the order to hunt down the supporters of Bonnie Prince Charlie after the Battle of Culloden in 1746. (5) It refers to the 'nine lozenges' in the coat of arms belonging to John Dalrymple, 1st Earl of Stair, who was 'justly held in abhorrence' for the 1692 Massacre of Glencoe. (6) Every ninth King of Scotland 'has been observed for many ages to be a tyrant and a curse to the country' – viz. Malcolm III was assassinated in 1046 by Macbeth; William (died 1214) was taken prisoner by Henry II; and James I was assassinated in 1437. Diamonds, apparently, 'imply royalty'. [Ebenezer Cobham Brewer, *Dictionary of Phrase and Fable* (Cassell & Co., 1898), pp. 318–19.]

Double carpet · This is also the traditional betting slang for odds of 33/1. In the sign language of the 'tic-tac' men it is signalled by crossing the arms over the chest. It seems likely that the etymology is linked to the 'double carpet' of prison slang, explored above. [See, for example, Ben Schott, *Schott's Sporting, Gaming, & Idling Miscellany* (Bloomsbury, 2004), p. 32.]